CRITICAL PRAISE FOR THE MYSTERIES OF LEA WAIT

"*Shadows at the Fair* [is] a polished first mystery that, with a good deal of charm and no more than a hint of malice, cannily draws on its author's professional experiences in the antiques trade.... [It] beckons like a weekend in the country, and the trade tips on everything from Colonial kitchenware to Victorian mourning artifacts are well worth the gate price."

—Marilyn Stasio, *New York Times Book Review*

"Wait knows her old Maine houses...[and] the rippling tremors former inhabitants seem to leave within the walls of such homes. *Shadows on the Coast of Maine* is a breezy page-turner.... Fun and compelling summer mystery."

—*Portland* [Maine] *Sunday Telegram*

"Enjoyable... Wait's knowledge of antique prints and American culture will entertain and educate readers."

—*Publishers Weekly* on *Shadows on the Ivy*

"It's hard to praise too highly Wait's skill at plotting, her ability at building suspense, and her ability to make so many diverse characters come alive."

—*Mystery Scene* on *Shadows at the Spring Show*

Shadows of a Down East Summer

BOOKS BY LEA WAIT

In the Maggie Summer "Shadows" Antique Print Mystery Series:

Shadows at the Fair
Shadows on the Coast of Maine
Shadows on the Ivy
Shadows at the Spring Show
Shadows of a Down East Summer

Novels for children and young adults:

Stopping to Home
Seaward Born
Wintering Well
Finest Kind

Shadows of a Down East Summer

An Antique Print Mystery

Lea Wait

2011
Perseverance Press / John Daniel & Company
Palo Alto / McKinleyville
California

A Perseverance Press Book
Published by John Daniel & Company
A division of Daniel & Daniel, Publishers, Inc.
Post Office Box 2790
McKinleyville, California 95519
www.danielpublishing.com/perseverance

Distributed by SCB Distributors (800) 729-6423

Book design by Studio E Books, Santa Barbara
Cover photo by Tammy Graham

10 9 8 7 6 5 4 3 2

LIBRARY OF CONGRESS CATALOGING-IN-PUBLICATION DATA
Wait, Lea.
Shadows of a down East summer : an antique print mystery / by Lea Wait.
p. cm.
ISBN 978-1-56474-497-5 (pbk. : alk. paper)
1. Summer, Maggie (Fictitious character)—Fiction. 2. Women history teachers—Fiction.
3. Antique dealers—Fiction. 4. Murder—Investigation—Fiction.
5. Prints—Collectors and collecting—Fiction. I. Title.
PS3623.A42S534 2011
813'.6--dc22
2010023677

For Maggie's many wonderful and devoted readers who've written and called and waited impatiently for her return.

And for editor Meredith Phillips, who brought her back.

Shadows of a Down East Summer

Chapter 1

THE DISTRICT OF MAINE. *Map of northern Massachusetts (when it still included Maine) engraved by John G. Warnicke. Published in Casey's General Atlas, Philadelphia. One of the earliest commercially available maps of Maine. Editions in 1796, 1802, 1814, and 1818; this map's edition is unknown. Hand-watercolored lines divide the District into six counties. Warnicke also engraved twenty of Alexander Wilson's ornithological prints. 12 x 17 inches. Price: $400.*

"Who is Carolyn Chase, and why is it so important that we meet her before Maggie's even had time to unpack?" Will Brewer asked his great-aunt. He sat close to Maggie Summer on the weathered wooden gliding rocker overlooking Maine's Madoc River.

Deep blue tidal waters stretched wide in front of them, the calmness of high tide interrupted only by the voracious cries of herring gulls circling an occasional lobster boat on its way to unload the day's haul. Maggie's hand squeezed his as cool, late-day salt breezes gently ruffled the escaping pieces of the long hair she'd pinned in a casual knot hours before.

"Carolyn's a very dear woman," said Aunt Nettie. Her back was cushioned by green-flowered pillows on the Adirondack chair, but her feet were planted firmly on the porch floor. Maggie suspected Aunt Nettie had sat in that very chair, in that very spot, on early August days like this for most of her ninety-one summers. "I know your drive from the Cape was long, Maggie, but I just couldn't wait for you and Carolyn to meet. You could be an enormous help to each other."

Maggie looked from Will to Aunt Nettie. "I thought I was coming

11

to Maine to relax. And do that antiques show you told me about, Will." And most important, spend time with the man she loved. Her back ached from the drive, and she didn't want to think about any more tasks. The Provincetown Show hadn't gone as well as she'd hoped. This trip to Maine might refill both her emotional and financial coffers.

"Don't get your knickers in a knot," said Aunt Nettie. "Lord knows I'm tickled to have both of you as guests. Will's been a widower so long I'd about given up hope of his finding some woman worth paying attention to. When I met you last summer, Maggie, I knew you were the right one."

Maggie kicked Will lightly in consternation. Will just grinned and squeezed her hand.

Aunt Nettie turned to Maggie. "Now, I'm an old woman, and know enough not to get in the way of young love, but you have to understand I have a few little things for Will to help me with this summer. You'd just be bored watching him work. I thought you could help Carolyn with her research while Will's busy."

Aunt Nettie had plans to fill not only Will's days, but hers as well.

Will winked at her, clearly not intimidated by his great-aunt. "I've always spent part of my summer helping Aunt Nettie with chores. When I got here two days ago she gave me this year's list. It seems I'm to paint her house, replace the gutters, and repair some shutters."

Maggie swallowed. A few little things! Visions of romantic walks on the beach and picnics on the rocky Pemaquid shore were dissolving before she'd recovered from her drive north.

"Don't be complaining, Will Brewer. You know I've got to keep this place in order or else someone's going to declare me incompetent and ship me off to some nursing home. Your cousin Shirley's already dropping assisted-living brochures on my coffee table. I plan to die in this house, and I intend for it to be in good order when that day comes."

"You're in perfect health," said Will. "As healthy as an ox. I'll talk with Shirley. But what about this Carolyn Chase? There have been Chases in Waymouth for generations. Who's Carolyn, and how does she fit in?"

"She's Helen Chase's daughter, of course," said Aunt Nettie.

"Helen was my dear friend Susan Newall's cousin. Surely you remember Susan, Will."

Maggie, who'd lost the genealogy thread several names ago, dropped Will's hand and sat up straight, ending the gentle back-and-forth movement of the glider. "Helen Chase. The artist, Helen Chase?"

"That very one," nodded Aunt Nettie. "I knew you'd be interested! Carolyn's heard of *you*, too. She read an article you wrote about Winslow Homer in some artsy magazine. She was very impressed when I told her you were my Will's lady."

Maggie ignored the references both to her relationship to Will and to her academic publications. She was with him now, although what their futures held she didn't want to guess. It had been a stressful spring, and she wasn't up to making any long-term decisions. Not that Will was suggesting she do so.

As a professor of American Studies, occasionally she had to prove she could publish. As an antique print dealer on weekends and vacations, topics related to nineteenth-century American artists were obvious choices for scholarly articles. "I don't know as much as I should about mid-twentieth-century artists." Maggie searched her brain. "Wasn't Helen Chase from New York City? And didn't she die about ten years ago?" If Helen Chase were the artist Maggie was remembering, her idiosyncratic oil paintings of New York City and its residents had found homes in some of America's top museums.

"Exactly right," Aunt Nettie nodded in approval. "I was sure you'd know who Helen Chase was. She did live in New York City. But her family history is here in Waymouth, where her grandmother was born, and her great-grandmother before that. Her daughter Carolyn used to spend summers here with my friend Susan. Now do you remember her, Will?"

Will shook his head. "I remember your friend Susan, but not a relative from New York."

"Carolyn's a few years older than you. I guess your paths didn't cross. Still, she and her mother, Helen, have roots in Maine, and Maine roots run deep. That's why Carolyn's here." Aunt Nettie leaned back in her chair and sipped her iced tea as though she had now explained everything.

Maggie smiled at Will and gently shook her head.

No matter what Aunt Nettie had planned, it was good to be in Maine. She was with Will, away from the tensions and decisions of life in New Jersey. Winslow Homer, her cat, was comfortably sharing summer quarters with Uncle Sam, the American Studies department cat, at her secretary's home. Her new red van had made it to Maine after the disastrous antiques show in Provincetown where she'd barely made enough sales to pay booth rent, but at least she'd been able to spend time with her best friend, Gussie White. Her bank account might be too low for comfort, but on the whole, life was good.

Maggie's antique print business was named Shadows. Prints are images of the past, bringing reflections of earlier lives and images to the present. Here on the coast of Maine, sitting on a nineteenth-century porch overlooking a river harbor once filled with three- and four-masted schooners, Maggie felt closer to that past than she ever did at home in suburban New Jersey. She glanced down at her worn jeans, wishing they'd magically transform themselves into a long, lace-trimmed linen skirt.

The air smelled of salt water and of clams being fried at a small restaurant on the next block, and the man she loved was beside her. Maggie tugged teasingly at his soft, gray beard. He pulled her wayward hand to his lips.

Aunt Nettie pointedly looked out over the porch railing at a bright blue kayak making its way through the wake of a small motorboat.

This was the first time Maggie had stayed at Aunt Nettie's house. She'd have to be on her—their—best behavior. She might be thirty-nine years old, but she'd already noted that she and Will had been assigned rooms at opposite ends of the second floor. Aunt Nettie's room and the one small bathroom in the house were between them. She hadn't felt so adolescent since she was in junior high school.

"When will we get to meet Carolyn, then?" asked Maggie, pulling herself back to the moment. "What research is she doing?"

"I'll let her explain. She should be here any moment now," said Aunt Nettie, looking toward the road. "I invited her for haddock chowder and blueberry pie. Even being from New York City, I'd expect her to remember that in Waymouth supper means six o'clock."

As though on cue, a tall, almost stately woman strode around the corner. From a distance she reminded Maggie of Katharine Hepburn: someone confident, and comfortable with herself. Her gray hair was short, but fell softly around her face, and her jeans and sweater were clearly from Madison Avenue, not L.L. Bean. She was perhaps in her late fifties. No wonder Will hadn't remembered her. Despite his gray beard, he was at least ten years younger than she was. As children vacationing in Maine they would have had very different interests.

Carolyn joined them on the porch and handed Aunt Nettie a bottle of Australian Chardonnay.

"I hope I'm not too late?" she asked, with a relaxed smile.

"You're right on time," said Aunt Nettie approvingly. "This is my nephew Will, and his friend, Maggie Summer, who I told you about. Will and Maggie, this is Carolyn."

Her handshake was firm. "Pleased to meet you both. I'm sure Nettie's told you all about my summer's quest. I've been longing to talk with someone who understands my project and can give me some advice and counsel."

Aunt Nettie took the bottle of wine and headed into the house. "You young people talk, while I check on the supper. Will, you come on inside in about ten minutes. I'll need you to open the wine and heft the chowder pot. After supper I have some pictures to show you all." The screen door banged as she disappeared into the house, clearly having left them an assignment.

"I just got to Waymouth an hour ago," said Maggie. "Aunt Nettie said you were Helen Chase's daughter, and I've always admired her work. I'm afraid Nettie didn't tell us what you were doing here, except that you were doing research."

"Nettie's a special lady, for sure," said Carolyn. "She probably just assumed you would figure it out. I've been in town several months now, and everyone seems to know. No secrets in Waymouth. My Aunt Susan is in a nursing home, and not doing well. Her mind is fine, but at ninety-seven her body is giving out. She was living at home, with help from a local home health aide, Joann Burt, until she fell last spring and broke her hip. She knew I was writing a biography of my mother, so she suggested I come here, stay in her house, and finish up my research. Between us, it was a way she could ask for help, and be giving help, too."

Will and Maggie exchanged smiles. That was just what Aunt Nettie might have done.

"Of course I came as soon as I could. On Tuesday nights the Waymouth Library hosts people doing genealogical research. It's a good way to learn where records are in Maine, and compare notes with others searching for their roots. Nettie comes once in a while. She's lived here all her life, and she remembers so much she's often a help to people."

Will nodded. "She once told me she did that. She enjoys sharing memories and stories of the past."

Carolyn agreed. "I've seen her identify faces in old photographs, and suggest directions to look when someone hunting for genealogical information comes to a dead end. She's the only one left who remembers that 'Ruth's youngest girl married a young man over to Camden'—which can be critically important for someone trying to trace their background. Anyway, Nettie told me you were coming to Maine and—click! Here I am. If I'm interfering with your plans, just tell me."

"So you're looking for your family history," said Maggie.

"Mother seldom talked about where she came from. I don't think she knew much, except that her grandmother was born in Waymouth. And the little she said didn't add up. For example, she'd always told me her grandparents died in an accident, but I can't find any record of that, although I did find their graves over in Sprucewood Cemetery. Susan has hinted she knows more, but she's never told me anything. And now that I'm actively looking I keep running into dead ends." Carolyn shook her head. "What's most surprising is that I'm finding connections with other artists. Mother never mentioned Waymouth's being a town of artists, like Monhegan or Ogunquit. But there have been artists here for years. In fact, Betsy Thompson, who I met at the genealogy group, is quite positive that her husband, who's an artist, is a descendant of Winslow Homer. Her father-in-law was an artist, too. His family has apparently been bragging about the Homer connection for years. Certainly Betsy lets everyone know about it!"

Maggie tried unsuccessfully to stifle a laugh. "That's amazing! So far as I know, Homer never married, or even had a serious romantic relationship with a lady friend. Or gentleman friend, so far as that goes."

"That's what I'd heard, too. But it seems there are a lot of family stories in town that support the Homer–Thompson connection. Kevin Bradman, a Harvard grad student, is here for the summer working on a history of Maine artists' connections to Waymouth, so he would love to prove that connection, too. It would make his doctoral thesis publishable, so he's hanging on Betsy's every word."

"'Publish or perish' is not just an old saying. Scholars would kill for proof that Winslow Homer sired a line of Maine artists!"

"Then you understand why Homer is a hot topic on Tuesday nights at the library!" said Carolyn.

They laughed, and Maggie shook her head. "I know a little about your mother's work. I've never heard of the Thompsons. But the twentieth century isn't really my field. You haven't told me what you think I could help you with."

"I'm not looking for help with the twentieth century. I know the artists who were my mother's contemporaries. Many of them were her friends. And rivals. I hoped you could help me with some information from the late nineteenth century."

Maggie looked thoughtful. "I know late-nineteenth-century prints and publishers. And I know the major painters, like Winslow Homer, of course. But the wood engravings he did between 1857 and 1874 are what I know best. He did them before he lived here in Maine, in Prouts Neck, where he did some of his greatest paintings."

"I'd love to chat, and share what I've found with you. I know you've just arrived, but would you be free for lunch tomorrow?" asked Carolyn.

Maggie looked at Will questioningly.

He nodded. "Go ahead. I have to measure and then get paint samples tomorrow morning." He looked at Carolyn and grinned. "My paint will go on the outside of Aunt Nettie's house. I'll leave the fine arts to you ladies." He looked at Maggie. "After you've had an artistic lunch with Carolyn you and I can spend the afternoon together." He got up. "Right now I'd better go and see how Aunt Nettie is doing with our chowder."

"Lunch sounds like fun," agreed Maggie. "Noon, at the Waymouth Inn? I've always wanted to eat there."

"Aunt Susan asked that I visit her at the nursing home in the morning. But I never stay long; she tires easily. Noon sounds fine."

Chapter 2

THE FAMILY RECORD. *Winslow Homer wood engraving published in* Harper's Bazaar, *August 28, 1875. Man sitting at a small wooden table entering a name in the family Bible while his wife looks over his shoulder. A baby lies in a cradle next to them. 12 x 8.125 inches. Price: $350.*

After supper Will and Maggie sat on one side of Aunt Nettie and Carolyn on the other side as the elderly woman carefully opened the worn red morocco leather cover of an old photograph album.

"Carolyn's been the one asking about her past, but Will, it's time you knew who you came from, and Maggie, you're a part of Will's life now, and you're going to be helping Carolyn, so I want you to see these, too," she said. Her tiny body looked as though it could hardly support the weight of the album she was balancing, and Will and Carolyn each reached out to hold a side of the large volume.

"Who are these people?" Maggie asked.

"This was my family." Nettie replied. "Some of yours, too, Carolyn. In the days people think were simpler." She pointed at the picture on the first page. "These are your great-grandparents, Will. My parents." The couple was posed formally, the woman seated, wearing a high-necked white dress adorned only by a cameo brooch on the pleated bodice, her husband standing stiffly behind her, his hand on her shoulder. Neither smiled. "Handsome, both of them. Could smile if it was required. But that wasn't often."

Nettie turned the page. "This is the year I was born, and your grandmother, Kathleen, was married, Carolyn. She's the tallest girl, over there on the right."

Carolyn leaned over the book, clearly fascinated. "I've never seen a picture of her before. She has light hair, like mine. Who are the others?"

"She does look mighty like you. Those are her cousins with her. That little one is your Aunt Susan. Susan's mother took Kathleen in after her parents died, and then had five little ones for her to look after. I don't have any pictures of Fred Chase, the man Kathleen married, but I remember people talking about how handsome he was. Wouldn't surprise me none to think Kathleen was happy when Fred Chase asked her to marry him and go away to New York. But life doesn't always turn out the way you think it will."

She turned a page. "Will, here's your grandfather, all dressed in his uniform, set to fight in Germany. Next to him is his brother William, who insisted on going too, even though he was a bit younger. He's the one you're named for, you know."

"I know," said Will, softly. "He didn't make it back."

"He didn't. Your grandfather never quite got over it. Said he couldn't stay here in Waymouth without his brother, so after the war he moved 'way out there to Buffalo in New York State, thinking that would stop the memories. Then he met your grandmother, and that's how your father and then you ended up being born there."

"Who are the two girls in that picture?" Maggie asked, pointing. "Is one of them you?"

"I'm the baby," said Aunt Nettie. "A late-life blessing, my mother always said. I hardly remember William, to be truthful. I was so young when he died. That's my sister Sally, holding me. She married Silas Leary, who took to fishing instead of to war. When you were here last year you met her grandchildren, Maggie."

"I remember." Maggie did remember all of them, although she'd never pass a test on how they were all related. How strange to look at these browned photographs and have met the adult grandchildren of the children pictured.

What had her own grandparents and great-grandparents looked like as children, she wondered. If there had been photographs, what had happened to them?

She'd been thinking of adopting. Adopted children would never be able to see their faces in a hundred-year-old photograph album. But, then, she wasn't adopted, and she'd never seen pictures like these either. And maybe some ancestors were best forgotten. Maybe it was easier to start fresh, without the weight of all these lives to live up to. Or live down.

She refocused her thoughts as Aunt Nettie turned another page.

"Carolyn, here's your grandmother Kathleen, back home visiting your Aunt Susan, during the hard times, in 1931, I think it was. The girl standing between them is your mother, Helen." She paused. "Your grandfather, Kathleen's husband, had died by then. Influenza took him in 1918. Your grandmother was working as a waitress, as I remember, but she brought your mother to Waymouth most summers. Helen must have been twelve or thirteen then. I'm the girl with the big bow in my hair. That bow was blue and just matched my eyes. I was right proud of that bow, and insisted I wear it in the picture."

"So you knew my mother and grandmother as well as Aunt Susan?" asked Carolyn quietly. "You knew my mother when she was a child?"

"There weren't that many children to play with. We all knew each other, even when some lived away and came only in the summers. That's why I have photographs of your family as well as mine."

"You never told me that before!"

"You never asked," said Aunt Nettie.

"Mother always said she didn't spend much time in Waymouth," Carolyn said in disbelief, staring at the photograph.

"Well, in truth, she didn't. Kathleen used to bring Helen up on the train and leave her with her Aunt Sarah, or with my mother, for a month or two. The Newalls and Brewers lived close by each other, and there was always room for one more little one in the summertime. We all knew Kathleen was having a hard time in New York. She never stayed here long herself; said she had to get back to work. For ten years, or maybe twelve, Helen was here for part of the summer."

"What was she like as a girl?" Carolyn asked eagerly.

"Quiet, mostly," Aunt Nettie answered. "More used to New York City ways than to Waymouth. Shy. She drew some, even then. Spent time at the library. She liked the freedom of walking on the shore, and in the woods. Went for long walks alone." Aunt Nettie smiled in the remembering. "Drove my mother crazy, that girl did. Never knew exactly where she'd be. Helen always seemed to be on her way somewhere, at least in her mind. She was friendly with all of us, but not real close to anyone but maybe Susan. She wrote to Susan in the wintertime, I think. She wasn't real handy at berry picking or fishing or gardening—those were things we did a lot of, with jobs and food hard come by. But she was family, and she was welcome."

"And then she just stopped coming to Maine?"

"Exactly that. Don't know why. Once in a while we'd hear about her. We knew she'd gotten a scholarship to art school. Her family and friends around here were real proud of her for that. Then we heard she'd gotten married, right before the second war. Everyone was so worried, and stirred up about the war, I don't think we rightly thought a lot about her at that point. She'd been gone from Waymouth so long."

"Her husband died in the war."

"Many men did. From here in Waymouth, too."

Aunt Nettie turned another page, showing a handsome man in uniform standing next to a young woman who was proudly holding his arm. Maggie recognized her immediately.

"Who's the man with you, Aunt Nettie?" asked Will.

"The man I was to marry," said Aunt Nettie. She looked at the book for a moment more and then firmly closed the cover. "The past is over. And I think I've had enough talking for tonight. I'm feeling weary."

"And I must be going," said Carolyn.

Maggie walked after her, toward the door.

"What a fascinating evening," Carolyn said. "I had no idea Nettie knew my mother so well. Do you think she'd loan me a few of those pictures? I'd love to have copies. Perhaps I could even use one in my book."

"You could certainly ask her. Another day, of course. And I'll see you for lunch tomorrow?"

"Noon, at the Inn," Carolyn promised.

Chapter 3

AT THE PARK, *c. 1865. Scene from* La Mode Illustrée. *By the late 1850s sewing machines were widely available, and magazines for middle- and upper-class women pictured new fashions they could copy themselves, or give pictures of to their dressmakers. In the Unit-ed States* Peterson's *and* Godey's Ladies Book *were the standards; in Britain, the* Englishwoman's Domestic Magazine; *but* La Mode, *published in Paris from 1859–1914, was the queen of fashion engravings. This steel engraving depicts seven elegantly dressed children feeding a family of ducks at a pond in a formal Parisian park. 9 x 14 inches. Price: $250.*

It was a glorious morning. Maggie kissed Will demurely on his cheek and left him with Aunt Nettie discussing the appropriate shade of forest green to paint the shutters.

She decided not to tell them that in the nineteenth century New England shutters were painted emerald green, which contained arsenic, which reacted to air pollution and darkened to the forest green used as the classic shade for shutters today. Of course, that same arsenic, used to preserve bodies of Civil War soldiers sent home for burial in family graveyards, was still polluting wells all over the north. Decisions made in the past still influenced the present in so many ways.

Commercial Waymouth was basically two blocks of small businesses on and off Main Street. If you wanted to buy groceries or hardware you'd have to drive ten miles or so to a larger town. The windows of the gift shop were filled with thermometers in the shape of lighthouses, stuffed toy moose, lobsters, and puffins, pine-needle-filled pillows, and souvenir T-shirts, sweatshirts, and baseball caps sporting a choice of Red Sox or Sea Dogs logos. Maggie paused, looking at the toys and children's clothing.

Last winter she had almost decided to adopt a child. She'd learned adoption took more than love, and now she was having doubts about what was right for her. This summer she'd vowed to focus on herself. And on Will, who didn't want children.

Putting off a decision about adoption had seemed very sensible and sane in June. But sometimes a moment as unexpected as looking at children's T-shirts could bring all her maternal longings back. Maggie shook her head slightly to chase those feelings away, and moved on to the next window.

An antiques shop featured folk art—samplers, stenciled Boston rockers, a sea chest in the original blue paint, and an iron horse weathervane. Nineteenth-century weathervanes brought high prices today. So high that many New England barns had lost their original weathervanes to thieves, and the market had been filled by modern "aged" weathervanes that looked very much like the originals. The merchandise in this window looked authentic. She wondered if the dealer offered a written guarantee of age with every item. For someone making a major investment in folk art, and that weathervane would be a major investment, buyers would be looking for provenance that told the history of the item, and a guarantee that it was as old as it was represented. Twenty years ago that wouldn't have been necessary. Today all buyers, including dealers, had to be more cautious.

The small bookstore on the corner featured an enormous gray Maine coon cat dozing in the window and books on Maine history, cooking, and children's books featuring lighthouses and lobstering, seals and puffins, blueberries and beaches, by Barbara Cooney, Robert McCloskey, and contemporary Maine authors Cynthia Lord, Lynn Plourde, Toni Buzzeo and Kevin Hawkes. Children again.

Across the street was the post office, a brewpub she didn't remember from last summer, and just a block ahead, the Waymouth Inn, across from the library. Built when this street had been on the Boston Stage route in the 1830s, the Inn had sheltered travelers for almost two hundred years. Today it offered a few rooms for overnight stays, but most of the high-ceilinged rooms had been turned into restaurant seating.

The young waitress, her hair pulled up in a conservative pony-tail, but with six piercings in each ear and a nose ring, found a table for two overlooking the village green. Maggie ordered a glass of Diet Pepsi and looked at the menu. Crab cakes and a salad would be perfect for her first Maine lunch of the summer.

What had Will planned for the afternoon? He hadn't told her; just said it had nothing to do with art or antiques. She smiled to herself. When she and Will were together they always seemed to end up at antiques shops or shows or auctions. But maybe today they'd drive to Pemaquid, to climb the rocks and see the ocean, or down to Boothbay Harbor and play tourist at the gift shops, or take the ferry to Squirrel Island and back. Will had been here for two days. He'd probably already scouted his favorite buying sites.

"Maggie!" Carolyn was carrying a large leather bag full of papers as well as her pocketbook. "Apologies for being late. My visit to Aunt Susan turned emotional, and I couldn't get away before this."

"I didn't even notice you were late," said Maggie. "I took advantage of the weather and walked here, window-shopping along the way."

"Waymouth's a beautiful little town, isn't it?" agreed Carolyn. "Lots of places to spend time and money, too, which is just what the locals are hoping we tourists do this summer."

"Have you decided what to order?" The waitress was standing, notepad in hand.

"Another diet soda," said Maggie, "and the crab cakes with a small salad."

Carolyn closed the menu she'd been skimming. "I'll have the crab cakes, too. But with iced tea."

"How is your aunt?" asked Maggie.

"Weak, but knows her mind. She's a dear old soul," said Carolyn. "Like Nettie, but with a harder crust. I spent summers with her when I was growing up. From what we heard last night, I guess the same way my mother did when she was young. I loved Waymouth and learned some of the old ways. Aunt Susan taught me to embroider. I wasn't too successful, I'll admit, but the summer I was twelve she actually insisted I produce a sampler of sorts. She walked me to the library once a week. When I was little she read to me, and then when I could read books on my own we had 'reading time' in the late afternoon. She served tea, and I felt very grown-up." Carolyn took a deep drink of the iced tea the waitress had brought. "As I think back, she must have been lonely, and very patient to take me in summer after summer. I wasn't always easy. Like my mother, I liked to take long walks by myself, and I loved to row on the river, which has a dangerous undertow. She'd worry. I cherish the memory of those summers. Now she's weakening every day. I never know when I'll be visiting her for the last time."

"She sounds like a wonderful woman. She had no children of her own?"

"She never married, so, no. Although not being married didn't stop my mother!"

Maggie looked at her.

"No secret! I thought you'd know, since you knew my mother's work. Mother was married once, just before the Second World War, but her husband was shot down over Europe. She never used his name. After that she had a lot of 'gentleman admirers,' but didn't marry again. I never knew my father. I never even asked who he was. Somehow Mother convinced me it wasn't important." She looked out the window for a moment. "Now, as I'm writing about her life, I wish I knew more."

"It must have been hard for both of you, not having a husband or father." Maggie thought about her own hesitation about adopting as a single parent. It couldn't have been easy to be an unmarried mother in the nineteen-fifties.

"Perhaps for her. I don't know. I don't remember it being a problem. We lived in Greenwich Village, and most of our friends were artists or writers or musicians. A lot of them lived in what the world considered 'untraditional situations.' I've had fun trying to remember those days and recreating the way we lived for my book. My summers in Maine were an important counterpoint to living in New York City. It was like traveling from one world, maybe even one century, to another each year for two or three months."

"From poetry readings in Bleecker Street coffeehouses to embroidering samplers in Waymouth." Maggie shook her head. "Two worlds indeed." She took a bite of her crab cake. Delicious, with bits of fresh scallions and parsley.

"Memories. If you're interested I'll share more when we have time. But now I have to tell you what happened this morning at the nursing home. It involves you."

"Me?"

"We've just met. So I want you to know that what I did this morning can be undone. "

What could Carolyn have committed her to? She'd hardly met the woman, and was looking forward to an uncommitted late summer.

"Aunt Susan's lawyer, Brad Pierce, was with her at the nursing home. He's been her friend for years, as well as helping her with legal issues. It seems he's been holding a trunk of old papers for her. She'd asked him to keep them until she was ready to, as she put it, 'cope with the situation.'"

Maggie put her fork down. Papers. Old papers. This was getting interesting.

"Aunt Susan said she'd decided to leave her entire estate to me. There's no one else left in the family she's close to, and she hoped I'd be able to keep her house as a summer home. Or sell it, if I chose to do that."

"How wonderful of her!"

"To be honest, I'd suspected she might do that. I'd already decided I'd keep the house. She was pleased when I told her. The house will need some work, but will make a wonderful retreat full of memories."

"You're lucky. Not many people today live in a house more than two or three years, much less keep a home in the family for generations." Maggie wondered for a moment what would happen to Aunt Nettie's house after her death. One house that had been in the Brewer family for two hundred years had been sold a year ago, and the ensuing complications had not been pleasant.

Carolyn continued, "Some families don't seem to break ties to places like Waymouth. Your friend Will, for example. I didn't catch everything Nettie was saying last night. Was he born here?"

"No; his grandfather, Aunt Nettie's brother, was. Will grew up in Buffalo. Like you, Will spent his summers here in Waymouth."

Maggie paused a moment. "Now that I think about it, I suspect he feels Waymouth is more home than Buffalo is."

Carolyn nodded. "I understand that completely. It's good to have roots; to know who your people were, and how they lived. It can give your life structure; make it feel part of a pattern."

"I envy you that," said Maggie. "I know very little about my family."

"Then you should do some research! Although that's harder than I imagined, even when the family comes from one small town. But let me tell you about the trunk of papers."

"Yes?"

"Aunt Susan was the only one of her brothers and sisters who didn't marry. She inherited the family house."

Maggie remembered Will's family house: always left to the unmarried daughters. Maybe it was a Waymouth tradition. Or just a practical solution.

"She found a trunk full of papers in the back of the attic, far under the beams. In it was a journal written by my great-grandmother, and letters my grandmother wrote after she moved to New York. Susan's mother had kept them all."

"What wonderful materials for your book!" said Maggie, leaning forward.

"Exactly what I said! I asked why she hadn't told me about the trunk before. She's always known I'm interested in family history, and I've been working on my mother's biography for five years now. But I've always felt my mother's life somehow wasn't attached to the past. There was the world of Waymouth, where her family had lived and worked and died in the nineteenth century, and there was the world of twentieth-century New York, where my mother and grandmother both struggled as single parents. The connection between the two was a blur."

"Yet she sent you back to Waymouth every summer, so you'd know the family you had here."

Carolyn nodded. "Part of it was convenience, of course. But clearly it meant a lot to Mother that I knew and loved Maine. She lived in New York, and she's known for her paintings of the city. But after I was in college she came back here a few summers herself, staying with Aunt Susan. Maybe she was trying to recapture her heritage. During that period she painted a number of seascapes and New England landscapes. I have some of them. She gave a half dozen to Aunt Susan, too, but this summer I've only seen four in her house. I don't know where the others are."

"They must be worth a fortune!" Maggie blurted.

Carolyn smiled. "The reaction of a dealer! I know their value. But I don't intend to sell them. Maybe someday I'll hang mine in the house here in Waymouth. That's where they should be."

Maggie reddened in embarrassment. Of course, value couldn't always be measured in dollars. She changed the subject quickly. "I don't understand why your aunt kept the letters and journal a secret. Why didn't she give them to you, or to your mother, when she was visiting here as an adult?"

"She said the papers contained Waymouth family secrets. That secrets of the past were best forgotten. She admitted she hadn't even read all of them. Just enough to know there was information in them that would be embarrassing to our family, and to other families in town."

"How curious! I'll admit I'd have read them."

"So would I. And I will." Carolyn looked straight at Maggie. "I'd like you to read them, too."

"Carolyn, it's not my family," Maggie said quickly.

"No. I'm serious. I want you to read them. I need the opinion of someone who's not emotionally involved with the family. Aunt Susan has already told me one reason she stopped reading."

"And?"

Carolyn took a deep breath. "Do you remember my telling you yesterday that my great-grandparents died in an accident, but I couldn't find any record of it?"

"Yes."

"This morning Aunt Susan told me it wasn't an accident. My great-grandfather shot his wife, and then killed himself. He believed his wife had an affair. That my grandmother, Kathleen, was the daughter of another man."

Chapter 4

---⊂⊃∞⊂---

FALL GAMES: THE APPLE BEE. *Winslow Homer wood engraving published in* Harper's Weekly, *November 26, 1859. A popular nineteenth-century New England custom was for young ladies to peel an apple in one long strand and then throw the peeling over their shoulder. If they were lucky the apple skin would form the initial of the man they would marry. 9.125 x 13.75 inches. Price: $325.*

Maggie sat back. "Your great-grandmother's having an affair would have been scandalous. Especially back in the eighteen-nineties! But I can't see it would be all that shocking to us, over a hundred years later, or that knowing it could do any damage to anyone today. It is a mystery, though: who was the *real* father?"

Carolyn didn't smile. "That was my first reaction, too. I thought, 'What great material for my book!' But Aunt Susan and her lawyer were all taking it very seriously. I couldn't help wondering what else was in the papers. Then she made me promise that after I'd finished with the papers, especially an early journal she said was important, I would destroy them, or make sure they were in the hands of someone who would understand how sensitive they were, and would take care of them. She didn't want them to end up in an auction, or in the hands of someone who would sensationalize them."

Maggie shook her head. "Your aunt sounds a little melodramatic. Family papers are important to the family, of course, and your mother *was* a well-known artist. But I can't imagine anything that would be devastating enough that those papers would be judged sensational. Not today."

"She's kept them hidden for so many years. She's passing on that

29

responsibility, and she wants me to understand how important it has been to her." Carolyn put her fork down. "She kept saying that knowing more about their history could change people today."

"I suppose that's true. Think of how some people reacted when DNA evidence confirmed Thomas Jefferson had fathered children with Sally Hemings, one of his slaves," Maggie said thoughtfully. "Although, of course, Thomas Jefferson was one of our founding fathers. And a man with strong public opinions about slavery."

"We're certainly not rewriting American history here in Waymouth. But Aunt Susan was very clear that it was a major decision for her to decide to trust me with the documents. I told her I would treat them with respect. But she was still nervous about what would happen to them if something happened to me, so I told her about you. She'd heard about you from Nettie, of course, because you're Will's friend. I said you were an academic scholar and antique print dealer; an expert on American art and history and a very caring person. I told her that if anything happened to me, you would take the papers."

"Me?" Maggie gasped. "You're giving me responsibility for journals and letters that are a part of your mother's history? American art history?"

Carolyn paused a moment and then looked directly at her. "I already have. That's why I was a few minutes late. This morning Brad Pierce wrote a codicil to Aunt Susan's will saying I am the sole beneficiary of her estate, but that when I die, you get any family papers that still exist. My current will leaves everything in my estate to the Portland Museum of Art. I thought they could use the money, and would value my mother's Maine paintings. But Aunt Susan's papers bypass my will and go to you."

Maggie just looked at Carolyn.

"I'm thinking I may add a note to my will saying you also get the notes for my biography. The notes and papers should really stay together, in case I don't get a chance to finish the biography." Carolyn shook her head as she saw Maggie's expression. "Don't panic, Maggie. I'm feeling fine, and plan on spending the next few years writing that book myself! But I'm not getting any younger, and none of us can predict the future." She grinned and raised her glass of iced tea in Maggie's direction. "To whatever life brings!"

Last summer Will's family home had been sold. That had been

upsetting. How would this family feel about their papers being left to Maggie? Especially if those documents contained sensitive information?

Maggie sat, stunned. "I don't know, Carolyn. I've just met you. You're trusting me with a big responsibility."

Carolyn put down her glass. "You won't do it?"

"Of course, we may read the journals and letters and decide there's nothing really important in them. No one today may care anything about long-ago scandals. And I'm assuming you'll live for many years and finish the biography yourself."

"I certainly plan to. But this morning I needed to reassure Aunt Susan. I know your reputation, and Aunt Nettie recommends you." Carolyn leaned toward her. "In Waymouth, that's high praise."

"What about other people in your family? How will they feel?"

"There's no one else. Susan had four brothers and sisters, so I have a few distant cousins, but none of them live in Waymouth, and no one has kept closely in touch with Susan. The papers are about *my* great-grandparents and grandmother. Since my mother and her mother were only children, I'm the only one left in that line."

"I see." Maggie drained her second glass of diet soda.

"Aunt Susan may be over-reacting. You're right. There may be nothing of interest in the papers. I might even decide to destroy them. Or, on the other hand, I might add them to what I leave the Portland Museum. But until I—until *we*—have a chance to sort through everything carefully, Aunt Susan was relieved, and I certainly would be, if you'd agree, to know that a trusted and intelligent friend of the family will be watching out for whatever secrets they contain."

"I understand," Maggie agreed, somewhat reluctantly. She hadn't been in Maine for twenty-four hours and she'd already taken on partial responsibility for a whole family's history.

"I have the trunk in my car. I'm going to the library to make a copy of the first journal. That's the one Aunt Susan seemed most concerned with. Tonight there's a genealogical meeting at the library. Why don't you come, and I'll give you a copy? That way we can read the journal at the same time and compare thoughts."

Maggie's curiosity was already thoroughly aroused. "I'll admit I'd love to read the journal. And maybe I should learn more about genealogy. What time is the meeting?"

Chapter 5

⸻

THE BUDS. *Winslow Homer wood engraving published in* Harper's Weekly, *March 3, 1860. Garden scene of two young ladies and a handsomely attired gentleman. He is handing one of the ladies several budding flowers, clearly (in 1860) a sign of emotional flowerings to come. 4.5 x 3.5 inches. Price: $140.*

"Your lunch with Carolyn went well, then?" Will had refused to tell Maggie their destination, but his car was headed north on Route 1.

"I think so," said Maggie. "I promised to meet her at the Waymouth Library tonight for a genealogy meeting. Her aunt gave her a trunk full of family papers, and she'd like me to look at some of the early ones." Maggie didn't tell Will more. Whatever secrets the papers held were Carolyn's. At least for now.

"Old papers sound right up your alley," said Will, slowing up. The car ahead of them had a Florida license plate and was going twenty miles under the speed limit. On two-lane Route 1, that meant it now led a caravan of more than a dozen drivers. No doubt a retired couple, returned from their winter down south and enjoying the cool breezes.

Locals ground their teeth and kept their brake lights blinking. Summer residents brought welcome dollars to Maine.

Will and Maggie weren't in a hurry.

"Did you get the appropriate shade of green chosen for the shutters?"

"I think we're set. Had to order the paint from Boston, but it'll be in tomorrow. Painting the house shouldn't take me longer than a week or two, even including the gutters and shutters. Aunt Nettie's grown used to depending on me for chores like that."

"I know," said Maggie. "And she's a dear. I really don't mind. But I'd hoped we could spend more time together. You're doing an antiques show this weekend, too, aren't you?"

"An outdoor show. The kind print dealers like you avoid like the plague. I agreed to do it when I was here last summer, so I'm on the hook."

"A one-day show?" asked Maggie.

"Right. Set up from five-thirty until nine in the morning. It's only about an hour from here though."

Maggie winced. "I hate one-day shows. You have to get up before dawn. But I'll join you if you'd like the company. I might manage some buying. Otherwise that's one more day we won't have together."

Will reached over and touched her hair.

"Always appreciate your company, my lady. And before you complain about my schedule, remember you're the one planning to spend this evening at the Waymouth Library rather than with me," he reminded her.

"Carolyn's going to give me a copy of an old journal that sounds intriguing," said Maggie, intentionally leaving out how eager she was to read it.

"I'm glad Aunt Nettie's managed to connect you with a project you're interested in."

"Me, too," said Maggie. "You can climb those ladders and fix the gutters by yourself, Will Brewer. The chores won't last forever. In the meantime, we're off this afternoon! No Carolyn and no Aunt Nettie." They passed an old mill that had been converted into an antiques mall. "No antiques?" she added, a bit wistfully.

"There'll be plenty of time for antiques. When have we ever *not* found time for antiques? But this afternoon I wanted to do something else." Will turned his head slightly and winked at her. "For your birthday."

"My birthday! That was back in May."

"So I recall. I also recall we spent that day with you hobbling around with a cast on your foot, looking for vans in used car lots."

"I had to do that after my old van blew up."

"And then we spent a romantic evening ordering out for pizza."

"It was good pizza," smiled Maggie, with a sideways glance. "As I recall the rest of the evening was even better."

"Indeed. You're a wicked woman," agreed Will, with a friendly leer. "But you've now recovered enough to get a real birthday gift. I was going to pick one out before you got here, but I thought you'd have more fun doing it yourself."

Maggie looked at the gold Victorian "regard" ring Will had given her last fall, which she wore on her right hand. *Regard* was spelled out by a band of small stones—a Ruby, an Emerald, a Garnet, an Amethyst, another Ruby, and then a Diamond. She rarely took it off. Will had found one at an antiques show after she'd admired one on someone's hand. Victorian sentiment rings were getting harder to find every year.

Since they'd met fifteen months ago at an antiques show where they were both exhibiting, he'd also given her a coffeepot for her kitchen (because he drank coffee and she didn't), and flowers, and had often brought wine or champagne to share. He'd never asked her to pick out a gift for herself.

Where were they going? How serious was this? Maggie realized she was clenching her left hand without noticing it. It couldn't be that. Neither of them was ready.

She felt like a flustered teenager, wondering what her boyfriend would give her for Valentine's Day.

Carefully she unclenched her hand. She was all grown up. She and Will had both been married before. Why was she reacting so foolishly?

But how much money would he spend? What if she didn't like what he'd picked out?

She barely noticed the vistas of pine trees and sparkling rivers and narrow streets lined with green-shuttered white houses. Occasional ANTIQUES signs caught her eye, but she refused to react.

"You're awfully quiet," Will commented. "You couldn't be nervous, could you?"

"Will, you don't need to get me a birthday present."

"Then it will be a 'welcome to Maine' gift," he agreed easily. "In fact, that's probably even more appropriate."

Maggie forced herself to smile. "Are we going out to eat lobster?"

"An excellent idea, and one we'll definitely explore at a later date. But not today." Will glanced at her again and grinned. "I've really got you worried, haven't I?"

"You can read me too well," admitted Maggie.

"Relax. I promise this will not be painful," said Will. "And we've only a few more miles to go."

Traffic was almost stopped in the classic Maine village they were passing through. In Maine pedestrians have the right of way. As long as they're in a crosswalk, all vehicles have to stop. In this small town there were three crosswalks.

"Now where are we heading?" said Maggie as Will turned off Route 1. She watched the narrow road twist around an inlet, following the shoreline almost too closely for comfort.

"Taking the back road to get us on Route 27," said Will comfortably.

"Route 27 goes to Boothbay," Maggie remembered.

"Give the lady an A-plus in geography," said Will as they made a right turn and headed down the peninsula. "You do remember what you saw last summer."

"Yes." Maggie remembered all too much from last summer. Amy, her former college roommate, had been arrested, and was currently living in a mental hospital in Augusta. Amy's husband had sold their home back to the family who'd originally owned it, and moved to "The County," as Mainers call Aroostook County, the northern part of Maine, to teach in a small school there. She hoped he'd found the peaceful life he'd been looking for.

"Almost there," said Will.

"Are those llamas?" Maggie asked, as they passed a field where several animals were grazing.

"We have just about everything in Maine, if you look in the right places," said Will. "Here we are."

He pulled into the parking lot outside several buildings whose sign introduced them as EDGECOMB POTTERS. Maggie remembered seeing their ads in *Down East* magazine.

"You want to buy me a piece of pottery?" Maggie asked, as she looked around, stunned at the iridescent colors of the pottery displayed on tables outside the showrooms.

"Actually, no," said Will. "Although their pottery is spectacular. But there's more than pottery inside."

There was. Individually blown glass vases and goblets; hand-woven blankets and rugs; sculpture; hand-crafted furniture. "Over here." Will gently directed Maggie toward the glass display cases in the back of the room.

The cases were full of jewelry. Maggie glanced quickly. The case Will was pointing to didn't contain rings. She breathed a little easier.

"Your eyes are such a beautiful shade of green," Will said, tilting her chin and looking down at her. "I wanted to get you a pair of earrings that would really show them off, but I got confused. I thought it would be best if you picked them out yourself."

Maggie looked. The case was full of pink and green and blue earrings and pendants of all shades. "These are...?"

"Tourmaline. The Maine state gem," said Will. "That's why this *is* really a 'welcome to Maine' gift. Tourmaline comes in reds, pinks, greens, and even blues. Sometimes the pinks and greens are in stripes. Those are called watermelon tourmalines." He pointed at one pendant that did, indeed, look like a slice of watermelon. "Take all the time you need. I don't want you to look at the price tags. But choose your favorite pair of green earrings. I've been imagining you wearing them for months."

Maggie's green eyes looked into Will's blue ones, and she gently kissed him. "They will be a wonderful birthday present," she said quietly. Then she turned back to look inside the case.

Chapter 6

⸺⚬⚬⚬⸺

UNTITLED, C. 1870. *Beautiful German chromolithograph of four snakes. Realistically unlikely to be together in any similar wooded scene: an Indian cobra, a viper, a python, and a grass snake. (Python is holding a frog in its mouth.) Light fold mark vertically down the center. Originally published in an unidentified natural history book. 12.5 x 16 inches. Price: $75.*

Carolyn and several other people were already gathered around the table in the Waymouth Library's seminar room when Maggie arrived, her new tourmaline earrings catching the light as she walked.

"I couldn't believe the number of papers in the trunk," Carolyn was saying to a heavy woman in her forties whose curly blond hair fell over her face.

"What period are they from?" the blonde asked.

"Do they mention other families in Waymouth?" asked a young man with interest as he opened his laptop.

"I don't know yet; I've only looked at a few. But I'm so thrilled. I wanted to share the news, since you've all been so supportive in helping me with my research. I know how important newly discovered papers can be." Carolyn beckoned to Maggie. "Everyone, this is Maggie Summer, the professor from New Jersey who's going to help me make sense of the new information. Especially anything to do with nineteenth-century art."

Maggie joined them at the table. For years Aunt Susan had kept the existence of those papers, and whatever secrets were within them, hidden. Now Carolyn was almost flaunting her possession of them. What if there *were* something significant in that old trunk?

37

Clearly her aunt had thought there was information that might be upsetting to people in town. What was Carolyn thinking?

"Maggie, I want you to meet some wonderful people. This is the director of the Waymouth Historical Society, Allison Griggs." Allison nodded and smiled and then turned her attention back to the papers in her briefcase. "And Kevin Bradman, who's writing his Harvard dissertation on Maine artists."

The young man stuck out his hand. "Pleased to meet you, Dr. Summer. Princeton?"

Maggie managed not to giggle. "No. Somerset County Community College."

"Oh." Clearly dismissing any contribution a community college professor might be capable of making, Kevin Bradman turned back to his laptop.

"And this," said Carolyn, as a red-haired woman wearing an orange-and-green paisley shawl that contrasted with her hair, but did somehow match her orange slacks and green fingernails, entered the room, "this is Betsy Thompson. Her husband is an artist, and so was her father-in-law. Betsy, this is Maggie Summer, who's going to help with my research."

Maggie reached out to shake Betsy's hand. So this was the woman who was going to prove that Winslow Homer was in her husband's family tree. Very interesting.

"Betsy, I've had the most marvelous luck! Aunt Susan's found a trunk of old papers and letters and diaries from my family."

Carolyn was conveniently not mentioning that Susan had found the trunk fifty years ago, and chosen to keep its contents private. Why hadn't Carolyn waited to share her news at least until she'd had time to read through the papers? Researchers could be predatory.

But maybe Carolyn didn't know that. She didn't work in ivy-bound halls.

"Carolyn, these papers would certainly be a wonderful addition to the Waymouth Historical Society's collection," said Allison Griggs.

"Possibly. But right now I want to go through them quietly, myself," said Carolyn.

"I didn't mean this moment, of course. After you've finished your research. They might contain information invaluable to other people interested in Waymouth and its families."

"They might," said Carolyn. "Especially the journal that starts in the nineteenth century. I can hardly wait to read it!"

Betsy Thompson moved closer. "A nineteenth-century journal? What years does it cover?"

"It begins in 1890. I haven't looked at it in detail yet," said Carolyn. "Maggie, I tried to make you a copy this afternoon, but the ink is faded, and the machine here won't make a clear copy."

"Carolyn, dear, you mustn't try to copy such a precious document on an ordinary copying machine," Allison put in. "Bright lights will fade the ink even more. And that beautiful nineteenth-century script is hard enough to read when it's clear. If you want to make a copy, why don't you bring it over to the historical society? We could scan it and put it on a disc for you."

"I think I'll just read it as it is," said Carolyn. "But, thank you. I'll remember that for the future."

"Henry!" Betsy called to an elderly man standing in the doorway, "Carolyn has made a real find! A whole trunk full of papers from her family here in Waymouth! She thinks most of them are late-nineteenth and early-twentieth century."

Henry was perhaps in his late seventies. His glasses were tortoiseshell-rimmed, and his jacket was tweed. He reminded Maggie of a slightly pretentious history professor from her undergraduate days. But Henry's best days were clearly behind him. He leaned on a walker, on the front of which was clipped a small basket filled with papers and a cell phone. The cuffs of the off-white shirt he was wearing were frayed, and it was a good guess he'd eaten eggs for supper, based on the crusted yellow stain on his tie.

"Hi, Henry!" said Carolyn, turning to greet him. "Come and meet my friend Maggie." She turned to Maggie. "Henry used to teach math here in Waymouth. He's writing a history of the schools in town."

Maggie smiled in greeting. Her vision of Henry as a professor had been right on the money. But she suspected that other stereotype, "absentminded," also fit. She wondered whether Henry drove himself to these meetings, or if he had a wife or son or daughter who kept an eye on him.

"Eighteen-ninety is a critical year for the research I'm doing," Betsy Thompson reminded the room in general. "Carolyn, if the journal you've found was written by someone in Waymouth, it might have the key to what I'm looking for. You have to let me see it!"

Betsy's interest was Winslow Homer, Maggie thought. When had he lived and worked in Prouts Neck? His brother Arthur had honeymooned there in the mid-1870s, she remembered.

All three Homer brothers and their parents had bought land there in the early 1880s. Winslow had made Maine his permanent home shortly after that, and had lived in Prouts Neck, a particularly scenic peninsula of Scarborough, off and on from then until his death in 1910. Anyone interested in Homer's relationship with someone in Waymouth would definitely be interested in a diary from the late 1880s or 1890s.

"I won't forget you. I know what you're looking for," Carolyn was assuring the persistent Betsy. "But Maggie and I are going to read the papers before I show them to anyone."

Betsy shot Maggie a look of pure hate. "I know this town as well as anyone, and I'd be very happy to help you understand any information you might find in those journals. Someone from away couldn't fully appreciate local references."

Before Carolyn or Maggie had a chance to respond, Henry clip-clopped his walker over to the table and sat down heavily. "Betsy, you've made your point. And you're not an expert on this town, much as you think you are. If Carolyn wants an expert she can come to Allison at the historical society or to me. You've only lived here since you married Win. When was that, six years ago? Besides, you're not going to find a Winslow Homer connection to your family. It never happened. I don't care what your husband's name is, or who he was named for. There's absolutely no proof Winslow Homer had a relationship with any woman in Maine, much less had a child with her."

"You're just an old know-it-all, Henry Coleman. I've been married to Winslow Thompson for eight years, for your information. Homer might not have put his name on a birth certificate, but who knows what really happened? There are people in this town who'll swear he was my husband's grandfather. There's family evidence, too. Why do you think every generation of Thompsons has a Winslow or a Homer in it? The Thompson family is just like the Wyeths. Three generations of Maine artists."

"You just go on believing that, Betsy dear," said Henry. "But don't expect the world to march to the same drum you've been beating all over Waymouth."

"Of course, we know all three generations of the Wyeths could actually paint," Maggie heard Allison Griggs whisper to Carolyn.

How much would a Winslow Homer pedigree add to the value of a mediocre twentieth-century artist, Maggie wondered. She'd never heard of either of the Thompsons. She suspected few people outside Waymouth had.

Everyone had heard of the Wyeths: the *paterfamilias* N.C., Andrew, and now Jamie. Of course, as the historical society director had pointed out, the Wyeths could paint.

Maggie focused back on the conversation.

"There was a television character called Homer Pyle a while back, wasn't there? Do you think he was a relative of Winslow Homer, too?" asked Henry, clearly enjoying the confrontation.

"That was *Gomer* Pyle. The only Homer I can think of on television is Homer Simpson. Although watching *The Simpsons* is probably below you, since you're such a celebrated high school math teacher. And you needn't be facetious. Family stories are often based on facts. Even *historians* know that," said Betsy, her voice rising with the color in her cheeks. "Isn't that right, Kevin?"

"Believe me, Betsy, if you can prove Winslow Homer fathered a child I would be more than happy to rewrite Homer's biography, and American art history. I want to believe your family's stories. A Homer dynasty could be the center of my dissertation." Kevin shook his head. "We just haven't found the proof yet. Family stories aren't always myths. Many are based on facts."

"Whoa!" said Allison, maneuvering her wide frame between Betsy and Henry. "What's important tonight is that Carolyn's made a discovery that may mean a lot to historians and genealogists in this area. We thank her for letting us know about it, and look forward to hearing more once she's had a chance to examine the papers."

"Well said," added Henry. "I believe you were going to bring us some information tonight about the Maine Historical Society's online Memory Network." He looked at his watch. "My son and his girlfriend are going to pick me up in an hour and I'd like to hear what you've got to say."

While the group talked about downloading and search tools, Maggie tuned out. She was familiar with on-line sources, and generally found them too limited for her research needs, except when she needed to check a current art gallery or auction price for a print. Then Google was her best friend. Even then, you couldn't take one source as truth. Cross-referencing was essential. She'd seen too many student papers containing factual errors downloaded from the web. The closest guarantee of truth was a primary source, and even primary sources differed, just as three people who viewed the same crime would describe a suspect differently.

Truth was harder to find than most people thought.

But, truth or fiction, the papers Carolyn Chase now owned would be fun to read. Old diaries and letters were windows into the past, like antique prints.

Just as she was beginning to wish she'd stayed at home and shared a cognac with Will, Carolyn slipped her a note. "Would you take the 1890 journal and start reading it? You'd understand it better than I would. I'll start with the letters."

Maggie looked back at Carolyn and nodded. Would she like to take the journal? Would she! She wrote, "YES!" on the note, and added, "Lunch tomorrow to compare notes?"

Carolyn nodded back.

Chapter 7

⸻ ∞∞∞ ⸻

SEA-SIDE ATTRACTIONS, *1869 wood engraving by John Felmer. Three vertical fold marks, enabling it to be folded into* Appleton's Journal. *Fully dressed people on sandy beach, beach houses in distance. Gentleman courting lovely woman while small boy and girl empty pail of sand into the man's pocket. 11 x 15 inches. Price: $70.*

Journal of Anna May Pratt

June 2, 1890
I have decided to begin a journal, since I have now passed my eighteenth birthday and am ready to begin my life as a woman. I intend to keep these pages so that when I am an old woman of perhaps fifty, too aged to care about anything but the past, I will be able to remember how exciting it was to anticipate the possibilities of life.

My sister Sarah, who is still a child who has not yet pinned up her hair, thinks I am foolish. But all spring, as the snow melted and the mud dried and the spring peepers began to sing, I felt certain my life was about to change. Sarah says I will marry and have seven children and gray hair and sun-darkened skin by the time I am thirty, like most women here in Waymouth.

But I am not like those women. I feel certain I am destined for a life of importance. A life that will be remembered.

I will not allow my youth to be wasted through waiting for others to act. I have resolved to set the course of my own future, and am determined to record and savor every moment of it. Yesterday may have marked the beginning of that adventure.

I attended church as usual with Mother and Father and Sarah. I wore my soft gray shawl against the coolness of the building, but

43

outside the early June sun warmed the air enough so I could remove the shawl. Since I am bound to be truthful in these pages, I will admit to wanting to show off the new ruffled yellow dress Mother helped me to make. I wanted to remove my hat, too, so I could feel the warmth of the sun full on my head as I did when I was a child, but of course, a young woman of eighteen should not be without a hat. Especially when her hair is light brown and her skin is pale, as mine is. My hopes for the future do not include freckles.

My dear friend Jessie Wakefield and her family then invited me to join them in a picnic down on Ferry Beach at Prouts Neck. My mother was concerned for my dress, but agreed when assured they had packed quilts for us to sit upon. The Wakefields' carriage is very wide, and we had plenty of room on the journey.

Jessie and I talked little in the carriage, since her parents were present, but we squeezed each other's hands in happiness at being together and admired the scenery on the ride. Fields are now greening, and lupine and bluettes are starting to bloom. Picnics with only one's own family, no matter how lovely the location, are dreary when you are young women.

We found a scenic spot, and Jessie and I shared the lemonade and biscuits and pickles and ham that her mother had packed. Her parents let us sit apart, so we could chat, and then agreed we could walk a little on the path above the beach that leads to the top of the ledges overlooking the ocean. Of course, all Jessie wanted to talk of was Luke Trask. She and Luke have been sweethearts since they were children, but her father wants her marrying better than a Grand Banks fisherman.

I must be honest within these pages: it has been difficult for me to hear Jessie's talk of Luke for so many years since I, too, have seen him growing into a man many women would find worth having. Although he vows his heart beats only for Jessie, I am certain he covertly admires me, and that I could win his love were Jessie's affection elsewhere.

For the moment I must suffer my longings in silence, and look for my heart's desire in places further from home than Waymouth.

It was while we were walking on the rough path along the top of the cliffs, when Jessie was telling me yet again how wonderful Luke was, that our lives took an exciting turn. My hands tremble to write *it! Not far down the path we were set upon, in a fashion, by a small, white, black-headed terrier.*

Clearly trying to be friendly, he jumped up on my dress, leaving paw prints that I hope can be cleaned. He was followed by a young man, racing along the path, calling, "Sam!" which it seemed was the name of the dog. The man was quite tall and handsome, with dark hair and eyes, and dressed in a fashion more common to the town than the shore. He was appropriately embarrassed when he saw what Sam had done to my skirt. We introduced ourselves, quite properly.

His name is Mr. Micah Wright, which I think a very elegant name. We chatted a bit, and continued walking and admiring the ocean view, when we came upon a most remarkable man.

He was even older than father, with very little hair, and what he had was covered by his straw boater. Sam went right up to him, and lay down at his feet, as though that were his rightful place, and I know now that was so. Mr. Wright introduced the man to us as Mr. Winslow Homer. He was sitting on a folding chair and painting a canvas set on a wooden easel. When he stood up to greet us we could see that he was much shorter than Mr. Wright, slight, and not much taller that I am.

We peeked at his picture of the sea, which appeared to amuse him. He then walked right around Jessie and me, looking at us closely, although not appearing at all forward, and then asked if we would consider posing for him!

He has been painting a young woman from Scarboro named Cora, he said, but is in need of other figures, and thought ours would do admirably.

We were, of course, very excited and flattered. Mr. Homer then walked back to where Jessie's parents were seated and spoke with them. He said he would send a wagon for us, and that we would be appropriately chaperoned, and would only model fully clothed. I had not even imagined another possibility!

While Mr. Homer spoke with Mr. and Mrs. Wakefield, Mr. Wright, who is Mr. Homer's assistant, assured us that the artist, strange though he appears, is quite well-known. He has studied in France and England, and has sold many paintings in Boston and New York!

After we returned to Waymouth Jessie's mother talked with my parents, and they agreed. We will begin posing next week! Mr. Homer will even pay us for the privilege of being immortalized!

I cannot help wondering if Mr. Micah Wright will be nearby when we next visit Prouts Neck.

Chapter 8

CHESTNUTTING. *Winslow Homer wood engraving published in* Every Saturday, *October 29, 1870. One boy is sitting up in a chestnut tree and shaking a branch; below him two girls and two boys hold a quilt to catch the nuts as they fall. One of Homer's most charming prints of rural nineteenth-century life. His wood engravings from* Every Saturday, *which had a limited circulation, are today much harder to find than those from* Harper's Weekly. *11.75 x 8.75 inches. Price: $500.*

Maggie was still thinking about Anna May Pratt's journal when Aunt Nettie handed her the telephone during the middle of breakfast. Clearly there had been a connection between Prouts Neck and Waymouth in 1890.

"No lady should call at such an early hour," Aunt Nettie sniffed as she went back to the griddle.

Maggie put her fork down. The wild blueberry pancakes with butter and Maine maple syrup were light and delicious. Perhaps the salt air had increased her appetite. She'd already eaten several more than she would have at home. "Hello? Carolyn! I've been thinking about you. I started reading the journal last night."

"Maggie, I've bad news," Carolyn interrupted. "It's Aunt Susan. She went to sleep last night and didn't wake up. The nursing home called to tell me two hours ago."

"I'm so sorry, Carolyn."

"It isn't a surprise, of course, but it's still a shock. I keep thinking of my mother's death. Now I have to plan Aunt Susan's funeral."

Carolyn sounded on the verge of tears.

"Let me come over and make phone calls, or do anything else that needs to be done. Maybe just keep you company."

"That's sweet of you, Maggie, but I'll be all right. The lawyer, Brad Pierce, is on his way here, and he'll help me make arrangements. She left instructions, so it shouldn't be too complicated. But I won't be able to meet you for lunch."

"Of course not, Carolyn. If you think of something I could help with, call me, please."

"I will. Maybe I'll see you tomorrow. The funeral won't be for a couple of days. Some distant relatives live in Massachusetts and New Hampshire and I want to give them enough time to get here."

"Know I'm sorry, and thinking of you." Maggie put down the telephone and turned to Aunt Nettie. "Carolyn's Aunt Susan died last night."

Aunt Nettie nodded sadly. "From your end of the call I was guessing that. Poor Susan. But she was getting on, and hadn't been well in a while." She started clearing the breakfast dishes. "I'll make a casserole and some muffins, Maggie, so don't you worry about that."

Cooking hadn't even occurred to Maggie. But food was the currency of sympathy in Maine, she remembered. "Thank you, Aunt Nettie. Can I help with anything?"

"Not a bit. I'll take care of it. I'll guess you won't be seeing Carolyn today?"

"No. She and Brad Pierce will be making the arrangements."

Aunt Nettie nodded. "He knows the way Susan would have wanted everything done."

Maggie looked out the window. It was a dank and dreary morning.

"You go find Will. He's out in the barn, puttering with all that paint we bought, waiting for the rest to be delivered. Looks like rain in any case. Too damp to start painting." She wiped her hands on her apron decisively. "The two of you go and look for antiques, or whatever you want to do. Leave me to think about Susan and put together some food."

Maggie resisted the urge to hug her. "Thanks, Aunt Nettie."

An hour later they'd organized the paint and tools Will had gathered, and as Nettie had predicted, it had started to drizzle. They decided to explore, and bring back lobster rolls for lunch.

"With butter, mind you. None of that celery some folks fill the rolls with to make you think you're getting your money's worth," advised Aunt Nettie. "A toasted roll full of lobster meat and a touch of butter. And some of those vinegar potato chips. I like those with a lobster roll now and then."

Will and Maggie promised, and headed out. Besides the three antiques shops Maggie had spotted on the main street Will knew at least a half dozen more hidden on side streets, but all within walking distance. That didn't even begin to count the craft shops.

"I remember Walter English's Antiques Mall from last summer," Maggie said, as they walked. "And his auction house. Will he be having any auctions in the next ten days or so?"

"I think there's one at the end of the week," Will said. "I'll check the local paper when we get back with lunch. Aunt Nettie always has a copy. If so, the auction preview will be in the next couple of days."

Maggie, wearing an old yellow slicker Aunt Nettie had urged on her, jeans, and a long-sleeved green T-shirt to go with her tourmaline earrings, was intrigued by a blacksmith's shop, so they made that their first stop.

"Morning, Tobias," said Will to the heavily muscled man who was working a piece of iron over a good-sized forge. "This is Maggie Summer. She didn't believe we still have blacksmiths in Maine."

"Aye, but we do," said Tobias, carefully putting down the long piece of iron he'd been holding into the flames, and taking off his gloves. "A number of us. I've been here for a good number of years."

"Do you shoe horses?" asked Maggie, looking around the small shop decorated with iron hooks and doors and gratings of various sizes.

"I don't. A farrier would do that. Back a hundred years ago, a smith and a farrier might be the same person. Not today."

Maggie nodded, hoping she looked intelligent. "So you make iron gates and fences and hooks and such?"

"And spiral staircases and fancy signs, and candlesticks and candelabras, and whatever the customer wants. Right, Will?"

Will smiled. "Tobias has done some custom work for me over the years. If I find an old fireplace set that needs a bit of repair work Tobias is the one who can make everything right without too much to show that the piece has been fixed."

Tobias grinned. "Although you always tell the folks, don't you, Will? That a bit of work has been done."

"I do," Will agreed. "I also tell them if they need any additional iron work, you're the man to see."

"Last summer I did quite a fancy archway for a young couple's garden, on your recommendation, Will. Thanks for the referral."

"Glad to know everyone was happy," Will agreed.

Out on the street again, Maggie asked, "Do you know everyone in town?"

"Not quite. Tobias moved to Waymouth about twenty years ago. He's a nice guy, and a good worker. We had a few beers, got along, and he made a set of wrought iron wheels for my wife to hang her copper pots in our kitchen."

Maggie blanched slightly. Her husband had been killed in an automobile accident eighteen months ago. Will's wife had been dead for nine years. But he still spoke of his wife in a tone that said she'd been loved, and was missed. Maggie's memories of her husband didn't inspire tones like that.

"There are other craftsmen, and -women, in town, too," Will continued, unaware of Maggie's loss of focus. "Up a couple of streets is a woman who weaves blankets and scarves like the ones we saw at the Edgecomb Potters yesterday. There are other potters, too. And smiths working in gold and silver who create jewelry and small sculptures."

"I saw three art galleries on Main Street."

"That's just the beginning. Two good-sized galleries are in Waymouth now. One in an old school, and one in a nineteenth-century sail-loft. During the twenties and thirties Homer Thompson even headed a small summer art colony here."

Homer Thompson! Betsy Thompson's father-in-law. Clearly, according to the journal entries, whether any rumors of paternity were true or not, there had been a connection between Waymouth and Winslow Homer. She was tempted to tell Will, but it was Carolyn's journal. She should be the first to be told. "I hadn't realized there was an art colony in Waymouth," said Maggie.

"Not a large one," said Will. "Your new friend Carolyn probably knows more about it. I never paid much attention. It was way before my time." He pointed up the hill and to his right. "The Thompson home is over that way. They have a big place, with a barn studio and a couple of cottages left over from that period, I think."

Maggie made a mental note to ask Carolyn more about the Thompsons.

"During the sixties and seventies a lot of counter-culture types moved to Maine, and some stayed. They ran organic farms, and spent the winters creating art and crafts for tourists to buy during the summer."

"Not a bad way to live," Maggie said.

"Not at all," agreed Will. "For those with talent, and the ability to market what they created."

"It isn't easy for an artist to make a living anywhere," Maggie said, thinking of Carolyn's mother. "At least here the cost of living is lower than in the cities."

"Maine is generally accepting of those whose lifestyles are not so conventional," said Will. "It's been the home of a number of characters over the years." He stopped in front of the door to an antiques shop. "Shall we check it out? I haven't been in this place for years."

The shop hadn't wasted any space. Or paint. The walls were rough wood covered with nails, on which hung everything from nineteenth-century iron ice skates to badly stained Currier & Ives prints to a Beatles poster to a crude modern painting that might have been of a bird. Or a moose.

Will and Maggie looked at each other, but carefully made their way through the narrow aisles between tables covered with miscellaneous china and glass and twentieth-century souvenir dishes and figurines.

So far this was definitely not what either of them were looking for. The back wall was covered with bookcases. From a distance none of the books looked older than 1930s *Reader's Digest* condensed editions, but Maggie headed in that direction to check.

Will went up to the elderly man, his head haloed by tufts of gray hair, seated at the counter which might once have been in a general store. "Do you have any early fireplace or kitchen utensils?" The man looked at him as though he hadn't heard.

"Old kitchen stuff." Will said it loudly this time.

"Don't have no copper just now," yelled the man. "Fine pottery mixing bowls on the floor under that far table. You like irons?"

Will shrugged and shouted back, "Maybe."

"Got a bunch of those, on the bottom shelf of the bookcase, over by the stairs." He pointed. "Go ahead and look."

While Will checked out the irons (most of which turned out to be electric) Maggie quickly perused the bookshelves. Most of the books were twentieth-century book club editions, or well-read paperbacks. She opened one 1908 children's book of poetry, but the illustrations were not good, and all of them had been crayoned over. When she reached the bookcase section where Will was looking, she whispered, "Find anything?"

He shook his head. "This guy must buy up everything no one else will buy at flea markets."

Maggie kept herself from giggling. "Agreed. I need to wash my hands after just looking at those books."

Will held his up. He'd been examining some fireplace tongs, and his fingers were black.

"Lobster rolls?" Maggie mouthed quietly.

"You've got it," Will answered, and they headed out.

"Find anything you like?" shouted the owner.

"Not today," Will called back. "Thank you!"

On the sidewalk outside they looked at each other.

"The term 'antiques business' covers a multitude of merchandise," said Will.

"Sometimes a multitude of junk," agreed Maggie. "How ever does he make a living?"

"Maybe he doesn't. Maybe he just supplements Social Security," said Will. "I'll bet he sells some of that china and glass to people trying to find pieces to fill in sets they already have, or just single dishes someone thinks are pretty. Years ago he had some good stuff in there. I don't think his inventory has turned over in a long time."

Maggie shook her head. "I wish him the best of luck. But right now I'm thinking lobster rolls. Does that place we're going have a bathroom so we can wash off the dirt of the ages before we order anything?"

"My dear Maggie," said Will, taking her arm, "Maine is now fully equipped with indoor plumbing. In the towns, in any case."

After lunch, Maggie thought to herself, she would treat herself to more of Anna May Pratt's journal.

Chapter 9

⎯⎯⎯⎯⎯ ⊱✽⊰ ⎯⎯⎯⎯⎯

THE ARTIST IN THE COUNTRY. *Winslow Homer wood engraving from* Appleton's Journal, *June 19, 1869. Cover art, self-portrait of Winslow Homer, back to viewer, painting on a portable easel on a hilltop. A lovely young woman is looking over his shoulder at his work. One of three wood engravings Homer did that are said to be self-portraits. 7.5 x 11 inches. Price: $300.*

June 10, 1890
This morning was foggy and damp, but I tried to ignore the weather's unfortunate effect on the appearance of my hair as I walked the blocks to Jessie's home. I could hardly sleep last night, my heart was pounding so. This was our first day to pose for Mr. Homer! I chose my good blue dress, and was glad to see Jessie had chosen a pink one, so we did not look too similar.

She was more distracted than I, but whispered that most of her distraction was in the shape of Orin Colby, who has been paying her attention in the past week. He visited her home last evening. Her parents think a thirty-year-old ship builder would be a good match for Jessie, but Jessie only dreams of Luke Trask, who is at sea, and says she does not like redheaded men. Orin Colby certainly has red hair. It covers his face and his hands as well as his head, and Jessie whispered that she suspects it covers parts of him a lady should not even imagine!

I was selfishly pleased her thoughts were on Orin Colby, since mine were on Micah Wright. And indeed Mr. Wright was driving the wagon which stopped for us at Jessie's house! It is strange: I have been waiting for so long for another man to capture Jessie's attention, and now, when her parents are introducing a man to do just that, my mind was drawn to the gentleman near to me, rather than to the man I have been dreaming of, who is on the cold north seas.

Very little was said on the drive, but I am sure Micah cast glances at me, and I immodestly returned several. The drive to Prouts Neck passed quickly.

On our journey I tried to imagine what sort of studio a famous artist would have. We passed several large hotels of the sort patronized by summer residents. At first I thought we were stopping at an elegant house overlooking the ocean, but instead Mr. Wright pulled the horse over at a small building to the rear of the grand one, but still with a view of the sea.

He informed us that the large house, which he amusingly called the Ark, is occupied by Mr. Homer's father, who must be very elderly, considering the advanced age of Mr. Homer himself, and by Mr. Homer's brother and sister-in-law. The artist prefers to live in the small building behind it, more like a carriage house than a home, and no larger than the parlor and dining room of my own home. A second floor, where Mr. Homer's bedchamber is said to be, also boasts a balcony. Several of his canvases were hanging from the railing there, which I thought strange.

Mr. Wright told us Mr. Homer preferred this method of drying his work, and also liked viewing his paintings from the distance of the cliffs. Artists have their own ways of doing things, I have already observed.

Micah helped Jessie and me down from the wagon, and we knocked on the door. We had to knock several times because of the noise from carpenters who were at work adding a small room to the rear of the building, away from the ocean.

Mr. Homer and his dog, Sam, admitted us to a room empty of furniture but for a large table on which stood a lamp, a bench, and four straight chairs, on which he suggested Jessie and I sit. Sam sat between us. He cocked his head and looked from one to the other as if to ask what we were doing in his home. For a few moments I wondered that myself.

Paints, jars of brushes, and a few books and dishes were on shelves near the fireplace, where a kettle and several pots were set, appearing to be used for cooking. There was no stove. Stretched can-

vases and paintings were stacked and turned to the walls. A banjo and several crates of liquor were near a side window. One corner was filled with fishing poles, nets, and other equipment one might normally find in a fishing shack or barn. The room smelled considerably of pipe tobacco. Jessie later said it made her head ache.

Between the tobacco smell and the stink of, I must say it, the dog, I was quite relieved when Mr. Homer said we would be posing outside.

We were joined by "Madame" Homer, a very elegantly attired lady. At first I assumed she was Mr. Homer's wife, but soon found that she was the wife of his older brother. Clearly she was to chaperone us, which I found reassuring, since Mr. Homer is indeed a bit strange. I imagined an artist would be romantically dressed in a shirt and pants covered with paint smears. Instead, Mr. Homer was dressed much as Father is when he attends church services.

Sadly, Mr. Wright then left us. I had hoped he would stay with us for the day.

Mr. Homer looked Jessie and me up and down as though we were horses he might be interested in purchasing. "You've worn lovely dresses," he said. "When next you come, leave your hair down and wear simple blouses and skirts. I need fishing women in my painting, not ladies."

Jessie and I exchanged looks of some dismay as he then led us down a rough path to a small rocky beach. Mrs. Homer followed behind carrying a wicker basket we found later was filled with bread and cheese and fruit. When we reached the beach Mr. Homer pulled an old fishing net, crusty with salt water and smelling of fish and seaweed, from behind some rocks, and asked us to hold it between us, as though we were inspecting it to see if it required repairs. Jessie and I looked at each other and wrinkled our noses. We were not fishermen's daughters! At home we would never have considered touching such a filthy net. He explained he was "working up" some sketches he had made on the coast of England a few years ago, and needed us to represent the women he had seen there.

This was hardly what we had supposed we would be doing! But we had agreed to pose, so pose we did.

"When you come again, be prepared to remove your stockings, and pose in your bare feet," he told us. Jessie giggled. I wondered

what Mother would think of that, but I was silent. It all sounded very improper, but in Mr. Homer's mind it clearly meant nothing.

We later agreed between us not to tell our mothers we were asked to remove any part of our clothing. Truthfully, I was increasingly glad of Madame Homer's presence.

Posing involves standing in one position for long periods of time. Several times I thought my arms would fall from exhaustion from holding the net and I would be embarrassed, but Mr. Homer seemed to know exactly how long we could stand without moving. We would pose for perhaps twenty minutes, and then he would allow us five minutes' rest, during which we could eat some of the fruit Madame Homer brought, or walk a bit on the beach. Madame Homer sat quietly on a large rock and embroidered for most of the morning. I do not think she and Mr. Homer exchanged more than a few words during the entire time we were there.

I was much relieved when Mr. Homer announced about noon that "The light has changed!" We soon discovered that meant our posing was over for the day.

We followed him back up to his studio, where he bowed graciously to us, gave us each fifty cents, and reminded us to come dressed less elegantly tomorrow.

Artists are not like other people, I have decided. But it was not bad work, and I now have fifty cents I did not have yesterday. We will return tomorrow. With our hair down.

Chapter 10

⌒⌒⌒

DEATH'S-HEAD HAWK MOTH. *Hand-colored steel engraving from the* Butterflies and Moths *volume of* The Naturalist's Library *(1843), a forty-volume set of small, delicately illustrated natural history books edited and published by Sir William Jardine and engraved by Scotsman William Lizar. As was popular at the time, only the subject of the engraving is hand-colored; backgrounds are left in the original black-and-white, giving the engravings a classical feel. The Death's-head Hawk moth is so-called because the coloring behind its head is shaped very like a human skull. 4 x 6.25 inches. Price: $60.*

Maggie reached down, put her arms around Will's neck, and gently kissed his forehead. "Haven't you finished that coffee yet? It's a beautiful morning, and the sea air is calling me."

"Is that it? The sea air?" Will grinned, put his coffee cup down on the kitchen table, and reached up to kiss her properly. "I thought it must be my magnetic presence. Or maybe my aftershave."

"I wish you didn't have to paint the house. It would be a perfect day to go to the beach, or climb the rocks at Pemaquid and look at the ocean."

"It will also be a perfect day for paint to dry. The faster I get the house painted, the sooner we'll have more time together." He kissed the end of Maggie's nose. "Remember, I have that one-day show to do Saturday. That's another day we won't be able to play."

"But I told you I'd help out! We'll be together."

"True enough. So we'll look forward to that. For now, I need to work." He grinned at her. "I checked Walter English's auction house. He's having an auction Saturday, and the preview is open today and tomorrow. Why don't I finish up painting by midafternoon and we check out the showroom then?"

"It's a date. At least Aunt Nettie's house doesn't have an ell and a barn to paint, too." Maggie touched his cheek lightly and walked to the window, hoping she didn't sound too petulant. "I'll call Carolyn and see if she's thought of anything I can help her with before the funeral. Maybe I can buy her a glass of wine and some lunch."

"Why don't you walk over? Her aunt's house is only a few blocks away. Carolyn spent a lot of time here as a child, but it's been years. I don't think she knows many people in town. She may need a friend. Even though her aunt was ill, dealing with death isn't easy."

Maggie poured herself more Diet Pepsi, and neither she nor Will spoke for a few minutes. Both were conscious they'd made funeral arrangements for spouses who'd died suddenly, too young. "At least Susan lived a full life," said Maggie. "She was in her nineties."

"In her prime, so far as I'm concerned," said Aunt Nettie, as she joined them. "Haven't you young people finished breakfast yet? It's almost nine. I've been up for hours and walked to the post office and back besides."

"We're about to get going," said Will, clearing the dishes off the table. "I'm planning to scrape and paint half of the back of the house today."

"I'm going to see Carolyn," said Maggie.

"Take the casserole and the muffins with you," said Aunt Nettie. "The casserole's a nice one, with shrimp and rice. Tell Carolyn it'll freeze if she'd like. The blueberry muffins, too."

Maggie pulled a navy cardigan over her red Somerset College T-shirt. When she reached the street she turned in the opposite direction from the main street of town. The air was crisp and cool. The sun hadn't yet warmed it for the day. She was thankful for both the sweater and the opportunity to do some brisk walking. Seafood was not virtuous when it was fried or dipped in butter, and she hadn't been virtuous since she'd been in Maine. Walking might burn off a few calories.

She shifted the casserole and plastic bag full of muffins in her arms. The glass casserole dish was heavier than she'd anticipated.

Waymouth's streets were narrow, lined mainly with white Colonial houses with dark green shutters, although every sixth or seventh house had been defiantly painted cream, or boasted a red door. Lawns were not wide or deep, but most lots included flower gardens. Yellow daylilies vied with tiger lilies for being the most dramatic early August blooms. A teenaged boy in shorts was mowing a lawn, and a young mother pushed a double stroller toward Main Street. The low hum of traffic from the center of town and the drone of an occasional motorboat on the river were in the background, but the sound of gulls crying, song sparrows twittering, and chickadees calling to each other filled the morning quiet. Maggie didn't remember hearing birds in New Jersey. They must be there. She was probably just too preoccupied, or moving too quickly between cars and buildings to pay attention. Here in Waymouth nature asserted itself.

Susan Newall had died, but life was going on in her small Maine community. Maggie hoped Carolyn was feeling the same sense of calm and continuity she was.

She made a left on Spruce Street and counted three houses in. Aunt Susan's house was small, and needed a coat of paint. Salt air was hard on paint, and many of the houses in town could have used a refresher coat.

Maggie walked up two granite steps onto the small front porch and knocked. After a few moments she knocked again. A yellow Nissan with New York plates was in the driveway. Carolyn was home, unless she'd also decided to go for a morning's walk.

After the third knock Maggie decided to check the back of the house. Carolyn could be lingering over a cup of coffee in the backyard.

The back door was half-open. Maggie knocked again. "Carolyn? Carolyn, it's Maggie!" When there was no answer she pushed the door open.

Carolyn couldn't have answered.

Her body was sprawled face down on the faded 1930s black-and-white patterned kitchen linoleum. Her head was lying in a pool of dark blood. A marble rolling pin smeared with blood lay on the floor a few feet away.

The kind used for pastry, Maggie thought automatically. But this rolling pin hadn't been used to roll out dough.

It had been used to kill Carolyn Chase.

Chapter 11

⊶⊷

AT SEA—SIGNALING A PASSING STEAMER. *Winslow Homer wood engraving published in* Every Saturday *on April 8, 1871. Although Homer was later known for his oils and watercolors of sea scenes, and did a number of engravings of beaches and harbors, he only did three engravings of ships at sea. This is a night scene, with rough waves threatening a schooner's survival. One mariner on a high deck is signaling for help with a lantern beam. 8.75 x 11.6 inches. Price: $275.*

Maggie stepped carefully around Carolyn's body, trying not to look at it too closely. She forced herself to focus on what she had to do, not on what had been done to Carolyn. She reached for the old-fashioned black telephone hanging on the wall. It had been a long time since she'd used a dial phone. Why hadn't she thought to bring her cell phone? She'd left it at Aunt Nettie's, along with everything else in her red canvas bag.

"Waymouth Police? This is Maggie Summer. I'm at Seventeen Spruce Street. A woman has been killed."

After promising the police not to touch anything, she looked around the room. Dirty dishes were in the sink and two navy place-mats and two white mugs were on the table. One mug had over-turned. Remnants of the dark liquid that had been in it had dripped through a crack in the table onto the floor. Dirty pans were on the cold stove.

Maggie's stomach began to turn. Those pancakes she'd had for breakfast were not agreeing with a murder scene.

Carolyn had shared her last meal with someone last night. Had she argued with her guest? Or left the kitchen to be cleaned up later, perhaps this morning? Maggie didn't know her well enough to guess.

But Carolyn wouldn't have left most of the cabinet doors open, and two drawers turned upside down on the floor, scattering their contents all over the floor. Maggie bent down to look. Most of the papers were Fair Point Telephone, Central Maine Power, and doctors' bills. She was careful not to step on any of them. Especially those soaked in Carolyn's blood.

The killer was probably not looking for an elderly lady's utility bills.

Maggie squelched her curiosity and didn't look in any of the other rooms.

Waymouth wasn't a large town. The police would arrive quickly, and she didn't want to be found somewhere she shouldn't be. She'd been in Maine before; she knew being from away would already make her a suspect in the eyes of many Mainers.

She stepped around Carolyn and waited on the back steps next to the food she'd brought.

The day no longer seemed sunny.

Who could have wanted to hurt Carolyn? She kept thinking of her face as she'd happily shared her news with the genealogy group Tuesday night. Now, just a day and a half later, not only was her Aunt Susan dead, but Carolyn herself was gone.

She tried not to think of the pool of blood on the kitchen floor of the house Carolyn had planned to restore and make a quiet country retreat. The house in which she'd spent so many happy summers.

"I remember you. Maggie Summer. Will Brewer's friend. You're back."

Maggie stood up. She'd been so preoccupied with Carolyn's death that she hadn't heard the police car drive up. "Good morning, Detective Strait."

Nick Strait was an old friend of Will's. She'd met him when he was investigating another homicide the year before. Under the circumstances it didn't seem right to say "Good to see you again."

"You called to report a possible homicide."

"Carolyn Chase. She's on the floor of the kitchen." Maggie pointed, and moved herself and the food out into the yard. She felt foolish carrying around a casserole and blueberry muffins, but they certainly explained her presence. Any Mainer would understand bringing food to the bereaved.

Strait and a younger cop went into the house. They returned almost immediately. "I assume you found her?" Detective Strait had his notebook out. "You called the police department."

"Yes. I came to keep her company. Her aunt, Susan Newall, died Tuesday night."

He looked down at the casserole.

"I was bringing her some food."

"When did you get here?"

Maggie checked her watch. "About fifteen minutes ago. I knocked on the front door. No one answered, but I saw Carolyn's car, so I came around to the back. The door here was open."

"And you walked in."

"Yes. After knocking first and getting no response."

"Did you touch anything?"

"I walked to the telephone to call the police, and then came outside to wait for you." Maggie didn't mention her few steps to look at the rest of the kitchen. What could they matter?

Detective Strait sighed. "I suppose you're in town with Will again?"

Maggie nodded. "We're staying at his Aunt Nettie's house. Nettie Brewer."

Detective Strait raised his eyebrows a bit. "At her house this year? Interesting."

Maggie felt herself blushing. It was no business of Nick Strait's where she stayed when she visited Waymouth.

"How did you know Carolyn Chase?"

"Aunt Nettie introduced us. Carolyn was writing a biography of her mother, Helen Chase, the artist."

"I know who Helen Chase was, and I know Carolyn's been staying at her cousin's house. What I don't know is your connection to them."

Maggie thought quickly. Everything had happened so fast. What would make sense? The truth sounded a bit strange, but it was just that: the truth.

"I was helping Carolyn with research for her book. I teach

American Studies in New Jersey, and I'm familiar with nineteenth-century American art. Aunt Nettie suggested Carolyn and I might have interests in common. We met Monday night at Nettie's house, and then had lunch Tuesday, and went to a meeting Tuesday night."

Detective Strait was taking notes. "What meeting was that?"

"A group of people who meet at the Waymouth Library to discuss genealogy."

"I'll check with the library. Did Carolyn mention, during this short acquaintance, that she was being threatened by anyone? Scared of anyone?"

"Not at all."

"Had you been to the Newall house before? Would you be able to tell if anything was missing?"

Maggie shook her head. "I've never been inside the house before."

"When was the last time you spoke with Carolyn?"

"Yesterday morning. She called to say she couldn't meet me for lunch, as we'd planned. Her cousin had died, and she had to make arrangements."

Strait put his pad in his pocket. "You'll be staying with Nettie for a while?"

"A couple of weeks."

The detective nodded. "I'll probably need to talk with you again. Be nice to see Will, too. Why don't you stay pretty close to Nettie's for the next day or so."

It didn't sound like a question.

Chapter 12

—⟨⟨⟨⟩⟩⟩—

HE SAYS YOU MAY GO AND OPEN THE CHEST IN THE CORNER AND YOU WILL SEE THE DEVIL CROUCHING INSIDE IT. *Tipped-in illustration (lithograph) by Arthur Rackham (1867–1939) for story "Little Claus and Big Claus" by Hans Christian Andersen in 1912* Fairy Tales. *Picture of older man talking to younger man at country table groaning with food while alarmed woman listens nearby. Rackham was one of the major artists of the "Golden Age of Illustration." Born in London, his highly detailed illustrations were known for their strange depictions of ogres, trolls, fairies, and strange unnamed creatures hidden in branches or roots of trees. 6 x 5 inches. Price: $65.*

"Not Carolyn!" Aunt Nettie, who normally took even the most devastating news with the grace and perspective of her years, sat down hard on one of the kitchen Windsor chairs. "Oh, Maggie. How could that have happened?" She looked pale.

"Let me get you a glass of iced tea." Maggie was glad to do something that might help. "Sit a moment. Then we'll talk."

She put the casserole and blueberry muffins into Aunt Nettie's freezer, feeling as though she'd been freed of a burden, and reached up into the cupboard to where she'd learned tall glasses were stored.

Spearmint grew just outside the kitchen door, lemons were in the Flow Blue bowl in the pine cupboard by the refrigerator, and within a few minutes she'd made a pitcher of iced tea and filled three glasses with ice. "I'm going to tell Will," she explained, as she handed one glass to Aunt Nettie. "I'll be right back."

He returned with her, wiping his paint-splattered hands on a

64

tattered cloth, and sat down at the table, careful that none of the wet paint on his coveralls touched the furniture.

Maggie explained what had happened. "I assume your friend Nick Strait is going to be in charge of the investigation, Will. By the way, he said he'd like to see you."

Will shook his head. "Maggie, why is it that when you're around Nick and I can't seem to have a beer together without the occasion's having sinister legal overtones?" He sighed. "At least neither you nor any of your old friends are suspects this time. You won't benefit from Carolyn's death." He paused as they all remembered the previous summer's events. "I can't imagine anyone would gain from Carolyn's death. Or who could be angry at her. She didn't even know many people in town."

"Actually," Maggie said, "I've been thinking about that. I don't know who killed Carolyn. Or why. But Carolyn did tell me a little about her will while we were having lunch the other day."

"Why ever would you be talking about *her* will?" asked Aunt Nettie, who'd recovered somewhat. "It was Susan we knew would be dying soon. Susan probably left her estate to Carolyn."

"That's right," said Maggie. "Carolyn just found that out, although she'd suspected it before. She'd met with Susan and Susan's lawyer, Brad Pierce, at the nursing home on Monday. It sounded as though her Aunt Susan's mind was sharp right until the end."

"Thank goodness for that," put in Aunt Nettie. "If my mind starts to go, Will, just smother me with a pillow and put me down in Spruce Point Cemetery with the rest of the Brewers so I'm no trouble to anyone. Having your body go is enough of a curse. If your mind isn't with you any more, you might as well just fold your cards and skedaddle." She looked straight at Will. "You remember I said that, young man."

"Yes, ma'am," said Will, winking at his aunt.

Maggie took a deep breath. "In any case, so far as I know Susan's mind was fine. Carolyn said she'd thanked her, and told her she'd be happy to keep the house. She planned to live in it at least part-time, during the summers. I assume she was also getting everything in the house."

Aunt Nettie nodded. "Susan told me some time ago that's what she'd planned. She had some lovely things, you know; a few of

Helen's paintings of Waymouth, and some family furniture and china that was good. I don't know the fancy names for things, the way you antiques people do, but a lot of her furnishings were old, for sure. Some of the pieces are in those old pictures I showed you. Susan inherited the Newall family house."

"Carolyn told me her mother had given Susan some Maine paintings, but she'd only seen three or four in the house," said Maggie.

"There were six, hanging on the living room wall, right there for anyone to see, last time I visited her," said Aunt Nettie. "Maybe Carolyn didn't recognize them. Or maybe Susan moved them for some reason. I haven't been in Susan's house for a year or so. She had home health aides in there to help her last winter. They may have moved things around so she didn't have to climb steps or could reach things more easily. Those health people do that sometimes."

"Maybe," said Maggie, looking over at Will. "But I'd think Carolyn would recognize her mother's paintings wherever she'd see them."

"Someone could have put them away in the attic, or a closet," suggested Will.

"That's possible," admitted Maggie. "And her lawyer has been in and out of the house. That's how he got the trunk of papers. He might have put the paintings somewhere for safekeeping."

"What trunk of papers?" asked Aunt Nettie.

"Susan gave Carolyn a trunk full of old journals, diaries, and letters. She said they were family papers that were important to the Chase family."

Aunt Nettie frowned. "She gave those to Carolyn?"

Maggie nodded. "Carolyn asked me to go over them with her. She even gave me the earliest journal, from 1890, and asked me to read it. That's why we were going to have lunch yesterday. To talk about the papers, and that journal."

Aunt Nettie looked at Maggie. "You have the 1890 journal? Here, in this house?"

"Yes."

"Have you read it?"

"Only the first entries. The penmanship is hard to read, and the violet ink is very faded."

"Maggie, that journal doesn't belong to you. Even if Carolyn said you could read it, she isn't alive any longer. You need to return it to whoever is going to inherit her estate. Don't read another page." Aunt Nettie's voice was rising, and her hands were shaking. "You're not from Waymouth, and you don't want to be involved in anything you don't understand."

Will put his hand on his aunt's arm. "Aunt Nettie, I'm sure it's all right. It's just an old diary. Nothing in it can be that important. Maggie will give it to whoever the current owner is whenever we find out who that is."

"You don't know." Aunt Nettie turned from Will to Maggie and back again. "You don't know, either of you, what you're dealing with. Susan should have burned those papers years ago. She left them to Carolyn, and now Carolyn's dead. You have to get rid of them before someone else gets killed."

Will and Maggie looked at each other. Certainly Aunt Nettie was upset at the deaths of two of her friends, but she seemed almost hysterical about the ownership of the old journal.

"No one else will be killed," said Will. "It's just a journal. We'll give it to whoever inherited it. Right now we don't know who that is."

"Actually," Maggie said quietly, "I do know. The Portland Museum of Art will get everything in Carolyn's estate. But Susan Newall added a codicil to her will this week. She left the papers to me in case of Carolyn's death."

Chapter 13

THE ROBIN'S NOTE. *Winslow Homer wood engraving published in* Every Saturday, *August 20, 1870. An attractive young woman sitting in a fringed Victorian hammock on a porch, looking into the distance. 9 x 8.875 inches. Price: $195.*

It took some time for Aunt Nettie to calm down. Finally, after she'd had another glass of iced tea and a piece of cinnamon toast, she agreed to go and try to nap, with the promise they would all go out for dinner that evening.

Maggie and Will sat in silence on the porch. He reached out and squeezed Maggie's hand.

"We can't just sit here all day. We have too many things on our minds. There's nothing we can do about Carolyn or her papers today. Before the world turned upside down we'd planned to go to the preview at Walter English's Auction House this afternoon. Clearly I'm not going to get a lot of painting done, so why don't we go ahead and do that."

"Good idea," Maggie agreed, still thinking about Aunt Nettie's reaction to hearing of the papers. "It's just an old journal. I don't see why she's so flustered about it. Is it because I'm not from Waymouth? What could possibly be in those pages?"

"We'll talk later," he replied, glancing toward his aunt's room. "Away from the house." He hesitated a moment. "I'll change out of my painting clothes, and you'd better get that journal and bring it with you, just in case Aunt Nettie gets it into her head to go on a search-and-destroy mission. I don't know what she thinks is in that book, but she certainly has strong feelings about it."

Maggie nodded. The old journal would slip easily into the faded red canvas bag she often used as a pocketbook.

A few minutes later, Maggie's hair newly pinned up, Will in clean jeans, and the journal tucked inside her canvas tote, protected by a leather folder she often used for class schedules, they were ready to leave.

"I wonder if the trunk of papers is still in Carolyn's car?" Maggie said as they headed out the door.

"Not your issue right now. Her whole house is no doubt a crime scene. That might include her car. The trunk isn't yours yet. I'm guessing Brad Pierce, that lawyer of Susan's, is already working with the police. He'll let you know."

"He'll be the one planning the funerals and such, right? He was helping Carolyn plan Susan's," said Maggie. "Carolyn must have friends back in New York. I wonder if he knows who to contact there."

"She probably left an address book and a computer. Lawyers know how to do these things," Will assured her. "After the situation has calmed down we can ask him, or Nick, about the trunk. In the meantime, hold on to that journal in case anyone realizes it's missing."

Maggie made two mental notes. One, to keep the journal with her at all times. And, two, to read more of it as soon as she could.

Right now there was an auction preview to attend.

Walter English's Auction House was several miles from downtown Waymouth. Far enough from town to require their passing three roadside stands selling WILD MAINE BLUEBERRIES, one HUNTER'S BREAKFAST CAFÉ, OPEN 4:00 A.M. TO 2:00 P.M. DAILY, and a hardware store specializing in STABLE EQUIPMENT, BIRD SEED, AND FOOD FOR ALL PETS that offered pre-season specials on wood stoves and snow blowers. One store advertised WYETH PRINTS—ALL SIZES.

"Your competition!" Will grinned as they passed.

"In some ways, I'm afraid so," said Maggie. "They're selling images on paper. Posters, really. Not even collectable prints. But most people don't know the difference."

"It doesn't matter if they just like the picture and want something to put on their wall."

"I suppose not," Maggie admitted. "I hung museum shop posters on my walls when I was in high school and college. Even in my first apartment. But then I grew up."

"You learned to value the difference in the paper stock and ink and the way the printing was done," Will pointed out. "You've told me you discovered nineteenth-century prints when you were still in college, so you already knew about lithographs and engravings and hand-coloring."

"You're right. And a lot of people don't care about that. They just want a picture on their wall that's an image they like, whose color matches their upholstery or drapes. Today some museums and botanical gardens sell reproductions of eighteenth- and nineteenth-century botanicals in a choice of sizes, and sometimes even colors. I've seen them in catalogs, too."

"If reproductions are in catalogs and museum shops, then people must be buying them. That should be good for your business," said Will.

"Unfortunately, no. People are buying the reproductions, not the actual prints. They don't seem to see the difference. In fact, sometimes they pay more for the reproduction than I would charge for the original, which would have some continuing value. Their reproduction is worth nothing in the long run. It's just a piece of paper."

Will shook his head sympathetically. "The same is true to some degree in my business, primarily with copper and brass fireplace sets. People buy contemporary Asian and Middle Eastern copper and brass. Sometimes the new ones are even labeled 'antique,' or 'antiqued,' meaning 'styled like antiques.' People don't seem to understand the difference, or if they do, they don't care. Those 'new antiques' are not as heavy, and not as well made, as the older ones, and they're not worn in the same ways, although some are produced to look old. I'll even admit some of the repros are pretty good."

"Ah," said Maggie. "And I'll bet those eighteenth-century andirons of yours aren't as pretty and shiny as the new ones. They might even have a pockmark or two. They need polishing, too."

"Of course. That's why the modern ones don't have the charm and elegance and dignity of the real thing," said Will. "You know that."

"As a print that is a hundred and fifty years old might have a small fox mark on it. And the paper might be off-white, which to some people is unacceptable. They want their 'old prints' to look brand new, so they buy reproductions. They buy 'eighteenth-century' andirons from Macy's, so they never have to be polished."

Will grimaced. "You're right. Handsome Victorian sterling silver is going for low prices at auction these days because so many younger people don't want to bother polishing it. They want stainless steel, even for their 'good' company table settings."

"I'd rather eat my food from sterling knives and spoons, or even good silver plate, than stainless, any day. But we're now in the older generation, Will," said Maggie, as they pulled into the parking lot at Walter English's Auction House. Red, white, and blue PREVIEW TODAY OPEN flags were flying. "I wonder what today's children will think of antiques."

Will opened Maggie's door for her with a flourish. "You mean, will they stop texting each other long enough to rediscover the joys of polishing silver and brass? I'm not sure I want to think about that."

"You never know," said Maggie, as they walked through the auction house doors. "Right now a lot of older people are selling family heirlooms instead of saving them to leave to their children because they know their children don't want them. Instead, they're de-accessioning their valuables and treating themselves to a trip to Paris or China."

"And auctioneers are loving it," said a middle-aged blond woman coming up to them. "Sorry to eavesdrop. Welcome to Maine, Will! It's good to see you again, too, Maggie."

Will reached down and gave her a hug. "Rachel! I didn't expect to see you here! Maggie, you remember my cousin Rachel Porter, from last summer?"

"Of course I do." The murder of Rachel's daughter had made last summer unforgettable. "You look great, Rachel. I love your hair!"

Rachel patted her new, sleek cut. "I spent last fall mourning and feeling sorry for myself after Crystal's death. Christmas was absolutely the worst of my life. But, Will, you remember I was seeing Johnny Brent? Well, Johnny convinced me to go with him to Quebec for New Year's, and begin the year with a new experience. He was right. Life has to go on."

"Are you still working at the library?" asked Maggie. She didn't remember seeing Rachel there Tuesday night.

"Part-time," said Rachel. "I'm still helping out here during auction previews and sales. I decided to keep busy until Johnny and I decide what we're going to do."

"'Going to do?'" asked Will.

Rachel flashed her left hand. "We're engaged, Will. Can you believe it? After all those years of being a single parent, I'm getting married. We haven't decided when or where. But sometime this fall, after the summer folks have left, and life calms down a bit, we'll have a quiet ceremony."

"Congratulations, Rachel." Will bent down and kissed her cheek. "I'm happy for you. I'm surprised Aunt Nettie hasn't told me. She usually fills me in on all the family news within ten minutes of my arrival."

"You're one of the first to know. We just decided a couple of days ago."

"Rachel! There's a line at your desk!" The summons came from a heavy-set man in his early thirties who looked more like a construction worker than an auction gallery attendant.

Rachel glanced back at the bidders' registration desk in the corner and lowered her voice. "That's the new guy. Lew Coleman. Walter hired him to do a friend a favor, and he's driving the rest of us crazy. A control freak. I have to get back to work. But I couldn't resist coming to tell you." She grinned at Maggie and glanced at *her* left hand. "Now, if you two should have any news to share, you'll know where to find me!"

Maggie found herself blushing, and closing the fist of that significant hand as Rachel walked back to her desk. No news of that sort, and not ready for any, thank you. She turned to Will. "Rachel looks terrific! I'm glad she's found someone. I worried about her last summer. She seemed so alone after Crystal died."

"She did," Will agreed, looking after his cousin. "Somehow I never thought she'd get married."

"Life works in strange ways," Maggie agreed. "Why don't we each buy auction catalogs and take off on our own? We'll meet back here in," she checked her watch, "say, half an hour?"

"Sounds good," Will agreed, as he put his hand on Maggie's

back and they worked their way through the crowded showroom to where a young man was selling lists of all the items to be auctioned, with brief descriptions and estimates of what they might sell for. "Two catalogs, please," said Will, handing him a ten-dollar bill.

He headed for the back of the large room filled with "Furniture and Accessories," while Maggie went toward a side room labeled "Art."

On the way she passed tables covered by cartons of leather-covered books. A quick glance told her these books were not of interest to her, but her antiquarian book dealer friend, Joe Cousins, would have coveted them, not for their literary value but because they'd be useful to a decorator.

Someone who wanted an elegant library would buy these books for their bindings, no matter what the pages inside looked like. She smiled, remembering Joe telling her that one of his decorator customers had bought a beautifully bound set of nineteenth-century laws of Connecticut from him, and then had "antiqued" labels printed and pasted on their spines, identifying the books as the complete works of Shakespeare. His client was thrilled. They looked distinguished in his library, and he had no intention of ever reading Shakespeare.

No doubt these leather-bound books would meet a similar fate and be sold as books-by-the-yard to someone feeling the need to appear more "old money" than literate. Or maybe they'd end up in an ad for Ralph Lauren attire. Or as background for an interior country estate scene in a movie.

The peg-boarded walls in the Art room were covered, floor to ceiling, with framed oils, watercolors, prints, engravings, and Art Nouveau and World War I posters. Unframed work was in boxes on tables in the middle of the room. Each piece, or group of pieces, was labeled with its lot number, the number which identified it in the auction catalog, and would indicate the order in which it would be auctioned.

Some of the lot labels already sported blue or green dots. Maggie checked the back of the auction catalog to see which code Walter English used. A blue dot meant the item already had one or more "left bids." Those were bids by people who would not be present at the auction and whose bids would be executed by the auction staff. A green dot meant a telephone bid: someone to be called during the auction so they could bid live from a remote location.

She glanced at the artwork on the walls, but didn't see any black dots. They would indicate Internet bids. Some auction houses put a new dot up to indicate each bid. Walter English was more subtle. He wanted to let prospective bidders know there would be competition for some items, but wasn't hinting at just how much competition there might be.

An auction was no longer just open to the people gathered in one room. For the right merchandise a good auctioneer could entice bidders who were collectors, dealers, and representatives of institutions on several continents.

Most of the lots in the Art room were oils and watercolors. If the price were right Maggie occasionally added a painting to her inventory to attract different customers to her booth. Some people would always prefer an inferior oil painting to an exceptional print, to her frustration. At least if they came into her booth she had a chance of showing them alternatives. An oil painting or two could be bait.

Today she didn't see any paintings that fit with her inventory.

She'd turned to leave the room when she spotted a familiar style on a large canvas on the wall to her right and went to investigate. Sure enough, it was a Charles Dana Gibson. She had a portfolio of his elegant cartoons of gentlemen and ladies from the early twentieth century, when his drawings for magazines like *Life* and *Collier's Weekly* earned him a thousand dollars each, making him a wealthy man. Those were the works he was most remembered for today.

Although they were black-and-white, prints of "Gibson Girls" playing golf and tennis and making buffoons of the wealthy men in their lives appealed to modern women, and Maggie usually had a few in her business. In excellent condition they sold for sixty to eighty dollars each.

Gibson was one of the many artists who'd loved Maine. In 1903 he'd bought land on the island of Islesboro and built a home and studio there. Later in his life he'd painted many oils of his wife and other members of his family in Maine. Maggie looked closely. This, she suspected, was one of those, dated in the early 1920s. That would explain how it had ended up in a Maine auction house.

Today Islesboro was still an island divided between the homes of wealthy summer people and those of year-round residents who'd made their living on the island or on the water. Now it was more a retreat for those who had made their money in Hollywood or New York than an art colony. She wondered if Gibson's home and studio were still there, or whether they'd been razed to make room for more modern residences.

She checked her catalog. Walter English was estimating this painting would go for thirty to forty thousand dollars. Out of her range, but a nice acquisition for a museum. Or for the living room of someone who could afford to enjoy it for a while, and then perhaps donate it.

She moved on.

Most of the rest of the art was too recent to interest her. There were three N. Curriers (Nathaniel Currier's company before he'd gone into partnership with his brother-in-law) and several Currier & Ives, but they'd been selling slowly recently, and the ones here were not in good shape. Not for her. Condition, condition, condition. Those customers who objected to a small mark on an otherwise pristine print would never tolerate a tiny tear, even if the tear were in the margin. The margins on these Curriers had been trimmed, killing their value for a collector.

A box of old maps, most of them backed in cardboard and shrink-wrapped, was on one of the tables in the center of the room. Probably the auction house had done the shrink-wrapping for the showing; backing with cardboard wasn't archival and wouldn't preserve the maps for any length of time, but for now it kept eager lookers from damaging fragile paper.

Maps were hot these days. They'd come back into style within the last ten years, and seemed likely to stay. As with other "old paper," the most popular and rare ones (early maps of Manhattan that appealed to Wall Street brokers looking to decorate their offices, for example) were being reproduced, although attractive nineteenth-century maps were still around and could be picked up fairly reasonably, if you were lucky.

Today Maggie wasn't. These maps were in poor condition, and

didn't have the elaborate borders that more desirable maps by publishers like Johnson or Colton did. Those maps, if they were of New England or of the mid-Atlantic states, where she did shows, would be worth pursuing. But a small, torn map of several western states from an 1880s school atlas? Not old enough to be interesting, and in that condition not even someone from one of the pictured states would want it.

Maggie took one more look around. She'd seen everything there she needed to look at.

Except… Two paintings were on the floor in the far corner, leaning against the wall. She hadn't seen them before because they'd been blocked by a large balding man in a dark green Notre Dame T-shirt.

As he moved away, pointing out a Lawrence Sisson seascape to the woman with him (a Sisson would go high, Maggie thought in passing; Sisson now lived in the Southwest, not in Maine, and wasn't painting as many seascapes and harbor scenes as he used to) Maggie maneuvered her way through the crowd. "Excuse me," she said softly as she squeezed past two young women examining the maps she'd just finished glancing through.

She looked at the painting in front, and bent down to examine it closely. Then she looked at the other painting, and checked both their lot numbers and descriptions in her catalog. She circled both, and left the room.

She had to find Will.

Chapter 14

AN AUCTION SALE. *Wood engraving drawn by W.L. Shepard, published in* Harper's Weekly, *April 30, 1870. Scene at city auction. Auctioneer standing on chair, gesticulating as he sells an oil painting to the crowd of elegantly dressed men and women, some of whom are bidding, some examining household furnishings yet to be auctioned. Two men are removing a painting of a ship sinking in a storm, with people on the beach trying to launch a dory in hopes of saving its passengers and crew. 10 x 15 inches. Price: $85.*

It took Maggie a few minutes to find Will.

The auction house was filled with furniture, from Queen Anne mahogany dining tables to 1950s Formica dinette sets to New England pineapple-stenciled chairs to a pine church pew to Victorian oak horsehair sofas and chairs to Mission oak china cabinets. A pile of oriental carpets (or oriental-style carpets) several feet high filled the center of the room.

Next to the carpets were two carousel horses, a captain's chest (mint condition, she noted, wondering whether it was really all original) and a pale blue Victorian wardrobe with sprigs of wild flowers delicately painted on its doors. Painted Victorian cottage bedroom sets had been going low in the past few years, especially the wardrobes that were part of them. The closets of the past were out of style unless someone turned them into entertainment or office-supply cabinets. That charming and lovingly painted wardrobe would probably go for a couple of hundred dollars.

She slipped past a line of women checking the case of estate jewelry and silver. Vintage jewelry often fetched bargain-basement prices at auctions. She was tempted to peek, but the size of the crowd was discouraging, and right now she was focused on art, not jewelry.

She passed a rack holding several elaborately embroidered black-and-red Japanese silk robes and three or four mink coats. In Maine, those coats would sell for a couple of hundred dollars each. Despite the anti-fur lobby, their purchasers would be warm next winter.

Where was Will?

Light fixtures, some of them Tiffany or Tiffany-imitation, hung from the ceiling. In the back of the long room Maggie could see two mantels most likely removed from homes that had either been updated or torn down. That would be the place to look for fireplace equipment. And Will.

She passed three beds, a triumvirate of modern sofas, a Barca-lounger, and a jukebox. Auction houses took items of value. Most didn't define of value to whom, or how old the items had to be. That's what made auctions, especially country auctions, interesting, and meant buyers who were looking for genuine age should beware. Not everything in this room that looked old, *was* old. That was certain. "Vintage" would be the most overused word at the auction itself, Maggie would bet. It sounded serious, and meant nothing.

There was Will, examining a set of electrified mirrored sconces hung next to the more elaborate of the mantelpieces. She walked faster, moving between two teenaged girls admiring a dressing table and their father, who was focused on primitive decoys displayed on a side table.

"Will, you have to come outside with me. Now." Maggie tugged a little on his arm, as Will turned toward her.

"What?"

"I need to talk to you. But not here, where someone could over-hear us."

Will looked around. The room was full of prospective bidders and auction staff, and although the noise level was low, there wasn't anyone close to them.

"You suspect someone is spying on us? I'm almost finished look-ing. Did you find anything you want to bid on?"

"No." Maggie hesitated. "I need to talk to you!"

"One more second." Will smiled down at her. "The antiques won't get noticeably older in another few minutes. I'll meet you out front, as we planned. We'll talk there."

Maggie nodded. Clearly she wasn't going to get Will to leave possible treasures. She hadn't even asked him if he were going to leave a bid.

The parking lot was busy. Cars and vans with licenses from states as far away as Wyoming and Texas parked next to vehicles from New England states. This was summer in Maine, and Walter English could count not only on local and regional dealers, but on dealers from out-of-state who were here to do shows or were here on buying trips. Even better for an auction house were collectors who were in Maine on vacation, or people looking for a souvenir to take home as a memory of a Maine auction ("Such a bargain I got!") or an item to furnish their home. Or their second or third home.

The dealers' mantra was "Somewhere there's a customer for everything." The challenge was to find that right customer. Here at a Maine auction in August there was a good or better chance of finding him or her, and auctioneers knew it.

Where was Will? Maggie paced the parking lot. She needed to talk with him. Now. If what she'd seen was what she thought it was, they needed to talk to the police.

Before this auction took place.

Chapter 15

---❦❦❦---

THE AUTHOR PAINTING A CHIEF AT THE BASE OF THE ROCKY MOUNTAINS, *1841 hand-colored steel engraving by George Catlin (1796–1872) depicting Catlin standing with palette and easel, painting a Native American chief in formal dress, surrounded by other natives watching the process. Catlin was the first artist to study and realistically paint representatives of forty-eight nations of Native Americans. In the 1830s he traveled throughout what is now the American West. In 1841 he published* Manners, Customs and Conditions of the North American Indians. *This engraving is from that work. 6.5 x 8.5 inches. Price: $400.*

"Will! Finally!" Maggie took his arm and towed him toward a quiet corner of the parking lot outside the auction house.

"Whoa! I haven't been that long!" He divested himself of her hand and looked down at her, his blue eyes looking directly into her green ones. "Calm down!" That look usually made her melt. Right now it made her angry.

"I think two of Helen Chase's paintings of Maine, the ones that should have been in Susan Newall's house, may be here, listed to be sold Saturday."

Will frowned. "How could that be? Aunt Nettie said they were hanging in Susan's house a year ago."

"Remember? Carolyn told me she'd only seen three or four. There should have been more. We wondered where they'd been put."

"Are you sure the paintings you saw were by Helen Chase?"

"Almost one hundred percent. But they weren't listed that way.

See," Maggie pulled out her catalog, where she'd circled lot numbers 107 and 108, "they're listed as 'OOC, oil on canvas, paintings of coastal Maine, c. 1960.'"

"They're not signed?"

"It doesn't say so in the catalog. But they're signed 'HC' in the lower left corner, which I'm pretty sure is how Helen Chase signed her work." Maggie kicked a small granite stone across the parking lot. "If only Carolyn were here. She'd know for sure. She never said anything about her mother's work being consigned."

"Walter English is estimating the value of the paintings at fifteen hundred dollars each. If they were confirmed Helen Chase paintings, what would their value would be? Ten times that?" Will asked, looking at the listing Maggie was holding.

"Try at least a hundred times that. Her oils have been going up every year since she died, and I don't think many people even know about her Maine work. There wouldn't be comparable listings to check with. These paintings would be a major discovery for a New York auction house."

"Could Carolyn's Aunt Susan have needed the money for nursing home expenses, and decided to sell the paintings without telling Carolyn?"

"I suppose that's possible," Maggie said. "But if that were so Walter English would have known they were Helen Chase paintings. And even if they weren't identified as such when they came to the auction house, they're signed, and this is Waymouth. Auction houses do research. Walter English stands to lose major dollars if the paintings only sell for what he's suggesting here. He charges a fifteen percent buyer's premium of the sale price. Helen Chase is an artist with local ties. I can't imagine anyone here not putting two and two together."

"There are three possibilities," said Will. "One, that you're mistaken; the paintings aren't by Helen Chase. In which case we're getting excited about absolutely nothing."

He looked at Maggie, who was beginning to pace again. "Let's assume you're right. The paintings are by Helen Chase."

"Thank you," said Maggie, nodding to confirm the intelligence of Will's judgment.

"Two, assuming they are by Helen Chase, then Walter English

and his auction house are woefully uninformed about art. That's hard to believe, especially considering Helen Chase's ties to Waymouth."

"And number three," added Maggie, "the paintings may have been consigned illegally. If so, then Walter English doesn't have the right to auction them."

"He has the right to auction them as long as they came from a source he had no reason to question," Will added. "We're the ones who don't have the legal right to question. But my old friend Nick Strait does."

They walked together toward Will's car. It only took them ten minutes to get to the Waymouth Police Department. Detective Strait was in his office.

"So, you're here because you think that *maybe* two paintings at Walter's auction house *may* be Helen Chase paintings that *may* have been stolen?" Nick Strait leaned back in his chair and looked at Maggie and Will. "Will, it's always good to see you again. But I will say, the last couple of times you've come to Maine you've gotten involved with some interesting situations." He looked directly at Maggie. "I suppose I could call Walter and ask him who consigned the paintings. Although I believe that sort of information is normally kept private, between the seller and the auctioneer, if the seller requests anonymity."

"From the police?" Maggie blurted.

"I could press the question," Nick agreed calmly. "If an investigation depended on the information. But at the moment I'm investigating the death of Carolyn Chase. If the paintings had been stolen from her at the time of her murder, that would be one thing. But that auction's been set up for some time. I'm not an antiques buff, but I know auction catalogs are printed at least a few weeks in advance. My sister works at Kennebunk Printing, and she mentioned staying late to get them finished several weeks ago. If those paintings were stolen, they were stolen from Susan Newall, and there's no question about the cause of *her* death. Susan herself could have consigned the paintings before she went into the nursing home. Or even afterward, with the help of a friend, or of her lawyer. Or Carolyn Chase could have consigned the paintings. She was the one living in Susan Newall's home. If the paintings were, indeed, in that home as you believe, then she was the one with the most access to them."

Maggie sat on the edge of her seat. "Carolyn told me she wouldn't sell her mother's paintings of Maine, and there were only three or four in the house. And it doesn't make sense for someone to consign them and then sell them for the estimates listed in the catalog! In New York those paintings would be worth over a hundred thousand dollars! A New York dealer or an auction house in New York would get a much higher price than Walter English is estimating. He's not even identifying the work as that of Helen Chase."

Nick Strait took his feet off the desk. "The paintings are worth that much money? Over a hundred thousand dollars?"

"Absolutely. Helen Chase's work is getting more popular, and more valuable, every year."

"Then that is curious. Someone from Waymouth might not know precisely how much the paintings were worth, but they would sure know who she was. At the very least I'd think Walter English would put her name on the catalog listings. He knows enough to check prices with galleries and auction houses in New York, and let interested buyers there know when he has an item they might be interested in." Nick took a few notes. "Last year he auctioned a sampler a friend of Paul Revere's daughter made. Perfect condition, with the history of the girl and her family and everything. Her father was the one who took Revere to his boat that night. Sampler went for four hundred and fifty thousand dollars." Nick shook his head. "I couldn't believe it. Made CNN when that happened. Walter English sure contacted the right people about that piece of embroidery!"

"Who's had access to Susan Newall's house in the past year besides Carolyn?" asked Will, trying to get back to the subject at hand. "Aunt Nettie mentioned Susan had a home health aide there before she went into the nursing home."

"I think that's right. And friends visited her. Probably the minister. Brad Pierce, her lawyer. Could be anyone. I'll give Walter a call and check into who consigned the paintings." Nick stood up dismissively. "But you understand my focus is still on the murder investigation, not on the possible misappropriation of a couple of paintings. Even valuable paintings."

Will and Maggie also stood.

"Thanks for listening, Nick," said Maggie.

"I'll be in touch." He turned to Maggie. "I understand you're one of the beneficiaries of Carolyn Chase's will, Dr. Summer."

"Indirectly," said Maggie.

"For people who'd only known her a few days, you both seem very interested and involved in this whole situation. You're staying in Maine a while?"

"I have an antiques show this weekend, Nick, and we're both do-ing one next weekend," answered Will. "We're at Nettie's."

Nick nodded. "I know where to find you. Don't worry."

Somehow neither of them were worried. Not about that.

Chapter 16

DISTRESSED SAILORS, *c. 1820. One of a series of six aquatints of street criers by George Cruickshank (1792–1878) the foremost political caricaturist of Regency London. Shows three sailors, one with a stump leg, two with crutches, one pulling a model of a ship, all begging for money in the streets. ("Distressed" meant drunken.) Several major artists illustrated "Cries of London," as Cruickshank did here. 3.5 x 6 inches. Set of six, in three frames. Price: $400.*

June 11, 1890
It rained and the wind blew dreadfully today; almost a nor'easter, which is most unusual for June. A young man (I do not know if it was Mr. Micah Wright) delivered a message early this morning, before I had even risen from bed, saying that there would be no posing today. Instead, a wagon would be sent for Jessie and me tomorrow, should the weather warrant. Today Mr. Homer would work on canvases inside his studio.

Although the skies finally cleared in time for there to be a sunset, it was a long, dank day indoors. Mother set Sarah and me to embroidering pillowcases for our hope chests. Sarah finds such work more tedious than I, but that is because she does not see a need for such items. She is too young to be interested in men or marriage, and certainly she is not interested in pillowcases.

Mother sat with us and talked about the need to be prepared for whatever the future might bring, and be content with our fates. I kept my eyes lowered and focused on the pink and blue wildflowers I was stitching. I wonder what kind of flowers Mr. Micah Wright prefers? Or Luke Trask? Or perhaps men do not have preferences of that kind. I wish I had a brother of whom I could ask questions of that sort. There are moments I feel I know so little about men. But, oh, I imagine so much.

June 12, 1890

A beautiful day followed the deluge of yesterday. The wagon arrived for Jessie and me at seven this morning, but it was not driven by Mr. Micah Wright, and the aged gentleman holding the reins said little.

I wonder where Mr. Wright is? I wore my lavender skirt, which is last year's, and has a gray bodice to go with it, so as not to look too elegant. I also took a grayed apron from the kitchen, thinking the combination might appear more likely to suit a fisherwoman in Mr. Homer's eyes. And my eyes do reflect well in lavender, I am told, although Mr. Wright was not to see how the outfit set me to advantage.

I wore my hair down. Mother questioned my hair, but I was able to tell her the truth: Mr. Homer had asked for it to be worn that way.

She shook her head, but did not interfere.

Jessie did not take the pins out of her hair until we were well on our way. She said her mother was not as understanding as mine. She would never approve of Jessie's being seen in company with her hair flowing like that of a young girl.

We both felt quite reckless and free.

Jessie is worried because there has been no word from Luke Trask. Yesterday's storm would have been a rough one in the north sea.

I assured her Luke would send word with another fishing vessel, as he always has, but now I am worried as well. Luke is at sea and Micah Wright is not here. There is only old Mr. Homer on whom to practice lowering my eyes just the right distance.

Jessie prattled on again about Orin Colby, and how boring he was, and how dreadful it was to endure his attentions.

I will admit to feeling jealous of Jessie, despite our close friendship. Jessie has Luke's affections, which I have always envied, and now she has the admiration of Orin Colby. I would not have Orin, but he is considered a fair and honorable man, and I told Jessie so, but quietly, for she does not wish to hear well of Orin from me.

And I, for all Mother ensures I have lovely clothes and embroi-

dered pillowcases, have no beaux at all. If only Micah Wright were to pay attention to me, then perhaps I could put my envy of Jessie to rest.

The day went by without Mr. Wright's appearing at Prouts Neck. Mr. Homer hardly said a word to either Jessie or me as we posed again with the smelly kelp and net on the beach. My arms ached from holding it, and my mind ranged in directions a young woman's should not.

By the time the wagon returned us home I was weary and not in good temper. I told Jessie it was the wrong time of the month for me, but it was not.

I will need to hold my tongue in the future. Jessie and I need to remain friends for any of my plans to work.

Chapter 17

—⊙⊙⊙—

A Maine Sea Captain's Daughter. *Illustration by N.C. Wyeth for* Kenneth Roberts's *Trending into Maine, 1938, book of essays on the history and culture of Maine. N.C. Wyeth and Kenneth Roberts were friends, and the very proper mid-nineteenth-century lady in this lithograph holding her teacup while looking out a window at rooftops and a Maine harbor is said to be based on a family portrait of Kenneth Roberts's grandmother. 5.75 x 8.75 inches. Price: $70.*

Maggie woke Friday morning to the distant ringing of the house telephone. She opened her eyes enough to see the 1950s beige plastic alarm clock on the pine table next to her bed.

Seven o'clock. Too early for someone on vacation. She pulled the feather pillow over her head for a moment, and then released it.

Someone had answered the phone. Aunt Nettie or Will, or both of them, were already up. With a deep sign she stretched and resigned herself to giving up another hour's sleep.

By the time she reached the kitchen Will was already outside, painting, and Aunt Nettie was pulling a pan out of the oven.

Maggie took a deep breath. "What is that wonderful smell?"

"My favorite blueberry cake, and the lemon sauce I always make to go with it," Aunt Nettie answered. "Sit yourself down. It'll be ready in a few minutes."

Maggie obeyed without hesitation. It had been a long time since a maternal figure in her life had given such calm and explicit instructions, and she found herself luxuriating in the feeling of being cared for.

"Everyone makes blueberry pie, but my mother's recipe for

blueberry cake is a favorite of mine, and I wanted you to try it," Aunt Nettie continued.

"Shall I call Will?" Maggie asked. Certainly he wouldn't want to miss Brewer family-heritage blueberry cake.

"Don't bother. He's trying to get part of the back wall painted before the rain starts. Forecast for this afternoon and the weekend is pretty dire. There'll be plenty of cake left for when he comes in."

"A rainy weekend? That's not good news for the outdoor show Will is doing tomorrow." And for me, who volunteered to help out, Maggie thought. Rain was one of the reasons print dealers didn't do outdoor shows.

She poured herself one of the diet sodas she'd stashed in the refrigerator two days before. Aunt Nettie, clearly in charge of her territory, removed the blueberry cake from its pan, cut two generous slices, and poured warm lemon sauce over them.

"This is fantastic." Maggie savored each bite. "The lemon sauce is perfect with the blueberries. Is it a lemon curd?"

"Not sure what you'd call it nowadays. I just know Mother always served it with blueberry cake, so I serve it with blueberry cake," Aunt Nettie said, taking another bite. "Doesn't seem like summer unless I make it at least once or twice."

"I'd love to have the recipe," Maggie said. "If you wouldn't mind."

Aunt Nettie paused. "There was a time I wouldn't have given it to you. But I'm getting along, and someone needs to be able to make it for Will. Mother wouldn't want her lemon sauce and blueberry cake dying with me. I'll write it up for you later. Just you remember, it has to be made with wild Maine blueberries, now, none of your big New Jersey blueberries. They don't taste near the same."

"I'll remember," Maggie promised. "May I have another piece?"

"Go ahead, dear. Cut yourself one. There's plenty," said Aunt Nettie, clearly pleased her blueberry cake had found a welcome reception. "Oh, and you had two telephone calls earlier. Before you were up."

"*I* had two telephone calls?" said Maggie, sitting back down with another generous slice of the cake. The calls must have been from people here in Waymouth. Her friends and colleagues in New Jersey called her cell phone.

"Brad Pierce called. He wants you to call him back at his office.

At your earliest convenience, he said. I wrote his number down over there." Aunt Nettie gestured at a pad of paper near the telephone on the counter. "Then Betsy Thompson called. She said she wants to see you. She left her number, too."

"Brad Pierce? He was Susan's lawyer. And was helping Carolyn."

"That's right. I asked him when Susan's funeral was going to be, since he should be the one to know. But, just like a lawyer, he wouldn't give me a straight answer. Said Carolyn's murder was holding things up and they might hold a joint funeral, but nothing's been decided yet. Something about trying to contact family members from out of state. Can't imagine who. There's no one left in that line I can think of who's taken the time to visit Susan in years."

"Maybe Susan or Carolyn had information in their wills."

"Perhaps so. If they did, he didn't share it with me. I asked him what he wanted with you, but he wouldn't tell me." Aunt Nettie smacked her lips quietly and patted them with her napkin. Every crumb of the blueberry cake on her plate was gone. "I can imagine what Betsy Thompson wants, but how does she know you have it?"

"Betsy Thompson. Isn't she the one who's convinced her husband's descended from Winslow Homer?"

"She's the one all right. She married Winslow Thompson a few years back and thinks she married not only his money, most of which she's already spent, but every one of his ancestors as well."

"She was at the genealogy meeting at the library Carolyn took me to."

"Of course. I should have thought. Betsy's a regular there." Aunt Nettie leaned in. "That journal you have, Maggie. That's what she's after. Don't let anyone know you have it."

"She said she was doing family research, and was interested in the 1890s," Maggie remembered. "Carolyn told her about the papers and the journal, and said I was going to help with the research."

"Well, you just play dumb. Don't get involved with that woman. Winslow Thompson's a harmless enough fellow. Likes to paint pictures of the ocean and the rocks and the fall foliage and keeps pretty well to himself. Spends most of his time in that old barn studio his father built."

"So his father was really an artist, too? I'd never heard of the Thompsons until this week."

"No, likely not. Winslow's father, Homer Thompson, was more of a host than an artist. Had lots of friends who were painters. Inherited money back in the twenties, and used his house and land to show it off. Winslow and Betsy still live in that place, along with Winslow's son, Josh, who's a whole other story. Not a story I'd care to tell, since I don't tell tales. Anyway, in his day Homer Thompson, the old man, imagined himself a patron of the arts. He painted some himself, and he invited other artists to come and stay with him, room and board free, and use his studio. Had half a dozen little cabins built for them."

"Like an artists' colony."

"So he imagined. Seemed to most of us in town that those who stayed in the cabins did more drinking and talking than painting. Weren't a lot of famous artists like in Ogunquit or Monhegan, but there were always folks hanging around who said they were artists. Especially during the thirties, when board and room was hard come by. I imagine the thought of a summer on a river in Maine with food and drink and art supplies included must have sounded pretty good. Weren't too many who stayed for winter."

"Did Helen Chase know him?"

"She did. But she didn't get involved with him or his friends. She came to Maine to get away from the art world, not bring it with her. But she knew they were here, and on one or two of her visits she went over to the Thompsons for an evening."

Maggie stood up. "There's a lot I don't know about this town, and about Helen Chase. I guess I'd better start by finding out what Brad Pierce wants."

He answered her call immediately. "Ms. Summer? I mean, Dr. Summer?"

"Maggie is fine."

"Then, Maggie." The voice hesitated. "We've never met, but we need to come to an understanding. I had a call from Detective Strait last night. He was asking about two Helen Chase paintings. He said you and Will Brewer thought they might have been removed from Susan Newall's home."

"I saw them at Walter English's auction house. Carolyn Chase told me none of her mother's Maine paintings had ever been shown or sold."

The lawyer's voice interrupted Maggie's. "I'm sure you meant to be of help, Dr. Summer, but please remember this is a small town, and there's a murder investigation going on. We don't need extraneous questions distracting from the crime that was committed."

"I understand, Mr. Pierce. But I thought the paintings might have some connection—"

"I want to assure you, I'm not aware of any Helen Chase paintings having being removed from the Newall home. To be sure, Detective Strait is following up with the auction house."

"I appreciate that. Those paintings are worth a great deal of money," Maggie put in.

"Dr. Summer, just because we're from Maine doesn't mean we're uneducated. Everyone involved with Susan Newall's estate and Carolyn Chase's unfortunate demise is quite aware of the value any paintings connected to Helen Chase could have. Frankly, your coming into our peaceful community and accusing local people of crimes is not very smart."

"Are you threatening me?" asked Maggie. Her voice stayed even, but she felt the muscles in her shoulders tightening.

"I'm telling you the truth. A murder has been committed. The police have a lot of questions to answer. I'm asking you to stay out of this investigation, Maggie Summer. Just stay out."

The connection clicked off.

"Well," said Aunt Nettie, who'd been listening to Maggie's end of the conversation. "That didn't sound like a courteous conversation. What bee has Brad Pierce gotten into his bonnet?"

"I don't know," said Maggie. "Right now I'm clearly not on the top of his popularity list. He's not happy I told the police about seeing those Helen Chase paintings at the auction gallery yesterday." She sighed, thinking of the journal she had. "And you were right, Aunt Nettie. I'm not going to tell anyone except you and Will that I have that journal."

"You're a smart woman, Maggie. I knew that from the start," nodded Aunt Nettie. "You'd be even smarter to burn the darn thing and be done with it."

"No. At least not yet," said Maggie. "Right now I'm going to call Betsy Thompson and see what she wants. I have a feeling that whatever it is, I won't have it."

Chapter 18

"GUIMAUVE" (MARSH MALLOW). *A lovely woman wearing a dress of marsh mallow plant leaves and roots is giving a cup of medicine to a frog who is in bed suffering from a sore throat. Delicately colored steel engraving. The herb marsh mallow (not like the sweet white marshmallows used in cocoa) is a plant whose roots and leaves contain a slightly sticky substance that, when mixed with water, forms a gel said to soothe painful throats and stomachs and allow swallowing, or applied to the skin, heal chafing. Drawn by "J. J. Grandville," (1803–1847) the name used by French caricaturist and illustrator Jean-Ignace-Isidore Gérard, whose drawings satirized political and social figures. "Guimauve" is one of* Les Fleurs Animeés, *his "animated flowers," published in Paris just after his death in 1847. 7 x 10.5 inches. Price: $150.*

What Betsy Thompson wanted was to meet with Maggie.

"At the library, or perhaps we could have lunch together," she'd suggested. "Or you could come by my home for tea."

"At first I thought tea at her house might be interesting," Maggie explained to Aunt Nettie. "I'd love to see her home, after hearing you describe it. But that might commit me to staying too long. And I'd like to check the archives of the Waymouth Library to see what information they might have on this fabled connection between Winslow Homer and the Thompson family that seems so important to Betsy. I'm going over to the library this morning, and she's going to meet me there at eleven o'clock."

"Be careful," warned Aunt Nettie. "Betsy Thompson gets what

she wants to get, and I imagine what she wants right now is that journal. Don't be letting on you know anything about it."

"I'll be fine," Maggie assured her. "I'll be back in time to help Will if he needs me to help prepare for tomorrow's show."

Anna May Pratt's journal was tucked carefully inside her bag. Will's advice to keep it with her was still good. She made sure she had a notebook for any information she wanted to write down, and she checked to see that the small tape recorder she always carried with her was working. Sometimes it was easier to speak notes than write them.

Will was painting the second floor of the house, and her view of him from the ground by the ladder looked good. Temptingly good, in fact.

Luckily, heights were not her favorite thing, so she didn't feel enticed to climb up after him. Instead, she blew him a kiss, glad she wasn't expected to help him with chores that involved climbing two-story-high ladders, and realizing, not for the first time, that bedrooms at opposite ends of Aunt Nettie's hall had definite disadvantages.

Rachel Porter was working at the front desk of the Waymouth Library. "Morning, Maggie! I didn't think I'd be seeing you again so soon."

"The auction gallery didn't need you this morning?"

Rachel shook her head. "Several of us alternate working the desks there in the days before an auction. There's enough work to keep several shifts busy. I'll be there this afternoon, and during the auction tomorrow, and then Sunday, to help with accounting and call people who left bids. I still work at the library mornings. Are you looking for anything special, or just for a relaxing vacation read?"

Rachel looked so helpful, and she was Will's cousin, and certainly knew this library and Waymouth, inside out. But she also worked at the auction house. Maggie hesitated. "I teach American Civilization, and I'm always fascinated by library archives. Carolyn Chase brought me to one of the Tuesday night genealogy meetings, and it intrigued me. I wondered if I could see your genealogy section, just to browse and learn something about the old families in town."

"Of course," said Rachel. "That's one of our most popular areas. We get a lot of people coming to Maine in the summer to look for their roots. Let me get the key." She went into a small office in back of the desk and came back in a moment. "We keep our archives room locked so children, or anyone else who can't be trusted with old documents and papers, won't go in there. Just sign our guest book, and you're welcome to make yourself at home. If you'd like, I'll take you up and give you a tour."

Maggie signed her name, noting that the names Carolyn Chase, Betsy Thompson, and Kevin Bradman appeared frequently in the register for the past month. Kevin Bradman, she thought. The young man from Harvard who was working on his thesis. "I'd love a tour."

She followed Rachel up the curved stairway to the second floor of the old library. Tucked in a corner of the long corridor at the head of the stairs was a door bearing the brass sign ARCHIVES. Inside, brown and green file cabinets of all sizes lined two walls, map and document cabinets filled spaces between the windows that looked down on Waymouth Harbor, and the inside wall was lined with bookcases. Several short aisles of additional bookcases took up half the room. The rest of the space was filled by an old oak table surrounded by chairs. Maggie resisted looking out the windows and focused on Rachel, who was proudly pointing out the resources they'd collected.

"Old Waymouth newspapers and maps are in the document cabinets," said Rachel, pointing. "The green file cabinets hold folders filed alphabetically and filled with whatever information we have about each family in town. For some names you'll see clippings from local newspapers going back into the nineteenth century, research relatives or librarians have done at some point in the past, and letters, papers, or journals that have been donated to the library. On other families we have very little information. For the history of the town, the schools, fire companies, libraries, buildings, and so forth, look in the brown file cabinets."

She pointed at a shelf of binders. "Those are listings of local men and women who fought in our nation's wars, and of the graves in local cemeteries. People want to know where their ancestors were buried, but that's hard if we're going back more than a hundred years. Markers or gravestones have been moved, and inscriptions have worn off. Some private burying grounds weren't cared for and have pretty much disappeared." She smiled at Maggie. "If there's anything specific I can help with, ask, and I'll see if I can find it." She pointed at a box of cotton gloves on the table. "I know you're a professor, so I'm sure you know to wear gloves while you're handling old papers. When you're through, leave everything you've looked at on the table. The librarian who's working tonight will file it. We find that's the best way to keep track of everything. Any questions?"

Maggie shook her head. "This is wonderful. Thank you, Rachel. I'm impressed that your archives are so open to the public."

Rachel shrugged. "We don't have the money to computerize them. We have to rely on people being careful. So far it's worked. By opening everything this way we also hope people doing research will share their results with us, and add to our resources when they find something new, or are able to connect data in their own files, or in other archives. We get a lot of new information that way."

Maggie took one more look around. "Is any of your material on microfilm? Or scanned? Or available on the computer in any way?"

Rachel shook her head. "Maybe someday. For now, we're among the many archives in the country available to scholars and genealogists only in person."

"My students believe anything worth knowing can be found on the Internet," said Maggie. "Your archive is a wonderful example of how a lot of history is still sitting in boxes and envelopes and old books, waiting for people to find it, and as you said, connect bits of information into a story that allows us to understand what really happened in the past."

Rachel laughed. "I don't know how many puzzles are in this room, but there are certainly untold stories! Enjoy your time here. I have to get back to the front desk in case someone from this century wants to check out a book."

Left alone, Maggie first looked out the window, toward the harbor. The Waymouth Library building had been a bank back in the nineteenth century. It sat high on a hill so it would have a clear view of vessels entering and leaving the harbor. Perhaps investors stood at this window, hoping for news of cargoes they'd invested in.

Several small sailboats and a lobster boat or two were on the river today. Two dozen boats of various sizes had tied up at the Waymouth Yacht Club or at private docks, but most of the river was empty.

What must it have looked like when it was full of three- and four-masted vessels that carried salted dried fish and lumber to the West Indies and Europe, and ice to China and India?

Rachel was right. Stories were hidden in these file cabinets and books. Will's family, Carolyn's, and so many others. If only there were a place she could find out about her own family.

Maggie brushed the thought away. Her fascination with history had grown in part because she knew so little about her own family's place in it. She felt an almost magnetic attraction to a town where so many people knew where they'd come from, and why. Surely they understood themselves better, and could better understand their motivations, and their role in the future, because they knew their past and that of their parents and grandparents.

Or maybe that idea was just a fantasy. After all, who knew better than an American Civilization professor that each generation of Americans created themselves? And that many Americans invented their own histories.

She glanced at her watch: 10:15. Only forty-five minutes before she was to meet Betsy Thompson in the reading room. Which folder containing family history should she start with?

She resisted the strong urge to look under "B" for Will's family, Brewer, and instead looked for the family of the girl who'd written the journal that seemed important to so many people.

Who was Anna May Pratt?

Chapter 19

"APRIL." *Sweet Victorian lithograph of little girl wearing pink dress and large pink hat, wiping away tears, in the rain. One of a series of* Babes of the Year *published by Frederick Stokes in 1888. Illustration by Maud Humphrey (1865–1940), one of the foremost American illustrators of babies and children in the late nineteenth and early twentieth centuries. Today Humphrey is best remembered as the mother of actor Humphrey Bogart. Her drawings were, and are still, reproduced in ceramics and as dolls. 7.5 x 9 inches. Price: $70.*

The folder for the Pratt family was not very thick. Maggie pulled it out and took it over to the oak table.

On a yellowed sheet someone had lightly penciled: "Caroline Smith, b. in Augusta, m. Albert Pratt, place of origin unknown, moved to Waymouth post–Civil War. On roll Congregational Church, 1868. Children: Anna May, b. 1871, d. 1893; Sarah, b. 1874."

There. That was her Anna May of the diary, and her younger sister, Sarah.

Anna May died only three years after she had written the diary. She'd been very young. No date of death was listed for Sarah. Perhaps she'd still been alive when this page was written.

Maggie turned to another page.

"Sarah Pratt, m. Enoch Newall, 1894. Children: Josephine, b. 1897; Louis b. 1899; Henry b. 1904; Margaret b. 1906; Susan b. 1909." Susan Newall! That would be Carolyn's Aunt Susan, who'd just died.

A grand old woman, the youngest of Sarah's children, and no doubt the last alive. Aunt Nettie would probably know more about the others. Again, no dates of death listed, or marriages for the children. But Anna May, of the journal, the excited young woman who had posed for Winslow Homer, would have been Susan's aunt.

On the last page in the file a yellowed clipping was taped: "United in marriage in Portland, September 13, 1891, Miss Anna May Pratt of Waymouth and Mr. Luke Trask of Waymouth." Underneath it someone had written, "Kathleen Elizabeth Trask, born April 2, 1891, Waymouth."

Kathleen. That would be Helen Chase's mother; Carolyn's grandmother! So Anna May had married Luke, the young man who was fishing in the Outer Banks, and given birth to baby Kathleen six and a half months later.

At the end of the folder was a note: "For Helen Chase, see Artists of Waymouth file." I'll do just that, thought Maggie. Thanks for the tip, Anonymous Librarian.

If there had been any doubt that Anna May Pratt of her journal was related to Helen, and then to Carolyn, this note was the answer. Anna May was Helen's grandmother, and Carolyn's great-grandmother.

But why was that important to Betsy Thompson? The journal did prove that Anna May was among the young Maine women who posed for Winslow Homer, but why should that be important to the Thompson family? Anna wasn't a Thompson.

Clearly there was more to know.

"Dr. Summer?"

Maggie looked up. "Yes?" The young man speaking looked very familiar but for a moment she couldn't place him. She was still back in the 1890s, wondering why Anna May had died so young. In childbirth? An accident? Fever of some sort?

"I'm Kevin Bradman. We met at the genealogy meeting."

"Of course." Maggie collected her thoughts. "You're writing your dissertation on Maine artists. I'm sorry to have taken a second to place you."

"I know what it is to get totally involved in these papers," Kevin said companionably, joining her at the table. "I've spent a lot of hours here. It's tempting to pick up just one more folder and see if you can find another story, or the continuation of one."

"Exactly. That's what I was thinking," agreed Maggie. "I'm

amazed at how openly the library shares information. You know what most university and historical society archives are like: they practically fingerprint you before you enter."

Kevin nodded. "I've had my driver's license and student ID copied. To access some stacks I've had to have a letter of introduction on file ahead of time from the head of my department. Here, you just sign your name and walk in." He looked at Maggie's hands. "At least you're wearing the cotton gloves. I've been here days when people weren't even using them."

She shook her head. "Well, I'm taking mine off now. I have to meet someone downstairs. I assume we put the ones we've worn in the basket over there?" She pointed at a brightly painted blue basket on the table just inside the door.

"Exactly," said Kevin, reaching over and pulling on a clean pair himself. "My turn to put some on."

"What are you researching today?" Maggie asked idly, as she picked up her canvas bag.

"I'm checking what buildings, inns, stores, and so forth were here in the 1920s and '30s. I'm writing about the artists, as you remembered, but I want to be sure I don't mention any of their local haunts in years the businesses weren't open, or name the wrong proprietors."

"Good luck with that! It was nice seeing you again."

"And you," said Kevin, opening his laptop.

The reading room downstairs was lined with bookshelves, but bright with sun from tall windows on each end. The windows were framed by the sort of inside shutters common in northern New England homes before such amenities as storm windows kept out the piercing winds of nor'easters.

Their views framed the Waymouth village green, still the center of the town, and the hill leading down Main Street to the Madoc River. The Waymouth Inn, where Maggie'd had lunch with Carolyn such a short time ago, was on the other side of the green, and the Congregational Church stood at the top of the hill, overlooking the village as it had for the past two and a half centuries.

I wonder if Anna May was married in that church, Maggie thought. She could picture Anna and her family stepping out into the sunlight after services on a summer day, and Anna giggling with her best friend about the adventures they were having that summer of 1890 with the old artist on Prouts Neck.

"Maggie! You've arrived ahead of me!"

Perhaps Betsy Thompson had just come from Cut 'n' Curl, the local hairdressing salon, which one of Will's many cousins owned and operated. In any case, every one of her various curls was certainly sprayed in place, and Maggie had to admit with a strange fascination, even her eyebrows looked as though either they, too, had been fastened in place, or not content with what nature had awarded her, she had drawn others on top of those already there. In any case, her eyebrows were memorable.

Maggie, in her relatively new jeans and T-shirt, had felt a bit "from away" at the auction house yesterday. Today, in a similar outfit, she felt what her secretary, Claudia, would have called "considerably unplanned." Which if, like Claudia, you were from Bayonne, New Jersey, was not a compliment.

Betsy was definitely planned. Her jeans were a shade of blue that, if not made to order, should have been. "Skybluepink," her father would have called them. And her tailored long-sleeved shirt, silk scarf, and hat all matched them. Maggie couldn't resist looking to see if her socks matched, too, but of course, that was a ridiculous thought. It was August, after all. Betsy was wearing high-heeled sandals. Her toenails matched. Betsy Thompson definitely would have stood out in a crowd. Particularly a Waymouth crowd. How long had Aunt Nettie said she'd lived here?

Betsy waggled her left hand at Maggie, perhaps for exercise, and perhaps to show off the rock that was somehow attached to the third finger of her hand. "How long have you had to wait? I hope not long. I had some errands to do, and then I stopped at the front desk to chat with Rachel for a while. She's the dear woman who works here. And here I am!"

Maggie nodded. Clearly, she was.

"Why don't we sit down?" Maggie gestured at several dark red leather chairs grouped comfortably near the fireplace on the center wall of the room. "You called me," she pointed out, once they were both seated.

"I did, indeed. This has been such a dreadful week for everyone. I heard you were the poor soul who discovered Carolyn's body.

What an awful experience! You must still be in shock. I would be in shock. I can't imagine anything worse than that."

"No," said Maggie.

"Whatever have you been doing since then?"

Playing it very cool, thought Maggie. She said, "Some antiquing. My friend Will is doing an antiques show tomorrow, and I'll be helping him. Maine is so lovely in the summertime; I'm very lucky to have friends here to visit. It's like living inside a postcard, isn't it? I was admiring the view down the street when you came in. I'm hoping to get down to see Pemaquid before I leave, and certainly eat more lobsters. And Maine blueberry pie is my very favorite."

"Yes." Betsy hesitated. Clearly she hadn't expected to discuss tourist attractions. "And Carolyn's estate. I understand you're inheriting some of Carolyn's papers."

"I didn't know Carolyn well, you know. Her estate hasn't been probated yet. I believe she said she was leaving most of her things to the Portland Museum of Art."

"Possibly. But that night we met here, at the genealogy meeting, she said she had a trunk of papers from her family. You were going to help her with them."

"She did say that, didn't she? She died so horribly, so soon after that." Maggie looked down at her hands. "It's sad to think of, Betsy. I would have liked helping her, of course. Now she's gone."

"And the papers?" Betsy leaned forward, as though Maggie was going to produce them at any moment.

"I assume they'd be in her house, which I understand the police have sealed. Or her lawyer has them. Wouldn't you think that's where they'd be?"

"I guess so. I just thought maybe…you might have them." Betsy looked unconvinced. "It sounded that night as though Carolyn was going to give some to you."

"Everything happened so fast. She wanted to read them first, before I looked at them. Wouldn't you have wanted to read them first?"

"Well, yes."

"By the way, at the meeting you mentioned that some people think your husband's grandfather was Winslow Homer. Do you have any proof of that?"

Betsy leaned over, and spoke in a stage whisper. "It was a deep family secret for years. My husband's father was conceived out of wedlock, you see. Winslow Homer never married."

"I knew that."

"So it wasn't talked about outside the family until it could be... until the people involved were dead."

"Winslow Homer died in 1910," Maggie remembered.

"True enough," Betsy agreed. "But the man who married his son's mother, who made the poor boy legitimate, Wesley Thompson, didn't die until 1925. It was after that his mother told him that he was Winslow Homer's son."

"No one knew until then?" asked Maggie.

"There were rumors, of course, but no one admitted anything," said Betsy. "But the Thompsons have talent. That's the real proof. Anyone looking at their work could tell that. It's only those stupid galleries in New York who don't believe their parentage without documents."

"Galleries?"

"They'd hang my Winslow's work in a minute if we could prove what everyone in Waymouth has known for years: that he is Winslow Homer's grandson. Maybe they'd do a retrospective of three generations: Winslow Homer; his son, Homer Thompson; and now, Winslow Thompson. But they won't even look at his canvases."

Maggie couldn't help being intrigued. "I'd like to look at his work, Betsy. Do you have any of your father-in-law's paintings I could see, too?"

"Of course!" Betsy broke into a wide smile. "Usually we have some of his oils displayed in one of our barn galleries, but this summer Winslow has been working so hard he hasn't even taken the time to hang anything. But I'd love for you to see what we have. You might even know some galleries in New Jersey or New York we could contact."

"My contacts are mainly for nineteenth-century prints," Maggie pointed out.

"But there's the nineteenth-century connection, my dear. Winslow Homer, remember! He's family! You must come! Perhaps tomorrow?"

"I can't tomorrow. I'm helping Will with the antiques show."

"Then Sunday. Do come Sunday afternoon. About four o'clock.

Bring your friend Will, too! We'll have tea. What fun! You can see where everyone painted, and lived, back when there was an artists' colony right here in Waymouth. Kevin can show you that part."

"Kevin Bradman? It's nice of you to think of inviting him, too. I'd like to get to know him better."

"Invite him?" Betsy's mouth laughed, although her amazing eyebrows never moved. "Maggie, I don't have to invite Kevin. He's living with Josh and me this summer. He's right there with us, all the time."

Chapter 20

—— ⚬⚬⚬ ——

COMING ON THE COAST OF MASSACHUSETTS IN A SNOW STORM.
Unsigned 1859 wood engraving from Harper's Weekly *showing three-masted schooner, displaying American flag, fighting to get to shore in a winter nor'easter. Shore, marked by a lighthouse, is on the right. 5.5 x 10 inches. Price: $95.*

June 15, 1890
After church today Jessie confided to me that she can wait no longer. She is going to write a letter to Luke. The seas have calmed, but no ships have yet arrived from the Grand Banks with messages from him, and she can hardly sleep for worrying. Orin Colby has invited her to the launching of the Lisa, *a fishing sloop his boatyard built this past winter for Captain Dodge. Jessie has ascertained that Captain Dodge is anxious to outfit the* Lisa *and sail for Yarmouth and Halifax within the week. Her plan is to send a letter for Luke Trask with him.*

I, of course, agreed that this was a fine idea, but suggested I deliver the letter to Captain Dodge, rather than have her do so in the presence of Orin Colby.

She readily accepted my offer. We are to meet tomorrow so she can give me her letter before the launching.

Jessie's confidences could make it all too simple for me to turn Luke's love for her toward me. At first I planned to merely destroy her note, which no doubt is full of sweet endearments and concerns. But then I devised a still better plan.

Luke shall receive two letters from dear friends in Waymouth. I shall write to him myself.

105

Chapter 21

⎯⎯⎯⊗⊗⊗⎯⎯⎯

A NOR'EASTER: SOME LOOK WELL IN IT. *Lithograph by Charles Dana Gibson, 1900. Four women in "Gibson Girl" attire, including hats (which they are holding on their heads) standing on a windy boardwalk with two dogs, looking out at a stormy sea. Hefty woman is looking askance at the shapely young lady whose wind-blown clothing is revealing her hourglass-shaped figure to advantage. American artist Gibson (1867–1944) is best known for his pen-and-ink drawings of the first American pin-up girl, known as "the Gibson Girl": the idealized American woman, who was young, smart, athletic, and stylish. His drawings often make fun of the upper classes. They were most popular from 1900–1910. 11.5 x 17 inches. Price: $60.*

Maggie woke out of heavy sleep to find Will's lips on hers, and his arms around her. She reached up and snuggled into his chest for a long, luxurious moment until she realized he was wearing a heavy flannel shirt. She blinked quickly and pushed him back a little as he laughed quietly into her long hair, now partially unbraided on her pillow.

"Wake up, Sleeping Beauty!" he whispered into her ear. "It's four in the morning, and we need to be on the road by four-thirty. I'm going downstairs to put coffee on for me, and make egg sandwiches for us to eat on the way."

"Ohhhh…" Maggie turned and pulled the pillow over her head.

Will pulled it off, and turned on the lamp next to her bed. "Afraid not. Get yourself up and beautiful. I'll see you downstairs." He paused a moment as they both listened to the howling gale-force wind and rain pounding against the windows and roof. "The morning seems to call for warm clothes, and whatever rain gear you brought. You can use Aunt Nettie's extra slicker. Do you have sneakers to wear during setup? The field is going to be muddy." He slapped her companionably on her rear. "Rise and shine, my lady."

Maggie sat up and shook her head. "This is why I don't do outdoor shows."

"I know. But I do. And you volunteered." Will pulled what was still intact of her long braid. "See you in the kitchen."

Within a few minutes the sound of coffee beans grinding filled the house. It was a good thing Aunt Nettie was slightly hard of hearing, Maggie thought, as she got herself up and washed, and pulled on jeans, sneakers and a long-sleeved T-shirt. A sweatshirt, too, she decided. It was chilly. She optimistically stuffed a long skirt, sandals, and a dressier top in her all-purpose red canvas bag, plus some lipstick and gray eye shadow and matte powder for later. Any attempts at makeup now would be farcical. Not to mention that it would smear or wash off entirely in the storm. As a last touch she added one of her signature rhinestone "M" pins to the sweatshirt for antiques show luck.

It had been raining for hours now. It would have to stop soon, wouldn't it?

By the time she reached the kitchen Will was sipping one cup of coffee and had filled a tall green L.L. Bean travel mug and thermos with a backup supply. He also had a cold six-pack of her diet soda ready and waiting. He knew his lady's preference for caffeine delivery.

"I made each of us two sandwiches." He handed her the six-pack and a paper bag. "We can get more food at the show if the vendors' stands haven't washed away. The folks from *Maine Antique Digest* usually arrive early and seduce us possible advertisers with free coffee, tea, doughnuts, and bagels before the show opens." He glanced around the kitchen. "I think we're set. I put my cash box in the RV yesterday afternoon, and Aunt Nettie knows we'll be home for dinner at about seven tonight. The show closes at four. With two of us we should be able to pack out in an hour or two, and get back to Waymouth by then."

He handed Maggie a slicker.

She put it on, leaving the top hook open. He reached over and carefully attached it for her. "It's *very* wet outside, Maggie," he said. He picked up the thermos and the travel mug. "Let's go."

Maggie had only one question as Will navigated the country roads whose twists and turns, some of them flooded, led them north and west toward the fairground where the antiques show was scheduled. "Your booth is under a tent, isn't it?"

"It is," he nodded, reaching over to pat her hand. "Not to worry. Some dealers set up tables around the rear of their van or truck, or bring their own tents. I don't know what they'll do on a day like this. The grounds will be very muddy. A few people may forfeit their deposits and not come. But the show contract said it would be held 'rain or shine,' so most of us will be there."

"Let's just hope some customers come, too," said Maggie.

"Did you read any more of the old journal last night?" Will changed the subject, as he wiped the inside of the windshield with his hand and turned on the defogger.

"A little. At least two young women from Waymouth posed for Winslow Homer: Anna May Pratt, who wrote the journal, and her friend Jessie. It's fun to read what they thought of the slightly strange old man (he must have been in his early fifties then) who dressed very elegantly while he painted and asked them to dress in fisherwomen's clothes to pose! Someone should transcribe the journal. I can imagine several museums, including the Portland Museum of Art, which now owns Homer's studio at Prouts Neck, that would love to publish the contents. But the ink is faded, and it's difficult to make out some of the words, so reading takes time. So far as I've read, Anna May is more focused on herself and her friend Jessie and their beaux, or lack thereof, then she is on an old artist."

"No mad love affairs with old man Homer as yet?"

"Not even close!" answered Maggie. "Although Anna May did think his assistant, or go-fer of some sort, was pretty hot. Or whatever would have been the 1890 equivalent of hot."

"Handsome and debonair? Maybe he was one of my ancestors!"

"Not a bad description," Maggie admitted. "But unless the Brewers had cousins with the last name Wright, I don't think he was a relative of yours!"

A line of vans and trucks had formed at the entrance to the fairground. "Not a good sign," Will pointed out, putting a card on his windshield that indicated his booth number and assigned parking spot. "It's after six o'clock, right?"

Maggie checked her watch. "Six-fourteen."

"Usually by now everyone's on the grounds unpacking. Something's not right."

"It's still pouring," Maggie pointed out, needlessly, as the windshield wipers continued their relentless rhythm.

A man in his seventies, wearing high boots and complete yellow sou'wester, from large hat to vinyl pants and jacket, slowly made his way down the line of vehicles from one driver to another. Despite his foul-weather gear, he was completely soaked; his beard and eyebrows were dripping, as were the edges of his hat.

"Sorry, folks." He looked at the card on Will's dashboard. "One of the access roads to the fairgrounds washed out, so we're moving people around a little. You're one of the lucky ones. Tent Four hasn't blown down yet. When folks in front of you start moving, stay over to the left. Park in back of Tent Three instead of where you usually park, okay?" He pointed.

Will nodded.

"Oh, and none of the porters who said they'd be here today have shown up. Hope that won't be a problem."

"No." Will glanced at Maggie. "Brought my own porter today."

"Good. Glad something's not a problem for someone," the old man muttered as he went on to the rental van in back of Will's RV.

"So far so good," said Maggie. "Have another half sandwich?"

"Good plan," agreed Will. "They'll be soaked as soon as we get out of here."

The spot where they finally parked was so muddy that Will was concerned about their being able to leave in the afternoon, but they had no time to think much about that. By the time they'd parked and checked out the booth location it was almost seven o'clock. Only two hours until show time.

Some helpful person had put boards down on the spaces between the booths where customers would walk, but even those walkways, inside the tents, were sinking rapidly into the mud. A torrent of muddy water ran down the slight rise outside Tent Four and right through it, leaving all the booths several inches deep in mud. Just walking was a challenge. Maggie's sneakers filled with mud almost immediately, and after four or five trips to the RV for cartons, she felt wet through to her underwear despite Aunt Nettie's slicker.

Of greater concern was the inventory itself.

Around them furniture dealers were drying sideboards with stacks of towels and propping the legs of mahogany tables and chairs up on blocks of wood, or putting them inside empty cans that they'd brought.

No one dared bring anything made of paper through the heavy rains into the show. Maggie saw one dealer using a blanket to mop water off what was probably a seventeenth-century oil painting.

She wasn't going to do much buying at this show unless the rain stopped. If anyone had prints, they were keeping them inside vans and trucks.

Will and Maggie put up the portable tables he'd brought ("theoretically portable," Maggie thought, her back already aching) and she covered them with the required inflammable ("just what we need today") tablecloths.

Will emptied a plastic bag onto one of the now-covered tables; it was full of old towels. "I'll bring in the brass and iron andirons and screens; you dry them with the towels. Dampness is the enemy."

"Dampness!" Maggie thought. Everything was dripping. Including her.

Above them the tent (the one that "hasn't blown down yet," she remembered) was billowing crazily in the wind, and rain was beginning to pelt into the booths along its seam lines. Two booths over, a china dealer joked, with an edge of hysteria, about setting out teacups to catch the drips and wondering if the splashing drops would play "Taps."

What about the dealers scheduled to be in the tent that *had* blown down? Not to speak of anyone who was supposed to set up outside. Maggie hoped they were sane enough to take one look at the fairgrounds and the sky and leave.

This was ridiculous.

She kept drying Will's iron and brass and copper, trying not to further smear price tags already almost illegible from rain. Nothing was really dry.

Will filled five tables with cast iron trivets and ice tongs, brass mortars and pestles, andirons, eighteenth-century iron skillets, match safes, S-shaped hooks for hanging kettles and pots, forks, knives, pairs of English bellows, butter presses, and tin, brass and early silver candlesticks. The two Victorian brass fireplace screens he put in front of one table immediately began sinking into the mud.

Will looked at the screens, and then at Maggie. "That's it. I have more, but I usually arrange items on the ground. Clearly I'm not going to do that today."

Inside the tent the ground was running with water. Usually dealers hid emptied boxes, bags, and packing materials under their tables. Today Will and Maggie piled them on the two folding chairs they'd been assigned. It didn't look artistic. But at least they'd be able to use the items later.

"What time is it?" Maggie opened her third diet cola of the morning. Anything could be borne better with a little caffeine. But if she were ever, ever tempted to do an outdoor show, she was going to remember this one.

"Show time in about fifteen minutes. We've done what we're going to do," Will said, giving her a hug. "Want to look at what the other dealers have brought?"

Maggie shook her head. "In a few minutes. There's no place to sit, so right now I just want to stand and drink my soda and wish I were somewhere dry and warm."

Just then the wind howled louder than usual and the tent swayed dramatically. Lights at the top of the tent blinked off and on. The soaked dealers stopped whatever they were doing, and their laughter filled the tent.

What could you do but laugh?

"The antiques business. Truly a glamorous profession, don't you think?" Will said. "Just think of *Art and Antiques* magazine. And Sotheby's."

"And the Park Avenue Antiques Show in New York," agreed Maggie. "And all those wonderful books on decorating with antiques."

"Maybe they don't tell the *whole* story," he pointed out.

"Possibly," Maggie agreed, trying to keep a straight face. She raised her can of diet soda to him. "May They!" she said. That's what she and her friend Gussie always said at the beginning of a show. It was shorthand for "May They Buy."

Only by intention did it sound very like the universal distress signal.

Chapter 22

NIGHT OF THE RAVEN. *Undated wood engraving (mid-twentieth century). Signed artist's proof by Margaret K. Thomas, listed American artist. Spooky landscape of dead tree, its branches silhouetted against a large full moon, the outline of a raven seen flying in the moonlight. Artist's proofs ("AP") are usually kept by the artists, or given to friends or to the producer of the engraving. They're run as tests before numbered engravings are made, and because of their rarity are considered more valuable than numbered engravings if signed, as this one is. 12 x 19 inches. Price: $350.*

A few hardy souls actually ventured out to attend the antiques show in the first hour or two, but they made very few purchases. Slogging through mud between tents that were waving uneasily in the strong gusts did not encourage customers to lengthen their stays.

At eleven-thirty Tent One groaned for the last time and sagged dramatically to the side, its center post falling on top of three booths, narrowly missing four people, ruining two Chinese screens, and smashing a showcase full of Chinese Rose Medallion and Japanese Satsuma porcelain. It left three dealers and the show manager calling their insurance agents or lawyers.

By noon the only people on the soggy fairgrounds were the dealers and the show manager. Food vendors had closed down and two of the parking lots had flooded. At a little after 1:00 P.M. a call from the state police announced that one of the two major roads to the fairgrounds had just been closed. A small bridge had washed out.

Even the show manager gave up at that point.

The words "The show is closed!" spread like a virus from one remaining tent to another.

Grateful dealers shrugged off their losses and began to pack, thankful no more tents had collapsed.

"At least we can be at Aunt Nettie's in less than an hour once we get this stuff back in the van," Will pointed out. "I feel sorry for those folks in the corner booth who drove from Minnesota and are staying in a motel. They lost a lot of money on this show."

Maggie nodded as she wrapped candlesticks and snuffers and butter molds and carefully repacked them in Will's cartons that, luckily, were plastic, so were not falling apart as the cardboard cartons of a dealer down the muddy aisle from them were.

"You've been really good about not saying anything about outdoor shows," Will said, as he folded the table covers and tried to find a dry plastic bag to put them in.

Maggie shrugged. "I know the business. This is part of it. Although," she glanced up at the tent swaying precariously above them, "I'll admit this is a pretty dramatic example of why I don't do shows like this. I assume on a lovely summer day we would have been complaining about the heat inside this tent."

"All too true. We would have been wishing for a few breezes, and the tent flaps would have been open. Although we also would most likely have had customers to talk to, which would have made the day considerably better." Will headed back to the RV with two cartons of inventory.

By a little after two-thirty they were back on the road, headed for Waymouth. The RV had not stuck in the mud, thank goodness, and they stopped at a small diner for two pints of fried clams, which they ate while they drove.

"All I really want is to get back, take a hot shower, and then a long nap," said Maggie, luxuriously popping a hot, freshly fried clam into her mouth. "A little cognac wouldn't be bad either."

"Ditto, ditto, ditto," said Will. "It would be even better if we could share that shower."

"I love Aunt Nettie, but..." Maggie agreed regretfully.

"When we get to be grown-ups," said Will, "it's going to be different."

Maggie almost giggled, but she was too tired. She hoped Will was more alert than she was, since he was driving. She was asleep before the clams were gone.

"Time to wake up." From somewhere deep in her dreams Maggie felt the RV stop and heard Will's voice. "We're back at Aunt Nettie's. And by some miracle the rain has just about ended."

She forced herself to surface. "What time is it?"

"Almost four o'clock. You slept most of the way home."

Will had already opened the RV door and picked up his cash box, not notably heavier than it had been when they'd left early that morning. "Aunt Nettie won't expect us this early, but she'll be glad to see us home from the floods. Maybe we can take her out to dinner again."

"Good idea." Maggie picked up her red canvas bag and jumped out of her side of the high vehicle.

The back door of the house was ajar. It was Waymouth, and that just meant Aunt Nettie was at home.

"Aunt Nettie? We're back!" Will called out as they hung their rain gear on hooks near the back door and walked through to the kitchen.

The kitchen light was on, and an empty teacup waited on the counter. The brass kettle was on the electric stove, and the burner below it glowed red hot.

Maggie picked up the kettle. It was empty; the bottom burned. The water had boiled away.

She turned off the burner and looked questioningly at Will. "A little longer and the heat could have eaten all the way through the kettle. The house could have caught fire."

"Aunt Nettie?" he called again, quickly looking through the other rooms on the first floor. Living room. Dining room. No sign of his aunt.

"Her car was in the driveway," Maggie pointed out, as she checked the downstairs bathroom. "Would she have gone for a walk and forgotten to turn off the burner?"

"A walk in the pouring rain? I doubt it. And so far as I can tell she's never done anything like leaving the stove on before," said Will as he took the stairs two at a time, heading toward the second floor.

Maggie followed.

The door to Aunt Nettie's room was closed and blocked by a

small marble-topped oak bureau that normally stood in the hallway to hold towels, soaps, and other toiletries. It wasn't large, but Aunt Nettie was ninety-one. She wouldn't have been able to open a door it was covering.

It took Will only seconds to push it aside and open the door to her bedroom.

Aunt Nettie was lying on the floor of her room, not moving. Every drawer in her bureau and dressing table had been dumped, and the contents scattered. Her wrists were duct-taped together in back of her, and her ankles were also taped. A third piece of the silver tape was across her mouth. A dish towel from the kitchen was tied around her head, covering her eyes, and the odor in the room said she'd wet herself. How long had she been like this?

Will bent to her and untied the dish towel. Her eyes flickered slightly. "I'll get this tape off, Aunt Nettie," he said, rising to look for scissors or a knife. "Maggie, call the police."

She backed out of the room, glancing at the other two rooms on the second floor as she did. It wasn't only Aunt Nettie's room that had been savaged. Every drawer in both Will's and her bedrooms had been overturned onto the floor. Pillows, sheets, and blankets had been pulled up, as though someone had been looking underneath the mattresses. Closets had been emptied, their contents dumped. Every box had been opened. Christmas ornaments stored for the summer were now on the floor, mixed with jars of buttons and sewing notions. Winter sweaters had been thrown from the pine trunks where they were normally kept and strewn throughout the rooms.

Had anything been taken? She didn't have time to look now.

Maggie dialed 911 and asked to be connected to the Waymouth Police Department.

If only Aunt Nettie was all right. What could anyone have been looking for? What if this wasn't a simple robbery? What if someone was looking for the journal she'd tucked in her bag and taken with her, even to the show? Was she somehow responsible for Aunt Nettie's being hurt?

Within a few minutes both an ambulance and Nick Strait were on their way.

Upstairs, Will had found Aunt Nettie's manicure scissors and was gently cutting the tape that held her ankles. He'd already freed her wrists, and Maggie started massaging them. Aunt Nettie's skin was pale and slightly blue.

Will had propped his aunt up against the bed, but she still seemed unresponsive. "Aren't you going to take the tape off her mouth?" Maggie asked.

"I started to," he answered, "but it tore her skin." He pointed at her cheek.

Aunt Nettie's thin, dry skin was no match for the heavy duct tape. "I'm hoping the medical folks will have something better that won't hurt her. She doesn't look as though she can talk now, anyway," he added.

"Fingernail polish remover might help," Maggie said, but then immediately realized that Aunt Nettie wouldn't have worn nail polish, and she hadn't brought any with her to Maine. "I'm worried about her breathing."

The screeching of sirens interrupted her thought, and she ran downstairs to greet whichever responders had arrived first.

Within five minutes local paramedics had carefully lifted Aunt Nettie onto a stretcher and carried her down the narrow stairway of her home.

Detective Nick Strait arrived just as she was being put into the ambulance.

"Whoa...did anyone take pictures of her?" he asked as he saw her, swaddled in blankets with an IV in her arm but with duct tape still firmly in place over her lips.

"Nick, she's my aunt. I got help. The paramedics got here first, and they're taking her to the hospital. I'm going with them. Maggie, stay and tell Nick what happened. Do you remember how to get to Rocky Shores Hospital?"

"Yes." Maggie remembered all too well, from last summer when her friend Amy's husband had been hurt in a mysterious car crash.

"Meet me there?"

She nodded. "I will." She looked at Nick, who had already gotten his notebook out and was jotting something down. "As soon as I can."

Will climbed into the back of the ambulance and the doors clanged shut after him. Maggie and Nick both watched as the ambulance maneuvered through the deep puddles on the narrow street, its siren sounding once more.

"How bad is she?" asked Nick.

Maggie shook her head. "I don't know. She wasn't responding."

"She's a tough old lady. I have to ask you: Had she been sexually attacked, could you tell?"

Maggie couldn't even think about that possibility. "She was fully dressed."

"Good," said Nick. "But I'll have one of the women on the force meet them at the hospital to take pictures and check for any DNA or other evidence on her body. I know you felt you had to get medical help for her, but…" He gave Maggie a long "if we lose evidence this is all your fault" look, as he called his office.

Maggie walked back into the house and sat down at the kitchen table. She could have used a little of that cognac she and Will had joked about on their drive home. Clearly this was not the time to pour any.

Nick joined her a few minutes later, notebook at the ready. "So. Talk. What happened this time?"

Maggie unclenched her fists and tried very hard to smile sweetly.

"Will and I left at about four-thirty this morning to do an antiques show."

"Was Nettie all right then?"

"So far as I know. We didn't see her. I assumed she was asleep. Her door was closed."

"Did you lock the house door when you left?"

Maggie hesitated. "I don't know. You'll have to ask Will."

"I'll do that." Nick made several flourished notes on his pad and turned the page. "Did you hear from Nettie during the day?"

"No. She didn't call, and we didn't call her. She expected us home by seven this evening, but the show closed early because of the weather, and we got home before four." Maggie paused a moment. Nick was clearly not an expert at shorthand, and was taking down her comments verbatim. Maybe she should donate her tape recorder to the Waymouth Police Department when this was all over? She immediately felt guilty for even thinking such a thing when she should have been focusing on Aunt Nettie.

"Was the door open then?"

Maggie was careful. "We came in the back way. Nettie's car was in the driveway. I think the back door was ajar. Will didn't seem to think that was unusual."

"Did *you* think that was unusual?"

"I come from New Jersey. We lock our doors there."

"I haven't forgotten where you come from." Nick cleared his throat a bit. "Believe me. Every time I see you I think about it. I know New Jersey is not Maine. I watched *The Sopranos*. Now, what did you see when you came in?"

Maggie swallowed a deep desire to tell him her cousin Guido was expected to arrive at any moment.

"The light was on in the kitchen, and the stove was on. The kettle on the stove had burned dry." Maggie pointed at the cup on the counter. "Aunt Nettie's favorite teacup was just where you see it. I turned off the burner on the stove and put the kettle on another burner."

"Did everything else downstairs look normal?"

"So far as I could tell. I don't know the house as well as Will does. We looked for Aunt Nettie. Will called her, and no one answered, so we went upstairs. Would you like to see the upstairs now?"

"Please." Nick followed Maggie up the stairs.

"We haven't touched anything except in Nettie's bedroom, to help her," Maggie explained.

"You stand in the hallway by the stairs," Nick directed. He took a small digital camera out of his pocket and started snapping pictures of the hallway and each bedroom.

"The oak bureau. That's the one you said was in front of her bedroom door?"

"Right. Will shoved it aside so he could open the door. Her room was a shambles, just as it is now."

"The drawers in the hall bureau weren't dumped," Nick commented, as he continued to snap his way through the upstairs.

"True," said Maggie, peeking over his shoulder to see him focusing on her new black lace nightgown, an adventurous splurge bought with a possible night away from Aunt Nettie's in mind. It now lay crumpled on the floor next to the front window in her room.

"Can you tell if anything's missing?"

"I could look through my things, if you're through in this bedroom," Maggie said. "I don't know what was in the other bedrooms, or even what Aunt Nettie stored in the closet."

Nick moved on to the bedroom at the other end of the hall. "Will was using this bedroom?"

"Yes."

"You weren't sharing a bedroom?" he asked.

"Why, Detective Strait," Maggie replied, "you know Will Brewer and I aren't married! I'm surprised at you, asking such a personal question!"

Nick just shook his head slightly. "Ms. Summer, you're from New Jersey; you're not Scarlett O'Hara. Don't patronize me." He moved on to Nettie's bedroom and looked at the mess there. "You and Will, and Nettie, if she's able, will have to come up with a list of any missing items. I'll need that as soon as possible."

"I understand," said Maggie.

"You're going to the hospital now?"

"Yes."

"Give my best to both Will and Nettie." Nick paused. "I don't know why it is that every time I see you there seem to be problems, Maggie Summer. Nick is an old friend of mine, and Nettie's a special lady. A lot of people in Waymouth will be upset when they find she's been injured." He hesitated again. "Or worse."

"No one is more upset than I am," Maggie assured him. "Are you going to dust for fingerprints? Or check for DNA?"

"Why don't you go to the hospital and see how Nettie is. Will needs you. For the moment, don't go into Nettie's room, even to look for missing items. In fact," Nick looked as though he were making a decision, "for tonight I'm going to make the entire house a crime scene. Tell Will you need to find somewhere else to stay tonight. Check with me tomorrow."

Chapter 23

A Gloucester, Massachusetts Fishing Schooner Discharging at Commercial Wharf, Boston. *Wood engraving on cover of Ballou's Pictorial, a Boston weekly newspaper, March 12, 1859. Includes article on Gloucester fishing smacks, or boats ("305 schooners, averaging 70 tons, employed in the industry,") and other facets of the fishing business. Drawing by Alfred Waud, who later worked with Winslow Homer and Thomas Nast as an illustrator for* Harper's Weekly *in New York City. 10.5 x 14.5 inches. Price: $95.*

Maggie pulled into the driveway of Rocky Shores Hospital, turned left, and parked near the emergency room. That's where the ambulance would have taken Aunt Nettie.

Why was it that she always seemed to know where the police stations and hospitals were in places she visited? A thought she didn't want to meditate on for the moment.

Will was sitting on an orange plastic chair in the emergency room waiting area, his head back against the wall, his eyes unfocused. Maggie sat down next to him. "How is she?"

"I'm glad you're here," he said, reaching for her hand. "The doctor said she's in shock. But they were able to get that awful tape off her face without tearing too much of her skin, and that's helped her breathing. A woman from the Waymouth Police Department is in there now taking pictures. They asked me to leave."

"Is she talking yet?"

"Just a few words. The doctor wants to run some tests to see if she had a minor stroke. The IV is already making a difference. She was dehydrated."

"I wonder how long she lay there?" Maggie wondered.

"I don't know. We left so early in the morning. Maybe someone saw us leave, and knew she was alone. But she'd gotten up and dressed, and she usually does that about six-thirty, so I'm guessing it was about seven in the morning."

"She hadn't had her morning tea," Maggie mused. "And there were no dishes out for any other food for breakfast. She might not have had time to get anything out if someone came in first thing. Nick didn't ask me any questions about her normal routine. He'll probably ask you those. "

"Did Nick give you a hard time?"

Maggie shrugged. "A few comments about my being not only from away, but from New Jersey. I felt a little sorry for the guy. It's true that every time I see him there's another crime."

"Maggie, that's his job. I'm sorry I didn't call him up to have a beer before you arrived, but I've been so busy with Aunt Nettie, and painting the house...."

"He asked me if you locked the door when we left in the morning."

Will shook his head. "I don't remember. Maybe not. Most of the time people in Waymouth don't worry about locking the doors, although I know Aunt Nettie locks them before she goes to bed at night. A couple of times she's asked me to check that everything is closed up before I go upstairs."

"Mr. Brewer?" A pleasant-looking woman wearing a white coat, her gray hair pulled into a ponytail, had walked into the waiting room. "I'm Dr. Simpson."

Will stood up immediately.

"The police are finished with your aunt for the moment. She's still drifting in and out of consciousness, and is confused about where she is. She doesn't have any bruises except those made by her struggling against the tape on her wrists and ankles. The good news is that she doesn't appear to have been assaulted in any way other than to have been constrained for a prolonged period of time. But for a woman of her age, that alone could cause a heart attack or stroke."

"Do you think—?" Will started.

"I don't think anything right now, except that we need to admit her and run a whole series of tests. I've called her regular doctor, but it's Saturday and I haven't heard from him yet. His records are computerized, though, and linked in to the hospital, and I can't see anything on her record that would be unusual for her age. Normally her blood pressure is slightly high, but right now it's low, which could be a concern. That's one of the things we're monitoring."

"I'd like to stay with her. If she wakes up I'd like her to be with someone she knows well."

"Your aunt will be having tests for the next several hours. Then we'll put her in a critical care unit near the nursing station on the second floor so we can keep an eye on her and monitor her for any changes. You're welcome to stay in the small waiting room on that floor, but I have to tell you, there are just a couple of chairs and a small couch there. It's not very comfortable."

Will looked exhausted. And Maggie hadn't told him yet they couldn't go back to Aunt Nettie's home that night. "Dr. Simpson, is there a motel close to the hospital?" she asked.

"There's one about a half mile south of here," Dr. Simpson said. "I'll be sure to call you myself, or have whoever is on duty do so, should Miss Brewer's condition change, or should she need you for any reason."

Will looked at Maggie questioningly.

"I think we should go to the motel," Maggie said, firmly. "It's close by, and you need rest, or you'll be no good to Aunt Nettie, or to yourself. Give Dr. Simpson your cell phone number, and we'll check back with her later."

Will dutifully wrote down his number, and Maggie steered him to the door of the emergency room.

"What was all that about?" he asked when they'd reached the outside. "Why a motel? Why can't we just go home?"

"Because it's a crime scene, and we're banned from the place tonight," she explained. "I hadn't had a chance to tell you. Besides," she continued, taking his arm and heading him toward her van, "the motel is closer to the hospital. Let's check in, and then get a decent meal and some sleep. We've been up since before dawn, our clothes and shoes are damp and muddy, and we're too exhausted to make any major decisions just now."

Will nodded. "You're right. I want to have my thoughts together before either of us talks with Nick, or the doctor, or Aunt Nettie again."

Luckily, the motel had one room free; on an August night in midcoast Maine, an open room was not a given. As Maggie tried to rinse the mud off her sneakers she longed for her clean clothes back at the now yellow-taped house.

But after they'd each showered they felt better, even having to put the same damp and dirty clothes back on.

"Is there some place we can go that just has simple food, and maybe a glass of wine? We had fried clams this afternoon, and I don't think I want anything else fried."

"I know just the place," said Will, pointing north on Route 1.

The restaurant he found for them was perfect: a view of the Madoc River, fresh homemade breads and chowders, and sand- wiches of all sorts as well as the ubiquitous lobster rolls and crab cakes that were *de rigueur* in August Maine. Plus a bar featuring lo- cal beers, ales, and wines.

"I didn't even know there were Maine wines," said Maggie, as she perused the wine list. "But now that we're here, I'm not sure I'm in the mood for wine tonight. I can't resist trying a light Maine beer, though. What great names! Which one do you suggest?"

"My favorite is Shipyard, but there are a lot of good ones. Gritty McDuff's, Allagash, Geary's, Pemaquid Ale. There's also a vodka made in Maine, and a great gin made by Back River," said Will. "But we can save those for another day. I think you'd love Back River's cranberry gin."

"Tempting," agreed Maggie. "But today, the Summer Shipyard and a large bowl of oyster bisque would be just right."

"Sounds good to me, too," he agreed. "A plate of onion rings to share?"

"They're fried," hesitated Maggie, remembering her earlier reso- lution, "but, still, onion rings...sound just like what we need."

They sat quietly, watching the early evening sun setting over the river. Will's hand was on Maggie's, and until their food arrived, they hardly spoke, enjoying the peace of the moment, and trying not to think of Aunt Nettie, and what the tests at the hospital might be showing.

As soon as the bisque and the chilled mugs of beer were on

the table their hands separated and occupied themselves with the important business of eating and drinking.

After a few minutes, her initial appetite satisfied, Maggie sat back. "I keep thinking it's my fault. Whoever broke into Aunt Nettie's house was looking for something. And we know Betsy Thompson wants that journal I have."

"Whoa, lady!" said Will. "To begin with, we haven't gone through the house, so we don't know if anything is missing. I'll do that as soon as Nick says it's okay for me to go back. Even then, I don't know if I'll recognize what's gone. What do burglars usually take? Electronics? Aunt Nettie has a twelve-year-old television no one would want, and it was still in her bedroom. She may have some jewelry, but I don't remember any real jewels. Only she would know. We know antiques, and I think you'd agree she has nothing of great value."

"Plus, whoever was there didn't even seem to touch the first floor, where most of her better furniture and china are. He or she totally tossed the three bedrooms, which just had clothes and bedding and the usual upstairs stuff." Maggie thought a moment. "People who break in look for drugs or liquor. Did she have any medications that were controlled substances?"

"Not that I know of. She hasn't had any surgeries that would require painkillers. She kept her blood pressure meds in the kitchen cabinet. I saw them there. I don't remember anything else. The wine and a few liquor bottles were in the kitchen, too, but you're right, that room seemed untouched. Besides, I can't imagine someone breaking in to steal a couple of half-filled bottles of liquor."

"And why didn't they choose a time when she was away from home? She goes shopping, and to visit friends, and to the library. Most of the time you can tell she's gone because her car isn't there. You and I are both visiting. That means two more vehicles are in her driveway most of the time. Even though you and I left this morning in your RV, it was dark then. Unless someone was watching the house, how would they know we'd both left? Wouldn't they assume that since my van and Nettie's car were still there, at least a couple of people were in the house?"

Will shook his head. "Nothing makes sense. But this wasn't just a burglary. A ninety-one-year-old woman was duct-taped. Maybe questioned. At least they didn't hurt her more."

They were both silent for a moment, thinking of what had happened to Carolyn.

"I wonder if she knows who it was?" said Maggie.

"She might. Or whoever it was *thought* she might be able to identify them. Otherwise they wouldn't have covered her eyes."

"I still think someone was looking for the journal," said Maggie, savoring her final spoonful. "And, by the way, this oyster bisque is fantastic. Sherry, I think?"

"Plus just the right amount of cream. They've re-introduced oysters to Maine in the past few years." Will munched on another onion ring. The pile was decreasing rapidly. "I know you think the journal is important. But the only person who's said they want to see it is Betsy Thompson. I can't see Betsy Thompson stomping up those stairs in her high heels, throwing Aunt Nettie to the ground, and then pulling out drawers and throwing pillows and blankets around."

"No," Maggie admitted.

"What's in that journal, anyway?"

"So far, all I've read is that Anna May Pratt and her friend Jessie are modeling for Winslow Homer. Jessie has a sweetheart fishing on the Grand Banks, but her parents want her to marry an old guy who's here in town, and Anna May also has a crush on the young man who's at sea."

"Sounds like a soap opera, with Winslow Homer as interesting historical background. Not something worth breaking into a house and knocking an old lady to the ground for."

"No." Maggie took another sip of her beer. "But I don't think Betsy Thompson really knows what is in the journal. She's just hoping it will help her prove her family's Homer connection in some way." She looked up. "In all the excitement, I just remembered. Betsy invited me to come for tea tomorrow, to see her house and look at her husband's work, and that of her father-in-law. I think she believes I may have some pull with getting their work into New York or New Jersey galleries. She invited you, too."

"I think I'll be busy. Do you want to go?"

"I told her I would, but that was before all of this happened. Oh, and she said Kevin Bradman would be there, too."

"The cast of characters is growing. Who's Kevin Bradman?"

"I told you about him before. He's the Harvard doctoral student who's writing his dissertation about Maine artists. Or Winslow Homer. I'm not really sure. I ran into him at the library again when I was there yesterday. Anyway, Betsy said Kevin was living with her this summer."

Will looked up at the ceiling. "As in *living* with her, or as in living at her house or in one of the artists' cottages on the grounds?"

"I have no clue," said Maggie. "But I'm curious. I think I will go for tea tomorrow, unless there's something I'm needed for at the hospital. Or at the police station. Or at the house."

They looked at each other and both grimaced.

"Enjoying your vacation, my dear?" Will asked.

"Worried about Aunt Nettie," said Maggie, "when it really comes down to it. And I want to know who killed Carolyn Chase. I came to Maine to see you, to relax, and do some antiquing. Not get involved with another murder. No wonder your friend Nick thinks I'm a little strange."

Will reached out and took her hand. "He doesn't know you as I do, Maggie. If he did, he'd know murders don't just happen when you're in Maine. They happen when you're in other places, too."

Maggie picked up the last onion ring and tossed it at him.

Then his cell phone rang.

Chapter 24

CLUSTERS, NEBULAE, AND COMETS. *Black-and-white lithograph from* Burritt's Atlas of the Heavens, *1836. Hole in margin that could be covered by matting. Thirty contiguous, white-framed drawings of comets (e.g., Halley's Comet, 1682; Great Comet of 1680), clusters (e.g., Cluster in Libra; Perpendicular view of our own cluster), and Nebulae (e.g., Great Spiral Nebula) against black background. 14.5 x 17 inches. Price: $75.*

It was Dr. Simpson.

Aunt Nettie's heartbeat was irregular. It wasn't serious, but the doctor thought Will should know. They would probably keep his aunt in the hospital for a couple of days.

"That's the best place for her, under the circumstances," Maggie said, knowing the words sounded artificial.

"Let's get out of here," said Will. "I can't stand not being able to do anything. We've finished eating anyway."

They stood outside the restaurant and watched the sun set. Cascading streaks of reds and oranges and blues filled the sky and its reflections in the water before disappearing below the hills on the west side of the river.

"Let's go back to the motel and get some sleep," Will said reluctantly. "I have a feeling tomorrow is not going to be easy."

The wide bed in the motel looked inviting, but the day's physical and emotional exhaustion had taken its toll. Maggie and Will found quiet comfort in each other's arms, but the black lace nightgown left on the "crime scene" floor was neither needed nor missed.

Will's first waking thought was for Aunt Nettie. He dialed the hospital. Her condition was the same.

"Drive me back to her house," he said to Maggie. "I can get my RV, so we don't have to be joined at the hip. And let's hope we can get back into the house to get some clean clothes."

On the way he gestured to Maggie to pull into a Dunkin' Donuts. They ordered two bagels, one with salmon cream cheese and one with chive, to go, and a cup of coffee, black. Maggie hoped she could retrieve a diet cola from Aunt Nettie's refrigerator.

If not, she'd make do with the bagel. They weren't New York bagels, but for Maine, they'd do.

Yellow crime scene tape was still around the house, and one crime lab van and two sheriff's department cars were parked in the street. Maggie found a place to pull over further down the street, silently thanking her years of parallel parking experience in New York City. About a dozen neighbors were standing around, watching to see if anything of interest would happen.

"Lookie Lous," Maggie commented, as she and Will walked past them. "They've probably known your aunt all of their lives, and want to know what's happened."

"Don't worry; they know what's happened," Will assured her drily. "In Waymouth, anyone at all interested probably knew about the break-in and Aunt Nettie's being in the hospital before we checked into the motel last night. Which no doubt they now know about, too."

Maggie stayed on the street, reassessing the joys of small towns, as Will stepped over the yellow tape and knocked at the house's open front door. "Hello? This is Will Brewer. Can someone tell me what is happening? Hello?" As he stepped inside he was pushed out by a uniformed man half his size.

Maggie couldn't hear what was said, but clearly it wasn't a pleasant conversation. After a few minutes Will stomped back down the stairs, glowering at the neighbors who were watching him closely.

"No news!" he shouted to the disappointed observers. When he got to where Maggie was standing he gave her a more detailed report. "That cop said they were going to need the house all day. That Detective Strait will let me know when we can 'reoccupy' the house.

What a pain! The only good news is that my RV is still mine. I'm taking it and going to the hospital."

"If I'm going to have tea with Betsy Thompson I'm going to need clean clothes," said Maggie. "Why don't I drive to Freeport and buy some in the outlets? I can get some things for you, too, so you can stay at the hospital."

"I don't mind L.L. Bean stuff, but this is ridiculous," Will groused. "We shouldn't have to buy new underwear because Nick and his pals are futzing around that house."

"Doesn't sound as though we have much choice."

"Okay, okay. I'll give you my underwear and jean sizes, and a few dollars. And I'll call the motel and tell them we'll need the room for another day or so." Will reached for his wallet.

Maggie hesitated. "You don't have to give me any money." Had she reached the point of being comfortable buying him underwear? Although she'd certainly noticed he wore briefs, not boxers. Tight briefs. In dark colors.

Will didn't seem to notice her hesitation. "There's an L.L. Bean outlet store and a store nearby that has the other stuff. Get a few basics. T-shirts, jeans. Nothing with fish on it."

He wrote a couple of notes, and handed them to Maggie with several bills. "Here are my sizes."

She nodded. Decision made. "I'll go to Freeport, go back to the motel to change, and then come to the hospital. If you need me, call. I'm not due at Betsy's until late this afternoon."

"Sounds like a plan." Will bent over and hugged her tight. "Have I told you how wonderful you are, special lady?" he whispered. Her ears tingled as his fingers traced their outlines.

Maggie leaned into his arms. For a moment everything happening around them could be forgotten. Then she reluctantly broke away.

"Tell Aunt Nettie to get better fast," she said. "We need her. But don't tell her how awful her house looks. We've got to get Nick's friends out of there so we can clean the place up before she gets home, or her heart will really have problems."

"Nick will probably call me about getting that list of missing items together," said Will, running his hand through his thick gray hair. "I'm going to have trouble doing that without her input. But I don't want to ask her what was in her jewelry box until we're sure she's going to be all right. Her health is more important than her belongings."

"Just go to the hospital and be there for her," said Maggie. "I'm on a quest to Freeport."

Each year between three and four million people made Freeport, Maine their destination. Maggie was convinced most of them arrived in August. Originally, and still, the home of L.L. Bean, Freeport's main street was lined with outlets of both major and minor specialty stores. Finding a parking space was a challenge.

She drove around and around, past cars and vans with license plates from as far away as California and Colorado, as well as from every state on the East Coast.

Finally she spotted a family of shoppers loading bags and boxes into a car from Ohio and waited for them to back out so she could pull in. Worse than Christmas shopping at the Bridgewater Mall at home, she muttered to herself as she headed back three parking lots on foot toward L.L. Bean.

An hour later, with jeans for Will, T-shirts for both of them, and a casual tan skirt and matching top she decided would do for her visit to the Thompsons in one large bag, assorted undergarments from another store in a second bag, plus a pair of leather sandals she'd glimpsed in an outlet window and couldn't resist in a third, she was back at the van, ready to head for Waymouth. Judging from the other shoppers she'd seen, not many visitors escaped from Freeport with fewer than three shopping bags.

A half hour after that she'd also stopped for toothbrushes, toothpaste, shampoo, deodorant, and a hairbrush she thought would get through her long hair. She'd had a comb and lipstick in her bag, and Will's beard didn't require daily shaving gear. With the additions to their wardrobe and toiletries they should be able to survive another day or two even if they couldn't get back into the house.

Which she certainly hoped they'd be able to do soon.

She put on her new skirt and top and sandals at the motel. Under the circumstances, she looked pretty decent. There was just enough time to stop at the hospital before she went to see Betsy Thompson.

Will was in the small visitors' room on the second floor. Sections of the *Portland Press Herald* littered the table in front of him, and the television on the wall was tuned to CNN, where they were reporting fires in Southern California and a record heat wave in Arizona. Will was reading the current issue of *Maine Antique Digest*.

"How is she?"

"Maggie! Hey, very nice. A skirt! Haven't seen you in one of those in a while. You should have gone to Freeport a while ago!"

"Thank you," said Maggie, spinning to model her outfit. "If I'd known skirts were so impressive I would have put one on before this. There's one back at the house, no doubt on the floor of my room somewhere. What's been happening here?"

"Aunt Nettie's sleeping most of the time. She doesn't seem to understand what happened, or where she is. The doctor said she may have had a mild stroke. It doesn't seem to have left any specific damage, but she's definitely not herself. At her age it's hard to tell how long it will take her to recover." Will looked exhausted.

"How do *you* think she is, Will?"

"I don't know. She isn't acting the way she does normally. I don't know if it's medical, or emotional, and I'm not getting any real answers from the doctors."

"Have you been able to talk to her?"

"I go in to see her for a few minutes every half hour or so, which the nurses seem to think is about right. I talk to her. But she doesn't really talk back. She just lies there, or mumbles a little. Nick called. He's anxious to talk with her. I've told him that the way she is now, she won't be able to help him at all. I don't know what she remembers or doesn't remember."

"And her heart?"

"They're monitoring it. The irregular heartbeat is about the same. Periodic. But it doesn't seem to be getting worse, and Dr. Simpson said she could have had it for years and never noticed it. So that may or may not be a problem."

"Is there anyone else who could help out...?"

"I've called some cousins to let them know what happened. But it's Tourist Time in Maine; most of them are working two or three jobs this time of year. If you're asking if there's someone else who could be here to take care of her, then, no." Will paused. "I've worried in the past few years, as she's gotten older, but she always seemed so together, and so healthy. Right now, I don't know what to do."

"She has to stay here now."

"And it's only been about twenty-four hours, so we don't know how she's going to be. It could go either way. Even if she's well enough to go home in a few days, I don't think I can go back to Buffalo, Maggie. It wouldn't be safe to leave her alone."

Maggie was silent. She'd wondered about that, too. "I've been wondering how she'll feel being back in her house after what happened to her there."

Will stood up and paced from one side of the small room to the other. He turned to Maggie. "I've always thought I'd move to Maine someday. Maybe this is the time."

"But your house in Buffalo. And how can you take care of Aunt Nettie when you're on the road doing shows most of the time?"

"I'll figure out something. She's family, Maggie. You take care of family."

Maggie just sat, silent. Families didn't always take care of each other. She wondered for a moment where Joe was. Joe, her brother who'd left home when she was six. She'd only seen him once or twice since then. Was he married? Did he have children? He was all the family she had, and she didn't know anything about him. She knew more about Will and Aunt Nettie than she knew about Joe.

Her parents had died in an accident eleven years ago. She'd thought about the responsibilities of having a child, but she hadn't considered the responsibilities Will felt now for someone at the other end of life.

"Carolyn said her Aunt Susan had a home health aide; someone to help her during the past year," she said.

"I should find out about that sort of thing," Will thought out loud. "Even if I move here, I'd have to settle my place in Buffalo. Put it on the market, and put my stuff in storage, or move it here. There are things to take care of." He kept pacing. "There's so much to think about."

Maggie glanced at her watch. "I have to go; I promised Betsy I'd be at her house for tea at four o'clock. I left your new clothes at the motel."

"Right. Of course. You'd better get going. Call me when you're through at Betsy's?" He held her for a long minute. "I'm so glad you're here, Maggie. What would I do without you?"

Outside, Maggie sat in her van. She didn't have to leave for the Thompsons quite this quickly. She'd just wanted to get away.

She'd felt entangled. She needed to feel calm; in control. To get her mind off what was happening. She reached for her red bag. She'd read a little more of Anna May Pratt's journal.

Chapter 25

MIRAGE. *Lithograph of men on camels, crossing a desert, seeing a lake filled with sailing vessels upside down in the clouds ahead of them. Animal bones litter the sandy foreground. By G.* Hathaway from The Aerial World, *a book on meteorology (1874). Background color: shades of tan, white border; sky pale blue-green. 5.5 x 8.5 inches. Price: $50.*

June 18, 1890
Although I do miss seeing Mr. Micah Wright, it is convenient that Mr. Homer planned to spend this week completing "studies begun in Florida last winter," for he had no need of Jessie or me, and there has been plenty to occupy me here in Waymouth.

Yesterday's ship launching drew most of the town's residents. My sister Sarah and I went with Mother and watched with others in the crowd as the Lisa *was pulled over logs down to the shore by the men at Colby's Boatyard and then slid into the Madoc River at high tide with great hurrahs from the crowd. Jessie stood with her parents, but near to Orin Colby, clearly in a place of honor on the grandstand.*

"Mr. Colby has made his regard for your friend Jessie very public," my mother said, nudging me. I nodded, knowing well that while Mother might not approve the public display, she did approve the admiration, and indeed, would wish such for me.

After the ceremony Jessie managed to slip away from Orin and pass me an envelope, which I quickly hid within the pocket of my skirt before anyone, even Sarah, who was standing nearby, could see.

"It was an exciting launch, wasn't it?" Jessie asked. She then

whispered, "Mr. Colby has said that 'Jessie' would be an elegant name for the next ship out of his yard."

I looked at her closely. Was she perhaps beginning to find Orin Colby and the life he could offer her attractive?

"I told him I believed a vessel should be named by its owner, not its builder," she continued. "How better could I have told him my affections cannot be bought with a ship?"

"No better," I assured her, although I wondered if perhaps Orin Colby suspected she was merely flirting. Mother has advised me many times that some men who feel they have much to offer cannot conceive of any young woman's rejecting their advances, and indeed, might take gentle rebuffs as teasing. Orin Colby must feel well satisfied as to the future, having won the respect and acceptance of Jessie's parents. Jessie may have pledged her heart to Luke, but her parents have clearly pledged her hand to Orin. I can only hope, for my sake, that is true.

"When will you take care of...my package?" she asked.

"Tomorrow, for certain," I assured her. "I will deliver it tomorrow."

June 19, 1890

Last night I kept my lamp burning late, long after Sarah and my parents had gone to sleep, as I wrote my letter to Luke Trask.

I wrote it several times, for I knew to be careful in the wording. I am not so naïve as to believe he might not show the letter to someone else, perhaps in disbelief, if he is confirmed in his love for Jessie. I finally decided to write merely as Jessie's and his dear friend, in concern at his long absence. Although I did point out that he needn't worry Jessie was languishing on his behalf. Indeed, her need for companionship was being attended to quite well by Mr. Orin Colby, whose attentions were particularly obvious to all of the citizens of Waymouth during the launch of the fishing sloop Lisa just this week, and to whose captain I entrusted this missive.

I also mentioned, quite poignantly, I believe, how much I, too, missed Jessie's company, and wished Luke would return soon so that we all could talk and be friends again as we had since we were children.

I debated some time as to how to sign it, but decided "Your sincere friend, Anna May Pratt" would do for now. The purpose of this *note is to alert Luke to his competition for Jessie's affections, and to my friendship for him.*

Any more direct interest could wait for another time. This morning I delivered both letters to the captain of the Lisa, *who added them to an already-bulging canvas bag of letters and packages he had readied in his cabin for Nova Scotians and Grand Banks fishermen. He told me he is well-pleased with his new sloop, his crew and supplies are ready, and he plans to make sail at the end of the week.*

Chapter 26

—————⚇—————

A DISTINGUISHED FISHERMAN ENJOYING HIS WELL-EARNED VACATION. *August 1884 wood engraving from* Harper's Weekly, *unsigned. Distinguished gentleman dressed in formal fishing attire (wearing tie) in chair, with rod and reel, in rowboat, accompanied by rustic, bearded, and "dressed down" guide, holding a net in anticipation of a fish being caught. A humorous view of late nineteenth-century "rusticators," city people who vacationed in rural areas and hired guides to take them hunting or fishing. 11 x 16 inches. Price: $70.*

Maggie kept thinking of Anna May Pratt's words as she drove toward the Thompsons' estate.

Many of her students at Somerset County Community College were the same age as Anna May and Jessie. Was Anna May a bitchy young woman trying to steal her best friend's boyfriend, or was she desperately playing for the high stakes of respectability in a small town that placed value on women only when they were married?

Or was she truly in love with Luke?

The descriptions of Winslow Homer's studio home and of those who surrounded him there in 1890 were priceless. Art historian Philip Beam had written an excellent biography of Homer that focused on his years in Maine, but he'd had to rely on secondary sources and interviews with those who remembered Homer and his family. The artist had granted few interviews during his lifetime, and even after his death his family had rarely spoken with media representatives or biographers. Primary sources related to Winslow Homer's personal life were rare.

She was carrying one in her canvas bag.

It was tempting to think that, as the one to inherit the journal, and whatever other papers were in Susan Newall's trunk, she'd be in a position to publish the journal either as it was, or footnoted and with a detailed introduction placing the information in it within the context of Winslow Homer's work and life. A university press would certainly be interested. Possibly even a trade publisher.

Maggie realized she was almost at her destination. She glanced at the directions she'd written to the Thompsons' home, and slowed up, just in time. Within twenty feet a small, faded wooden sign nailed precariously to a tree marked a narrow drive. MIRAGE, Homer Thompson's art colony.

Betsy Thompson's father-in-law must not have been looking to advertise his retreat for artists. At least not the way Betsy was trying to publicize his work, and that of his son, today.

Betsy had implied an elegant home, but the dirt drive didn't encourage that expectation. Winter frosts, spring thaws, and flooding had taken their toll, and Maggie's van jounced more than she liked, despite being heavily loaded with prints, stands, portable walls and tables, and all the other supplies necessary to set up at an antiques show.

As she continued down the narrow road, worrying about her shock absorbers, the top of the van scraped some low-hanging branches that looked as though they'd been bent by the heavy ice of winter storms.

The Thompsons need a gardener, Maggie cussed silently. Or at least a saw.

Negotiating this driveway in winter ice or deep snow would be close to impossible. She swerved, missing a deep-looking pool of water left from yesterday's rain. They lived here all year round. They must have heavy vehicles with four-wheel drive. And a generator and snow plow.

Maybe Will wouldn't mind living in Maine year-round. He was used to Buffalo winters.

New Jersey didn't look like a postcard, but at least roads and driveways were paved.

Finally the dark aisle of scrub pines and firs and bushes opened into a wider drive that circled somewhat unevenly around what might once have been a lawn.

Or not, Maggie thought. After all, this was Maine. Perhaps it had always been a field of waist-high grasses, goldenrod, and Queen Anne's lace. Like the field she and her friend Amy had pushed their way through a year ago, looking for Rachel's missing daughter.

Maggie repressed thoughts of that week. This was another field; another year. Another situation.

Betsy had said to pass the camps, and go on to the cottage. Maggie knew enough about Maine to understand that a "cottage" was a large home, usually built for summer use. Although Aunt Nettie had said the Thompsons lived here year-round, she'd also said that originally the house was a summer place. So, in Maine parlance, it was probably still a cottage, although over the years the Thompsons must have winterized it.

"Camps" were small, casual vacation homes; what those born in places other than Maine would probably call cottages. The camps here were probably the residences or studios used by the visiting artists.

As she continued around the several-acre field Maggie passed half a dozen log cabin–style buildings nestled among the pines. One or two had worn paths to their doors. Several looked vacant. Ahead of her, as she reached the far side of the field, was a large weather-grayed barn-shaped building, with glass panels in the roof and wide windows around the sides. Winslow Thompson's studio, Maggie decided, slowing down to look.

After a densely wooded area on her right the drive widened again, making space for the cars, trucks, and Jeeps parked in front of a sprawling rustic house, its brown roof spreading out to meet the branches of the maple trees surrounding it.

Maggie parked her van between a black Jeep and a faded green Ford pickup.

Like an aging dowager, the house was clearly past its prime. Many stained wooden shingles were missing. The shutters, originally painted, were now faded, and slats were missing. Several of the small balconies outside rooms on the second floor were listing precariously.

At least two dozen Adirondack chairs sat unattended on the wide porch that circled the first floor, like guests who had stayed too long. Maggie half expected someone in elegant attire, as in an

F. Scott Fitzgerald novel, to open one of the French doors and walk out onto the porch, sit down, and call for a gin and tonic.

Maggie looked up toward the attic, wondering if it held any interesting old furniture. Or prints. Or ghosts. More than anything, she wished Betsy Thompson would offer to give her a tour of the building. What a shame the house had not been kept up. It had once been a beauty. Maybe it could still be an inn, or a bed-and-breakfast. In today's world, large houses had to support themselves. How many rooms were there? Perhaps fifteen bedrooms? From the outside it was hard to tell. The heating bill must be incredible.

She walked up the steps, across the wide porch, and turned the old-fashioned round-handled doorbell. Its strident ring reverberated through the house. For a moment Maggie wondered whether the rooms were empty.

Then the door opened, and Betsy Thompson stood in front of her.

Maggie's L.L.Bean twill skirt and beige blouse, while appropriate for ninety-eight percent of Maine afternoon engagements, were clearly not what was expected of a guest for tea at Mirage.

Betsy's hair was piled high. She wore a long black skirt with a white lace sleeveless top, and a half dozen chunky gold necklaces. The effect was made even more dramatic by the embroidered Japanese black-and-gold shawl over her shoulders and her high-heeled gold sandals.

"Maggie, I'm so glad to see you," Betsy said, peeking beyond her. "Your friend Will wasn't able to come?"

"No; he's sorry, but he had another commitment," Maggie semi-fibbed. If Betsy was the only person in Waymouth who didn't know what had happened to Aunt Nettie, then she wasn't going to be the one to tell her. Perhaps living this far from town kept her from hearing the latest gossip.

"We'll miss him, but you were the one I wanted to talk with, in any case," said Betsy dismissively, guiding Maggie through the wide center hallway of the house, past the staircase that led to the second floor and the open second-floor balcony and into the sitting room to the right of the front door.

The room reminded Maggie of castles in England that had been owned by generations of one family. In the earliest days they'd hung tapestries on the walls, for decoration and to keep drafts and chill winter winds out of unheated rooms. In later years their descendants replaced the tapestries with oil paintings. The paintings were often marks of the family's heritage (portraits), importance to the kingdom (historical scenes), friends (portraits of and with famous people), wealth (homes, lands, hunting preserves), and then, after the Grand Tour of Europe became the style, scenes of Europe by fashionable and classical artists bought "on the Continent," to show their erudition and artistic sense.

To hang all of those varying facets of an entire family, for generations, took a great deal of wall space.

In this room the number of paintings hung from floor to ceiling monopolized and numbed the mind. There were windows in the room to be sure, a number of dowdily comfortable chairs, and at least two couches. But Maggie couldn't focus on what Betsy was saying, or on anything else in the room.

"The paintings and drawings," she managed to say, as she walked around the room. "Who did them?"

"Our guests," said Betsy, clearly proud of the impression the room had made on Maggie. "When Mirage was a famous art colony the custom was for every artist who stayed here, whether for a night or a summer, to leave one piece of artwork as a thank-you. They were all hung here."

Maggie looked closer. Many of the pieces of art were signed "To Mirage" or "To Homer" or "To the Thompsons." Most of them were dated in the 1930s.

Maine scenes of lighthouses and rocks and surf were popular themes, as were autumn colors and several scenes she could identify as Waymouth landmarks. Two she was sure were Pemaquid, and several were most likely Monhegan Harbor. Every artist who'd ever crossed the border from New Hampshire into Maine seemed to have made a pilgrimage to Monhegan. There were also abstracts that Maggie could not identify as having any particular subject or emotion. A few were most likely portraits.

"It's like a museum, isn't it," Betsy said softly, as she followed Maggie's journey around the room. "There's nothing else like it anywhere in Maine."

"I believe you're right," agreed Maggie. All she could think of, as her eyes raced from one horrendous, amateurish, insipid, hackneyed, incompetent, crude work to another, was how amazing it was that this many people had been here who had thought they could paint, and that not one had been successful. The very best she could think of to say of any of these paintings was that they were pretentious. That they had actually been framed and memorialized was, in its own way, absolutely amazing.

"At one time I actually considering selling them," Betsy was confiding. "Win isn't awfully good about money, and we were having some rough times, and I thought, maybe...so I called two different auctioneers to look at them."

"What did they say?" Maggie asked, tearing herself away from looking at the walls and curious to hear how a professional would have delivered the bad news.

"They both said the same thing. That the value of these works lies in keeping them right here, with this house. They're a part of this house's history. Away from this house, they wouldn't be worth nearly as much as they are right where they are now."

Maggie silently tipped her hat to the sensitivity of the auctioneers, whoever they were. "That makes sense," she agreed. "There's no doubt they captured my attention immediately."

"I'm so glad!" said Betsy. "Now, why don't we have the tea I promised, and then I'll show you some of Win's paintings, and his father's, too." She picked up a small mahogany-handled silver bell on the low table near one of the couches and rang it. "After seeing all these pictures, though, I hope you won't be disappointed. The Thompson family paintings aren't anything like these."

Maggie sat where Betsy indicated, on a chair next to what she now assumed would be the tea table, and waited to see what would happen next. Betsy arranged herself in the center of the couch, carefully ensuring that her shawl fell artfully.

A few moments later Kevin Bradman appeared through a door in the far end of the room. Contrary to expectations Maggie had of graduate students at any school, he was wearing a navy blue suit, and carrying a late-nineteenth-century mahogany tray with brass handles.

Seeing the tray, Maggie expected it to hold porcelain teacups and scones. Instead, it held a teapot and the sort of tiny Japanese pottery cups used for tea in American Chinese restaurants, a small pitcher, and a silver bowl full of potato sticks.

Kevin put the tray on the table in front of them, smiled at Maggie, and then sat beside her. Maggie watched in fascination as Betsy poured each of them half of a tiny cup of tea and then looked up.

"Maggie, do you take cognac?"

"No, thank you. I'm driving," she said.

Betsy nodded, and added more tea to Maggie's cup, while filling hers and Kevin's with light golden liquid from the pitcher.

"You've met Kevin, haven't you, Maggie?" she asked.

"Yes; at the library. Twice," Maggie answered, feeling as though she were at the tea party in Alice's Wonderland.

"Kevin, did you tell Win our guest was here?"

"I told him, but he was very involved with his painting," Kevin answered, sipping his tea.

"Are you sure you told him we had potato sticks?" asked Betsy.

"I told him," said Kevin.

"What about Josh?"

"He'll be here soon," Kevin assured her.

"Every afternoon we have tea together," Betsy explained to Maggie. "And every day I try to think of some little treat for Win. He's getting older, you know, and he does have his preferences. I'm sure you understand."

Maggie nodded. But she had absolutely no idea what they were talking about. Potato sticks? Weren't they a snack food you bought in cans at the grocery store? She was very sure she'd never connected them with a tea party of any sort. But she hadn't come here for the tea. She'd come here to find out about the Thompsons.

So far she'd found out quite a bit. But nothing that connected anyone at this strange old house either to Carolyn's death or to what happened to Aunt Nettie.

"Betsy, I'm glad you invited Kevin to be here, too. What I'm curious about is the connection you mentioned between your family and Winslow Homer. I'd always heard that although Homer had a crush on at least one woman, he never had a real romantic relationship with any woman...or man."

"It really is all very simple, Maggie. It happened in 1890."

Maggie put her tea cup down. Of course. That was the year of Anna May Pratt's journal.

"My husband's grandmother lived here in Waymouth, and she posed for Winslow Homer. Well, you know about artists and their models." Betsy actually winked, as she smiled at Kevin.

Maggie wondered again exactly what the relationship was between those two.

"His grandmother got pregnant. I can't imagine Winslow Homer not making a decent woman of her, but he didn't. Or maybe she didn't tell anyone right then that he was the father. In any case, her family sent her away to have the baby.

"She met Wesley Thompson in Boston, and he married her anyway, and gave little Homer his last name. Homer Thompson, they called him. His mother didn't tell young Homer his real daddy was Winslow Homer until after Mr. Thompson died, in 1925, and of course Winslow Homer was long dead by then."

"He died in 1910," said Maggie.

"Right," said Betsy. "So there was no way to prove it one way or another. But Homer Thompson was also a talented painter. He's the one who turned Mirage, his family's summer cottage, into an art colony. When he and his wife had a child they continued the family tradition and called their son Winslow. Winslow is my husband."

Maggie started adding up the years. "Pardon my asking, Betsy. But your husband...must be a few years older than you are?"

"My goodness, Maggie, I would hope so. He's almost eighty!" Betsy said, as though she'd just been accused of robbing a bank. "He and I have only been married a few years."

Just then the back door to the room opened and a young man about Kevin Bradman's age came in, wearing jeans and a very tight black tank top.

"Josh! I'm so glad you've come to meet our guest!" said Betsy. "Even if you didn't have the courtesy to dress appropriately."

Josh walked over to the group at the tea table, and poured himself a full teacup from the pitcher of cognac. "Always good to see you, too, Stepmum," he said.

Then he bent down and kissed Kevin dramatically on the lips.

"Josh! Not in public!"

"Artistic lives are lived in public, Betsy dear," he said, downing his "tea" and refilling his cup.

Maggie watched, fascinated, as Betsy's cheeks reddened, and then blanched.

"Maggie, would you mind awfully much if we looked at those paintings another day?" she said, standing. "I do believe I feel a dreadful headache coming on."

Maggie stood slowly, hating to leave the scene. "But you didn't finish the story," she said, as she followed Betsy to the front door. "What was the name of your husband's grandmother, who posed for Winslow Homer?"

"Jessica Wakefield," said Betsy. "Jessie was what her family called her."

Chapter 27

THE BRAIN AND THE NERVES. *Colored lithograph, 1909, showing longitudinal section through head and neck, including parts of the brain, nose, oral cavity, cavity of the jaws, and larynx. 8 x 10 inches. Price: $40.*

Maggie left. She'd accomplished what she'd set out to do: she'd found the connection between Anna May Pratt's journal and Betsy Thompson.

She'd also found that doctoral student Kevin Bradman clearly had a connection to at least one Thompson. Possibly two.

She didn't know whether Homer Thompson, founder of the Mirage art colony in the 1930s, was a great artist himself, but clearly his artistic friends were not going to go down in American art history.

So far the only Waymouth artist she was sure would be included in art history books was Helen Chase. What *had* happened to the two Helen Chase paintings she and Will had seen at the auction gallery? She hadn't even had a chance to think about that since Friday.

The concerns of the living always overshadowed those of the dead.

She drove directly to Rocky Shores Hospital. Will looked somber. The wrinkled clothes he'd been wearing for the past two days didn't improve the picture. Across from him in the small waiting room Detective Nick Strait was taking notes.

Neither of them looked up.

She was about to join them when a pink-outfitted nurse pushed by her. "Mr. Brewer? There's been a change. You'll want to see your aunt now."

Will got up immediately, and saw Maggie. "Good; you're finally here. Come with me," he said, sweeping her with him down the hall. "I was waiting for you."

"I just got back from the Thompsons'. A really strange experience. How's Aunt Nettie?"

"She's been about the same all day." Clearly Will wasn't expecting any miracles. Maggie noted that Nick Strait was following them.

Aunt Nettie's bed was in the area behind the nurse's station, one of several "observation" beds separated only by privacy curtains. The curtains in front of her bed were open, and the nurse was helping her to sit up.

"Will! Maggie! It's about time you two came to see me," she said. "This young woman's been telling me I'm in Rocky Shores Hospital. Would you please tell her there's been some mistake, and I'd like to go home now, please?"

"Aunt Nettie!" Will reached over and gave his aunt a hug and kissed the top of her head. "You're feeling better!"

"I'm feeling just fine, thank you. Now, why is this needle in my arm, and why am I hooked up to all these contraptions? Why am I here to begin with?" Then Nettie saw Detective Strait in back of Will.

"Nicky! You're here, too! Are you sick? I can't believe you just stopped in to have a beer with Will at the hospital."

"No, Miss Brewer." Even Nick Strait was grinning. "I'm fine. I'm glad to see you're feeling better. You don't remember what happened?"

"Miss Brewer, don't overdo. You've had a lot happen in the past two days," said the nurse who was checking Aunt Nettie's IV line.

"Stop fussing with that, girl, and leave me be. Seems to me I should know what happened if I can clear my mind a little." She hesitated. "Did you people drug me, or am I just an old woman who doesn't know her own mind?"

The nurse tried very hard not to smile. "I can see you know your own mind, Miss Brewer. You're on some medications. Your heartbeat was a little irregular, and your blood pressure was down, so we're monitoring you. You were dehydrated, so we're giving you liquids. You've been sleeping for a while. You may feel a bit confused."

"Confused? Never clearer in my life. Except I don't know why I'm here."

Nick spoke gently. "What's the last thing you remember, Miss Brewer? Before now?"

Aunt Nettie hesitated. "Are you asking me as Nicky Strait, or as Detective Strait, young man?"

"As Detective Strait, I'm afraid," Nick replied. "I hope you'd give me the same answer, either way. Do you remember Saturday morning?"

"What's today?" asked Aunt Nettie.

"It's Sunday afternoon," said Maggie.

"Sunday afternoon. Well, that's not so bad. I was afraid you'd say Thursday or Friday, or it was December instead of August."

"No, Aunt Nettie," Will said. "It's still August. Yesterday it rained a lot and Maggie and I left early to go to an antiques show."

She stared at her hands for a few moments, and at the red marks and bruises on her wrists. "I remember. It was raining hard. I heard you leave, and took another little doze, and then I got up, and dressed, and went down to make tea."

They were all silent.

Then, slowly, Aunt Nettie pointed at her left wrist with her free hand, the one the IV needle was not taped to. "That's what happened, wasn't it?" she asked. "Someone came into the kitchen, and grabbed me. I screamed, but he put that sticky silver tape over my mouth, and carried me upstairs."

"Aunt Nettie, did you see him?" Will asked.

She shook her head. "No. He covered my eyes with something. But it was a man. It felt like a man when he picked me up. He was taller than I am. And his legs should be bruised. I kicked him as hard as I could!"

"I'll bet you did!" Will reached out and squeezed her hand. "Thank goodness he didn't hurt you any worse."

"He put me on the floor of my bedroom and wrapped that tape around my ankles and my wrists. I tried to get it off. I tried so hard. I heard him…"

"What did he say, Miss Brewer?" asked Nick. "Did he ask you any questions?"

"He didn't say anything," said Aunt Nettie. "But I think he

messed up my house. I heard things falling, and doors slamming, or drawers closing. I couldn't tell. I was just trying to get free. I had trouble breathing, with that tape on." She was quiet, as she looked from Will to Maggie to Nick. "That was yesterday morning? It wasn't just a bad dream?"

"It was yesterday, Aunt Nettie. But it's over now."

"And my house? My things?"

"We'll clean everything up as best we can, before you go home," Maggie assured her.

"Did he take anything?" Aunt Nettie asked.

"We don't know," said Will. "You'll have to tell us that, when you get home."

Aunt Nettie was quiet for a moment.

"I've lived in that home almost seventy years. I've always felt safe there. Your home is a place you should feel safe." She looked over at Nick. "Will I be safe if I go home now, Nicky?"

Chapter 28

⸻⸱⸙⸱⸻

CRABE AND HOMARD (CRAB AND AMERICAN LOBSTER). *Hand-colored steel engraving; two separate drawings on one sheet, the crab above the lobster, both on seaweed-covered rocks, the sea and a small fishing shack in the background. Artist: Félix Édouard Guérin-Méneville (1799–1874), a French entomologist who had several beetles named after him. His beautiful natural history drawings, most of them combining unusual mixtures of plants, animals, and insects, often with scenic elements in the distance, were published without commentary (published separately) in his* Dictionnaire Pittoresque d'Histoire Naturelle *from 1836–1839. 11.33 x 7.75 inches. Price: $95.*

Despite Aunt Nettie's insistence that she needed to go home immediately, Dr. Simpson was definite. She must stay in the hospital for observation at least one more night.

Will decided she was well enough to ask for anything she wanted, and told her to rest. "I'll talk to your doctor on the telephone, and see you probably late tomorrow morning, Aunt Nettie," he said, bending to kiss her forehead. "Your job is to get a good night's sleep."

"She'll need some follow-up appointments, but clearly she's survived, and is ready to carry on." Will chuckled in relief, as he and Maggie left the hospital together. "We Brewers are tough. What I'd like now is to go back to the motel, take a quick shower, and put on some of those clean clothes you got for me in Freeport."

"What about the house? Did Nick say when we could get in to start straightening it up and get our own clothes?"

"The evidence crew should be finished tomorrow morning. At

least we'll be able to start sorting through things before Aunt Nettie's released. Despite her insisting that she's fine, the nurse on duty told me they won't let her go before tomorrow afternoon at the earliest."

"After you get cleaned up, I'm guessing both of us will be ready for dinner."

"Actually, I'm starved. I didn't have any elegant tea this afternoon."

Maggie didn't volunteer exactly what elegant tea at the Thompsons had involved. "Early dinner sounds good to me, too. What about the Waymouth Inn?"

"Fine. We each have our own wheels, so why don't you go ahead and get us a table. The Inn could be crowded on a Sunday night in August. I'll meet you there in thirty minutes."

"Take your time," said Maggie. "I'll order a glass of wine. I have a book to read." She patted her bag that held the journal.

She got them a table in a corner of the Inn, safely out of sight of prying eyes, and ordered a bottle of Champagne for when Will arrived, and a glass of sparkling water for now. And opened the journal.

Monday, June 23, 1890
With great delight I can write that Mr. Micah Wright was the driver of the wagon that came for Jessie and me this morning. The day was a perfect one; the fog had burned off by the time we drove through the marshlands leading up to Prouts Neck, and both Jessie and I craned our necks looking at all of the carriages now at the summer boarding houses and fine hotels. Summer visitors began arriving during the ten days since we visited here before.

Boys and girls playing with marbles and hoops, many of them dressed more elegantly than Jessie or I, were outside several of the houses on or near the cliffs or beaches, and horses were tied at the blocks outside the inns. Some of the houses which take summer guests are large enough to hold several families; others only offer their facilities to one group, particularly since most households come from Boston or Hartford or New York with their maids and nursemaids and butlers and drivers. Even the servants appear very elegant.

South Gate House and The Willows and West Point House and, largest of all, Checkley House, which is close by Mr. Homer's resi-

dence, are the grandest of all, and have dozens of rooms. Perhaps hundreds! I could not begin to tell. I wanted to ask Mr. Wright about those places, but there was no time during our drive, as Jessie and I were sitting in the back. Our eyes were wide open the entire time, I can assure you, and when one of us saw something, or someone, of particular interest, we poked the other. Ladies never point.

Although I had visited this area before occasionally in spring or fall, I had never been there in the height of the season, when it turns into a summer colony.

Posing for Mr. Homer is opening windows to worlds I had only imagined.

But my imagining those refined occasions ended when we arrived at his studio. Sam was barking furiously at a large white duck that Mr. Homer himself, despite being dressed in his usual city attire, was chasing around the yard, between stacks of lumber, while the carpenters working on the addition to his studio laughed loudly!

Mr. Wright jumped down from the wagon immediately and joined in the chase, which added to the amusement. Jessie and I laughed as much as the carpenters, I must admit. And I was much surprised when, finally having caught the duck, Mr. Wright carried it to the studio, and put it inside, shutting the door.

He then straightened his clothing, brushed off the feathers, and came to assist Jessie and me down from the wagon.

"What is the duck doing here? And why did you put him in the house?" I couldn't help giggling.

"His name is Duck," Mr. Homer answered, quite seriously. "And he is quite a good duck. Normally he does not run about so. He was startled by so many people appearing at once, with the men building, and then your wagon coming down the street, and Sam's barking. Sam," he addressed the dog, who wagged his tail wildly and did not seem at all contrite, "you must behave yourself around Duck."

"Mr. Homer wanted to paint a duck, so he asked me to get one to model for him," explained Mr. Wright, grinning. "He planned for me to kill the creature and stuff him, so he could be posed appropriately. But Duck has won everyone's heart, so Duck will be remaining quite alive, I believe."

"He most certainly will," agreed Mr. Homer. "Now, have you explained to these young ladies what we are to do this week?"

"No, sir; I believe you can best do that."

Mr. Homer explained that he needed us to pose in the studio this week, taking turns holding ourselves in various positions so that he could work on sketches and watercolors he had done some years ago in England, and a few he had worked on in Florida more recently. He is organizing his studio while the construction is going on, and desires to finish work he started earlier. His agent, he said, was waiting for new work, but this would have to do.

Mr. Wright stayed outside and helped one of the young carpenters who was making a special house for Sam, and enclosing a separate area for Duck, so Duck would not have to remain in the studio all of the time.

(Mr. Homer did not seem to care that Duck pecked at Jessie and me, but was quite aggravated when Duck decided that tubes of paint might be edible.)

Truthfully, it was an exhausting day, but one full of possibilities. I have determined to somehow see the inside of one of those grand inns this summer.

Prouts Neck is definitely a more interesting place than Waymouth.

The Champagne was chilled by the time Will arrived at the Inn.

"What are we celebrating?" he said, bending to give Maggie a kiss that lingered long enough to promise more.

"Aunt Nettie's recovery, and a quiet night just for us," she said, closing the journal and slipping it back inside her canvas bag. For now, the nineteenth century could stay in the past.

"Sounds perfect," he agreed. They ordered mussels steamed in white wine and herbs, and lobster. "To us," he proposed, as their champagne flutes clicked.

"And to Maine," Maggie added.

The mussels were seasoned with just the right amount of garlic, and the lobsters were sweet soft-shells. "They're calling these 'new shells,' now, I noticed at one of the restaurants," Will commented. "But I'm an old-timer. Lobsters will always be either hard-shells or soft-shells to me."

"Is there really a difference?" asked Maggie, picking carefully through the body of her lobster for the small pieces of meat in the body behind the legs. "Other than the hard-shelled ones being thicker and harder to open, of course."

"I like the soft-shells. I think the meat is sweeter," said Will. "Of course, since the lobsters have just shed their old shells and grown new ones, there's empty space in the shells and they're messier to eat. But for my five dollars, or whatever the going rate per pound is this year, they're definitely worth it."

"These are delicious," agreed Maggie. "Right out of the water."

"Every hour out of the ocean or deep salt river makes a difference," said Will. "Anyone who thinks a tank in a restaurant or supermarket keeps lobster fresh just because they're alive hasn't eaten the real thing."

They didn't talk much, as they dipped their meat in lemon butter.

"So, your visit to the Thompsons was interesting," said Will.

"I never did see the art I was invited there to see," said Maggie. "But I did look at a lot of art from the 1930s colony. Horrible stuff. Mirage was a good name for the Thompsons' place. That colony must have attracted every wannabe artist in the Northeast. It definitely was not Ogunquit or Kennebunk or Monhegan. I didn't meet the senior Thompson, either, who I gather is quite elderly now, although his wife Betsy is not over thirty-five. But I did meet his son, Josh."

"Josh?" Will thought a minute. "I don't remember a son. But I know he was married to someone a lot older than Betsy years ago. So I assume that was wife number one or two, and Betsy is the latest edition."

"Maybe. Josh looks like trouble. Doesn't look as though he gets along with his stepmum, as he called Betsy. And I wondered why the Harvard grad student, Kevin Bradman, was living there for the summer. I'm still not sure, but he might be Josh's boyfriend. Or maybe he's Betsy's boy toy. He certainly looked very friendly with everyone."

Will grinned. "Sounds like the current version of the artists' colony is still humming. Didn't those colonies all have pretty racy reputations?"

"Some did. But a lot of work was done in many of them. Good work. I'm not sure what kind of work, if any, is being done at Mirage right now."

Will took another sip of the Champagne. "When I talked with Nick earlier he said they hadn't found anything in Nettie's house that would help them identify whoever broke in. At least she seems to be better, and whatever damage he did wasn't worse. Nick didn't think he'd found a stranger's fingerprints; whoever was there must have been wearing gloves. Our fingerprints are on file, since we've both been teachers. We'll have to clean up the house the best we can, and hope Aunt Nettie can see whether there is anything missing."

"There doesn't seem to be any reason for someone to break in, then?"

"Not that Nick can figure out. I also had a call from Rachel. She wants to see us tomorrow. I have no idea what that's about, but she is family. Maybe she just heard about Aunt Nettie and wants to hear from us how she is."

Maggie shrugged. "There are too many things happening. Now that we know Aunt Nettie's all right, I want to know who killed Carolyn. No word on anything there?"

"You were going to talk with her lawyer tomorrow, weren't you? He may have heard something. I don't think they've even set a date for the funerals yet."

"Sounds like we have a full day lined up. Especially if we'll be bringing Aunt Nettie home. We've got to get her room looking decent before she sees it. Despite how she thinks she feels, she's going to be weak, and need someone to keep an eye on her at first."

"How about we end this day then?" said Will. "Champagne, lobster, and a lovely lady. I can only think of a couple of other possibilities to make the night sweeter."

"Chocolate?" teased Maggie, as they got up to leave the restaurant.

"Chocolate is one possibility," Will agreed. "Have you ever tasted Round Top's Chocolate–Raspberry Chip ice cream?"

"No, but if it's as good as it sounds, it might be the beginning of a serious relationship," Maggie said, putting her hand in his, as they walked together down the quiet street toward a nearby ice cream shop.

Chapter 29

⎯⎯⎯ ∞∞∞ ⎯⎯⎯

A NEW ENGLAND HOME. *Currier & Ives hand-colored lithograph, 152 Nassau Street, New York, c.1860. Idyllic picture of square, white, shuttered, two-story Colonial home with center chimney, front and side doors, front porch. Separate barn; cows, chickens, light carriage pulled by horses; several children playing in drive; hills in distance. Currier & Ives prints (first under the name Stodart + Currier, and then N. Currier) were published from 1834 until 1907. Calling themselves "Printmakers to the American People," they published over 7500 prints, most subjects United States–related. Their low prices (five cents to three dollars) made them affordable by average Americans. Small folio, 8 x 12.5 inches. Price: $450.*

The evening had ended in a most satisfying way. Maggie stretched as she began to wake the next morning. She peered at the motel's digital clock radio: 7:10. Uncharacteristically, she had wakened first. Will was still snoring softly on the pillow next to hers. He must have been even more tired than he'd let on.

She slipped out of the bed, made a bathroom stop, and decided to use the time until Will woke up to sneak in another chapter of the journal. After what she'd heard at the Thompsons' house about Jessie's future, or at least what family stories said was Jessie's future, she was anxious to find out what Anna May's version of the summer of 1890 had been.

June 27, 1890
I have not written in a few days because there has been nothing new to write. Jessie and I have been to Prouts Neck three days this week,

during which time Sam's house has been completed, and Duck's enclosure also.

Mr. Homer has a special garden next to his studio in which he grows all manner of vegetables and flowers, and at the end of today's work he bowed to Jessie and me and gave each of us a nosegay before wishing us well. Since next week ends in the Fourth of July, and all its related celebrations, and both of Mr. Homer's brothers are expected at the Ark (one of them traveling with his family all the way from Houston, Texas, Mr. Wright told us!) we are not expected back until July 7.

It will be a dull week in Waymouth with only the usual parade and fireworks and reading of the Declaration and such. But Mother is relieved I will be here to help her cook for the church picnic. I am also planning to spend some of the money I have earned on new ribbons for my hat in an attempt to make it a bit more stylish. After seeing those elegantly dressed women outside the inns at Prouts Neck (and I am sure they believe they are in their vacation attire) I am more and more conscious of how countrified we are here in Waymouth, no matter how many copies of the Boston Globe's *fashion pages we study.*

July 4, 1890

What excitement we have had! The wife of the captain of Luke Trask's ship received a telegram that the ship was indeed damaged in the storms some weeks past, but all aboard were rescued by a fishing ship out of Newfoundland, and survived, to the joy and relief of everyone here in Waymouth, since all seven are local fishermen, and many feared them lost.

The men are making their way south to Halifax, where they will find passage back to Waymouth. Their ship was lost, which is a considerable financial hardship to its owner and captain, but not a major concern for Luke, since he had no loss but his gear and time.

Jessie was the one to tell me the news. She knocked on our door early this morning. She was smiling so, my mother said her happiness would dim the sun.

She said it would take Luke another year to pay for new gear, but that was nothing in comparison with what might have been lost, which, of course, was the truth.

I also rejoiced, but more silently, since both my concern before and my rejoicing now must be private.

After Jessie left, Mother wondered out loud what Orin Colby would think when he saw her joy today. I lied when I told Mother I thought he would understand Jessie was relieved to hear that her childhood friend was safe.

We knew other men on board, of course, so there were happy tears throughout the town, and the Independence Day Parade celebrated the good news as well as our Independence from Great Britain. The whole town, it seemed, gathered as always on the village green for a picnic after the parade, while the children and some of the fathers and young men played games and the women chatted and gossiped.

Jessie stayed with her family and I with mine, while my sister Sarah sat with a group of young women of her age from the church who later entertained us with a selection of patriotic songs. The mayor, as always, read the Declaration of Independence, the school band played, and when it was dark enough for a few couples to be seen walking into the shadows at the side of the green there were fireworks over the river, provided by the two shipyards and the mill in town. As we walked home afterwards I heard several young men shooting their rifles, as they frequently do on the Fourth, especially after they have imbibed to excess in celebration.

Since I had no one to sneak off the green with, and Mother's friends' gossip held no interest for me, the day's excitement had come early. But I have next week to look forward to, when I return to Prouts Neck.

Will turned over and opened one eye. "Maggie? It's almost eight-thirty!" He sat up. "We have to get over to Aunt Nettie's house. Why didn't you wake me?"

"You needed the sleep," Maggie pronounced, not mentioning she'd been so focused on Anna May's lavender script that she hadn't looked at the clock in forty-five minutes.

"Maybe," Will admitted, pulling his new L.L. Bean jeans on, "but we have work to do." He looked at her. "You're reading the journal?"

"It's fascinating," she answered, putting the book down.

"That's good," Will said, obviously focused on the present, not on 1890. He walked around the motel room, throwing their dirty clothes from Saturday and their toiletries into one of the shopping bags Maggie had brought back from Freeport. "Make sure we have everything. We need to check out and get going."

Within fifteen minutes they were back at Aunt Nettie's house. The yellow crime scene tape had been removed, but the mess left by whoever had broken in was only the beginning. Investigators had left gray fingerprinting dust on every surface in the house, and moved the few things on the second floor that had not already been misplaced. The first floor hadn't escaped the rampage either.

Maggie walked through quickly to get an overview. "I don't know the house as well as you do, Will. But I can scrub woodwork and counters. I'll start on the downstairs woodwork and put the kitchen back together. If you throw Aunt Nettie's sheets and towels down the stairs, I'll start a load in the washing machine so we can have fresh sheets on her bed when she gets home."

Will looked more overwhelmed than Maggie. "I keep thinking of someone going through her things. The china figurines and souvenirs and pictures that would mean nothing to anyone but her. It's going to be hard for her to come back and see all this."

"That's why we have to get as much back in order as possible," Maggie agreed. "The bathroom upstairs, and her bedroom are the most important. For now we can close the doors of our rooms and she might not even have to see those."

"You're right," nodded Will. "I'll get the sheets." He headed up the stairs.

Maggie started the washing machine as soon as the first load of laundry arrived. The rhythmic sounds of water pouring in, and then the familiar side-to-side *whoosh*ing of the washer was soothing. She scrubbed the woodwork and counters and stovetop and washed the dishes that had been left out. Everything had acquired a veneer of fingerprinting dust in the past thirty-six hours.

A mop she found in the closet cleaned the floor adequately. You couldn't eat off the floor, she thought, but it would do for walking. Most of the muddy footprints had more to do with the heavy rains Friday and Saturday than with forensic evidence. There had been a lot of people walking in and out during the past two days.

The living room and dining room seemed to have been skipped

by both the intruder and the police. The only dust looked like the sort she would no doubt find in her own house once she got back home. She took a dishcloth to use as a duster, and cleaned off the table tops and open shelves. Might as well do some basic house-cleaning while they were at it. Aunt Nettie wouldn't be up to it when she got home. She found the vacuum cleaner in the back hall, and gave the carpets what Aunt Nettie would have called "a lick and a promise."

What women of 1890 wouldn't have given for an electric vacu-um she thought, as it roared away dust and stray crumbs and pieces of crumbled leaves and dirt that had been walked in on wet shoes and boots. Anna May and Jessie and their mothers would have had to take up rugs, carry them outside, hang them over clothes lines, and hit them with carpet beaters to get the dust and grime out of them in spring and fall.

When had they invented carpet sweepers? She couldn't remem-ber. In the 1870s sometime. They must have seemed revolutionary!

When the washing machine paused she could hear Will mov-ing about upstairs, putting drawers back in bureaus, and return-ing furniture to where it belonged. Maybe she should go and help him.

But now she was curious. In that book of old photographs Aunt Nettie had shown them that first night she was in Maine, the night Carolyn had come for dinner, had there been any pictures of Anna May or Jessie? There'd been a picture of Carolyn's grandmother, Kathleen, she was sure. Helen Chase's mother. Did the photographs go further back?

She couldn't resist taking a peek. It would be wonderful to find a picture of Luke Trask, too, or even of Orin Colby. Who were these people she was reading about? What had they looked like?

She was sure Aunt Nettie had put the red morocco photograph album on top of the bookcase by the fireplace. But there was noth-ing like it on the bookcase. Or in it.

Maybe she was mistaken. She checked another, smaller book-case, and the shelf under the coffee table. Nothing. No morocco leather photograph album anywhere.

She felt a chill. Could the person who broke into the house have taken it? Who would want a century-old photograph album? Maybe

Aunt Nettie had taken it upstairs to her room, to look at it again. It contained her memories, after all.

Sudden silence signaled the end of the washer cycle. Maggie shifted Aunt Nettie's sheets and other bedding to the dryer. She was about halfway upstairs when Will's phone rang.

"Rachel! I was going to call you as soon as I finished at Aunt Nettie's house." Pause. "No, she's a lot better. We're hoping she can come home today. Is it critical we see you now?"

What could Rachel want that could be so important? Aunt Nettie's health was the issue right now. That and solving Carolyn's murder, of course.

"I'm sorry, Rachel. But I can't imagine… How long will you be at the library? Then we'll stop there in about an hour. Take it easy. I'll take Aunt Nettie's car. See you then."

Maggie continued up the stairs. "What was that about?"

"Rachel. She says Lew Coleman, that young guy who works at the auction house, blames her for the police removing the two paintings we thought were by Helen Chase from the auction last week. Coleman's threatening to have her fired."

"What?" said Maggie. "Why? It would be illegal for them to sell stolen art. If the paintings weren't stolen, then they should have records to prove that. All reputable galleries are careful about that sort of thing. And why fire Rachel in any case?"

"Because she's my cousin, and you're my girl, and she was seen talking to us before the police came and checked on the paintings. We're both linked with Carolyn Chase. And, it turns out, Rachel took two calls from someone at Sotheby's last Sunday for Lew Coleman."

"So?"

"Lew didn't want anyone to know about the calls. Rachel picked up his private line, thinking she was doing him a favor, and left the message note on the auction staff bulletin board."

"Let me guess: where his boss, Walter English, saw it," said Maggie.

"Right." Will sighed. "I don't know what that's all about, but we're somehow mixed up in it, so she wants to talk with us." He stood in Aunt Nettie's room. The furniture was back in place, fresh sheets were on the bed, and drawers were back in the two bureaus, but Maggie suspected not everything was exactly as it had been. How could either she or Will know which drawer Aunt Nettie used for her unmentionables and which for her out-of-season clothes?

At least the room looked presentable on the surface.

"You've done a lot of work. The bathroom?"

"Clean as I can make it," he said, opening the door to show her. "Luckily, it wasn't as messed up in there. Whatever the guy was looking for, I don't think it was drugs. At least not Aunt Nettie's aspirin and cough drops, which were all that were in there."

Will picked up a pile of towels he'd folded and started tucking them inside the small bureau he'd restored to its usual place in the hallway.

"Speaking of things missing. Have you seen her old photograph album? The one bound in red leather that she showed us the first night I was here."

Will stopped for a moment. "Isn't it on top of the pine bookcase in the living room?"

"I checked there. And everywhere else I could think of. I don't think it's downstairs. I hoped she'd taken it up to her room."

"If she did, then I didn't see it." Will's shoulders sagged. "Hell. I hope we find it. That's the first thing we've identified that might be missing. And it's something that can't be replaced. Maybe Aunt Nettie won't notice it's gone right away. We may still find it."

"But why?" said Maggie. "Why would anyone want a book of old photographs?"

"Most of them were of my family," said Will. "But there were pictures of Carolyn's family, too, you'll remember. Things seem to circle back to Helen and Carolyn Chase."

"They do," said Maggie. "The journal, written by Carolyn's great-grandmother. Her mother's paintings at the auction house. Carolyn's murder, and her house searched. Now Aunt Nettie's house searched, too, and Nettie hurt, and all we've found missing so far are those photographs. But that doesn't explain why."

"Let's just be thankful only one person was killed," said Will.

Chapter 30

UPSET, *1936 lithograph by American regional painter Grant Wood (1891–1942). Born and based in Iowa for most of his life, Wood is best-known for his painting* American Gothic, *one of the most recognizable images in American art. He also founded the Stone City Art Colony in Iowa during the Depression. This print is from one of the few books Wood illustrated:* Farm on the Hill, *written by the wife of one of his fellow professors at the University of Iowa, Madeline Horn, and published in a limited edition. It has an orange background, and shows a dismayed boy covered with milk, holding a milking stool, in front of a cow who has kicked over a milking pail. 7 x 9.5 inches. Price: $70.*

Aunt Nettie was a great deal better, her doctor reported when Will called. She'd been moved to a semi-private room. But the doctor would, to his aunt's aggravation, like her to stay one more night to make sure all her systems were working properly and she was strong enough to go home.

"She's fussing like an old hen whose chicks have been taken away, but she's fine so far," the doctor reported.

"I promised we'd stop to see Aunt Nettie later this afternoon," Will told Maggie, as they headed for the library to meet Rachel. "Her staying in the hospital does give us one more day to clean the other rooms. I still don't think we should leave her alone right away when she gets home."

Maggie nodded. "Not until we see how strong she is." Will hadn't mentioned moving to Maine to take care of Aunt Nettie since Sunday night. She certainly didn't want Aunt Nettie to fall, or be left alone in a home where she had been attacked. But she had so little time with Will. If he moved to Maine, when would she ever see him?

Aunt Nettie was lucky to have someone like Will, who loved her, and was clearly willing to turn his life upside down if she needed him. Most women would kill for a man like Will. So why did she find herself feeling almost jealous of a ninety-one-year-old woman?

As they paused at a stop sign, Maggie put her hand on Will's for a moment and gave it a quick squeeze.

He looked at her and smiled. "What was that for?"

"Just because," she answered. "You're a very special guy. Aunt Nettie's lucky to have you as a nephew."

"And you?"

"I'd be lucky if I had a nephew like you, too," she teased, wondering to herself how she would manage if she were Aunt Nettie's age and in the hospital. She had no family. No close friends she could count on to help. There were assisted-living centers and nursing homes full of women like her. She was thirty-nine. How much would a long-term-care insurance policy cost?

"You look very serious," Will said, looking over at her as he pulled into a parking spot near the Waymouth Library. "And you haven't heard anything I've said in the past couple of minutes. Where are you, Maggie Summer?"

"Sorry! Daydreaming. Onward to meeting Rachel."

Rachel was at the front desk with another woman, but after a hurried conversation, she grabbed the key to the archives room, and gestured to Will and Maggie to follow her. She closed the door after them.

"Why all the secrecy?" asked Will.

"Because I don't know what's going on, and I don't know who's involved in it!" Rachel said. She put up her fingers and started counting. "First, Carolyn Chase is murdered. Second, you guys imply that Walter English is auctioning off stolen paintings, and then police swarm all over the auction house the day before a sale. Great for buyer confidence, I assure you. That alone got me in seriously boiling water. Then I hear Aunt Nettie got mugged in her own house Saturday. And then yesterday, to top it all off, I almost got fired because I took a couple of telephone messages. So." Rachel folded her arms as though she were a principal examining two truant adolescents and looked from Will to Maggie and back again. "You both owe me an explanation."

Will just looked at her. "Don't you want to know how Aunt Nettie is?"

Rachel relaxed a bit and Maggie thought she saw a hint of a grudging smile. "I heard she was doing better. True?"

"True. She's doing much better. If all continues well, her doctor says she'll probably be able to come home tomorrow."

"That's great. Now. What about all the other stuff?"

"Rachel," Maggie asked, "who blamed you for the police removing the two Helen Chase paintings from the auction sale?"

"Lew, mostly," Rachel answered.

"That's Lew Coleman?" asked Will. "The guy who told you to get back to work when you were talking to us on Thursday?"

"That's him. He knows you're my cousin. His dad told him that, I guess, after he met Maggie—"

"Whoa!" said Maggie. "I met his father? Who's his father?"

"Henry Coleman. He used to teach math at Waymouth High."

"Ah," Maggie remembered, turning to Will. "He was at that genealogy meeting I went to with Carolyn, here at the library. Henry Coleman. He was writing a history of the schools in this county, or region, or something like that."

"Well, anyway," Rachel continued, undissuaded, "Lew knew Will was my cousin, and his girlfriend was a friend of Carolyn Chase's, and knew about American art. So after he saw me talking to you both, and then Nick Strait came in, claiming some art expert had said there were unidentified Helen Chase paintings in the sale, and asking their provenance, Lew put it all together."

"What *was* their provenance?" asked Will. "Who was the seller? Because if whoever it was proved they owned the paintings, or had the right to sell them, then there was no problem in their being auctioned. The auction house could always say they didn't know they were Helen Chase works. 'Buyer beware' can also be 'seller beware.'"

"Not something the seller would like, certainly," Maggie added quietly. "Since the paintings would sell for a lot less than if they were identified. And the chance that Walter English didn't recognize them as her work seems rather remote."

"I know, I know," said Rachel. "All those things are problems. Walter is always very careful about keeping detailed paperwork about consigners. He has notes on who appraised the items in his sales, or what reference sources he used for his own appraisals. But in the excitement of last week's auction no one could find any of the paperwork for those two items."

Maggie and Will looked at each other. "There was *no* paperwork for the paintings?" Maggie asked. "Nothing?"

"The file was empty. It didn't even list the person who consigned them. Walter was furious at having to give both the paintings to the police, but without proof of where they'd come from, Nick said they could be evidence. Walter was furious. As soon as Nick left he yelled at Lew. He said Lew had been the one who'd been the contact for the consigner, so he was responsible for the paperwork. Lew kept saying he'd done it, and it had just been misplaced."

"Did he say who he'd gotten the paintings from?" asked Maggie.

"He said some young woman had brought them in. He didn't remember her name. And then as soon as Walter had gone back to his office, Lew turned around and blamed *me* for the whole mess. He said you were my cousin, Will, and if you hadn't brought Maggie to the sale, then this wouldn't have happened." Rachel looked as though her whole world was about to collapse.

"Sounds as though he was looking to blow off steam, and you happened to be in his line of fire," said Will. "I'm sorry about that. But you had nothing to do with what we saw at the sale, or what we did about it."

"I know that. But he really was ready to fire me when I left those two messages for him on the bulletin board yesterday. Here I thought I was doing him a favor. Instead, he hit the roof." Rachel shook her head. "I had nightmares all last night."

"What kind of messages were they?" Maggie asked.

"Nothing exciting. Or at least I didn't think so. We were all there yesterday, doing the auction cleanup. Calling everyone who'd left bids to tell them whether they'd gotten their items, and if so, when they could pick them up. Arranging shipping for the large pieces of furniture. Adding up the accounts for each of the people who'd had consigned items sold." Rachel looked at each of them. "There's an incredible amount of paperwork that has to be done before and after each auction. Everyone was so busy that when Lew's line kept ringing, I thought he'd appreciate my answering it."

"Do you usually answer the telephones?" Will asked.

"No. But as I said, it was crazy there, and I thought maybe a customer had a question I could answer. Instead, it was someone I didn't know. An Alex Daggett. He called twice; said he could only talk to Lew, and it was important. The second time he said he was from Sotheby's."

"Did you give the messages to Lew?"

"I looked everywhere for him, of course. But I had work to do. I wrote the message out and stuck it on the bulletin board right at the entrance to where the offices are. We all leave messages there for each other. I knew Lew'd see it whenever he went back to his desk."

"And did he?"

"He sure did. He grabbed it off the board, tore it into little pieces, and then came in and dropped the pieces all over my desk. He said he never wanted me to pick up his line ever again. It was private, and that I'd already done enough to ruin his life."

"Ruin his life?" Maggie said. "That sounds a bit dramatic."

"You're not kidding," said Rachel. "Luckily, it was close to the time I was scheduled to leave, so that's what I did. I'm not sure I ever want to go back. Walter English isn't bad to work for. But dealing with that Lew Coleman isn't worth the hassle." She twisted the ring on the third finger of her left hand. "I don't really have to work anymore. I'm doing it to be independent and to have some money in the bank that's just mine. I don't want to be yelled at and blamed for crazy reasons."

"No," agreed Will. He paused. "Had the paperwork on those paintings showed up by the time you left yesterday?"

"I don't think anyone was even looking for it," she answered. "That was Friday's problem. During the auction Walter just announced that those lots had been withdrawn. No one asked any questions." She looked at them. "I feel better, having told you both. I know you can't do anything about it. But I was so angry that I was being blamed for doing what I thought was the right thing."

"You didn't do anything wrong," said Will. "But I think Nick Strait ought to know about those phone calls for Lew."

"Why would Nick Strait care about them?" asked Rachel. "It's not unusual for people at one auction house to call people at another."

"No. But on the day after an auction... Do you know if the Sotheby's guy...Alex Daggett?"

Rachel nodded.

"If Alex Daggett bid on anything at the auction?" asked Maggie.

"Nothing I know about," said Rachel. "But I didn't see all the bids. There were left bids and phone bids and Internet bids. Not even counting the people who were there in person."

"Of course, he might not have used his own name," Maggie pointed out.

"No," agreed Will. "Rachel, are you going back to the auction house today or tomorrow?"

"I've pretty much decided to quit," she said. "I'll probably go back tomorrow to give notice. They may ask me to stay the next couple of weeks to do the Labor Day sale, though. That's one of the biggest sales of the year. It wouldn't be fair to everyone else for me just to leave."

"When you go back, would you check something for me?" asked Will. "Out of curiosity. And if you have any trouble doing it, don't go any further. But if the records are clear, I wonder if you could find out who placed absentee bids of any kind on those two lots Nick Strait removed from Saturday's auction."

"The two paintings?" said Rachel.

"Right. The names and contact information for anyone interested in them. It might be important."

Rachel looked from one of them to the other. "You're doing it again, like last summer, with my Crystal. You're trying to figure out what happened with those paintings, aren't you?"

"If we can," said Maggie. "Of course, that's Detective Strait's job. But if we have any ideas that might help..."

"I'll see what I can find out," Rachel promised. "I'll call you tomorrow."

Maggie and Will stood up to leave. "By the way, Rachel, how long has Lew Coleman worked for Walter English?" asked Maggie.

"Only about five or six months," said Rachel. "Before that he worked in New York City. He came back to Waymouth to take care of his dad, who was diagnosed with Alzheimer's about a year ago. He's not too bad yet, but Lew gave up his life in New York to come back here and watch out for him. Pretty nice, right? Even if he was mean to me."

"Very nice," said Maggie. "Not every son would do that."

"They would if they loved their father," said Will. "Maybe Lew's under a lot of stress at home; maybe that's why he's been so jumpy recently, and misplaced the papers."

"Maybe," said Rachel. "But I'll try to find out who was interested in those paintings."

Chapter 31

SHIP-BUILDING, GLOUCESTER HARBOR. *Wood engraving by Winslow Homer for* Harper's Weekly, 1873. *One of his most famous engravings. Boys building toy boats from discarded wood shavings next to a ship being built in Gloucester, Massachusetts. Homer's "Gloucester Series," picturing people on the beach and boating in the harbor, is considered his finest group of wood engravings, and was published shortly before he turned to painting in oils and watercolors full-time. Many images in the series reappeared in his paintings. 10.5 x 15 inches. Price: $600.*

"Will, would you drop me at home while you go to see Aunt Nettie?" said Maggie, as they left the library.

"Sure," he answered. "But why?"

"I could do more laundry. The sheets in both our rooms are still on the floors and our clothes from the past week need to be washed. I'd like to have all that finished before Aunt Nettie gets home. Our rooms need to be cleaned, too. While you're visiting Aunt Nettie I could get a lot done." She was justifying not going to the hospital, but there *was* a lot to do. She'd rather accomplish something than sit around a waiting room. And there was the journal to read.

Will agreed, reluctantly. "I hate having you do all the grunt work, though. I won't stay at Rocky Shores too long."

"Stay as long as you need to," Maggie urged. "I don't mind." She leaned over and kissed him on the cheek. "Aunt Nettie doesn't need both of us there."

Back at the house she gathered laundry, which turned out to be a bigger job than she'd anticipated, started the washing machine, and settled down at the kitchen table with the journal. Somewhere in that little book there must be answers.

July 7, 1890
Jessie could hardly stop talking during our trip to Mr. Homer's studio this morning. I had noted her family's absence in church yesterday, but had not dreamed it was due to an invitation Mr. Colby had issued, inviting all of them to his parents' home up in Augusta for the day.

Jessie was furious, for the invitation had been extended not to her, but to her father, on all of their behalves. It was clear the purpose of the invitation was for Orin Colby's parents to meet her and her family and determine whether she would meet whatever criteria would be required to become a part of their family.

Jessie said Orin (she is now calling him "Orin," I noted, and not "Mr. Colby," as she was only ten days ago) seemed quite perturbed at her excitement upon hearing of the rescue of Luke Trask's ship, and swiftly spoke to her father. She is afraid he will make an offer for her hand before Luke is able to return to Waymouth, and that her father will accept the offer for her.

She admitted that Orin's family seemed pleasant enough, but old and dull. She reported she hardly said three words in the day she was with them, despite significant glances from her mother. Orin said, indeed, she impressed his mother as being an "attractive and modest" young woman, which infuriated Jessie still more. I have never seen her less composed than she was this morning.

Micah Wright was, as I had hoped, our driver this morning, but I had little chance to speak with him, as had been my plan. Jessie's concerns filled my ears from Waymouth until we reached the shore of the Atlantic.

Mr. Homer was waiting for us. He is quite excited about an idea for a new painting. He did not explain it all to us, but said that on the evening of the Fourth, guests at the Checkley House had celebrated on the beach below the hotel, which is visible from the balcony above his studio. He watched the partying, and went down on the cliff walk above the partygoers to sketch them dancing in the moonlight. Now he would like to paint the scene, and he wants Jessie and me to pose as two young women dancing together on the beach.

We giggled as he strode back and forth amidst the carpenters, Sam and Duck having forgotten their quarrels and both parading after him as he explained what he wanted to do. He also had a plan for painting one, or perhaps both of us, sitting on driftwood by the dunes. Clearly our one week away from Prouts Neck had provided Mr. Homer with many ideas!

He conferred with Mr. Wright, and they both agreed it would be more peaceful to do such painting away from the studio, perhaps on Ferry Beach. That is the same beach where we picnicked on the first day we met Mr. Homer and Mr. Wright, so long ago.

Mr. Homer assigned Mr. Wright the task of finding an appropriate spot, away from vacationers, for such painting, to begin tomorrow.

Today he sat Jessie and me on a large rock near the road in front of his studio and sketched each of us in turn. While he sketched Jessie, I took advantage of the free time to walk closer to two of the summer inns so I could observe those seated on Adirondack chairs and enjoying the ocean breezes.

Before the end of our posing I will find a way to see the inside of one of the inns. I am most curious to see what those large, high-ceilinged rooms look like.

July 8, 1890

Today was our first day posing on Ferry Beach. Micah (for so he has told both Jessie and me we may call him!) has found an old float that was once attached to a pier, but which must have been loosened in a nor'easter, for it is in weathered condition. It will serve as our dance floor on the beach. A large log brought in by winter storms and left above the high tide line will serve as a seat for the poses Mr. Homer wants near the dunes.

Micah drove us directly to Ferry Beach today. Madame Homer, who has, since that first day, been in the background to provide lemonade, iced tea, fruit or cheese and crackers, was also there, although she left before we were finished. I overheard her tell Mr. Homer that she had guests to attend to. She asked Jessie and me if we felt quite comfortable staying by ourselves with Mr. Homer. We both assured her we did.

I trust Mr. Homer. If anything, I would like him to allow us more freedom to explore the beach and cliffs. We are never solitary. Jessie

and I are together, Mr. Homer is with us, and often Micah, or one of
the other men who help Mr. Homer at his house, is also with us.

On the beach families enjoy the sea air. Nursemaids watch out
for their little charges who have changed into beach attire in the small
houses at the top of the dunes. Not everyone changes. Many men
and women are dressed for day, as are Jessie and I. It is warm on the
sand even in the early morning, and Mr. Homer will not have us wear
hats, as our mothers would certainly insist we do, since he is painting
us in an evening scene. We are conscious of freckling and reddening
our noses.

Jessie jokes that perhaps she'll get such a bright nose that Orin
will decide she is too wild a woman to be Mrs. Colby, wife of the
owner of the largest shipbuilding company in town. But I know she
is only hoping.

Each day she asks how long I think it will be until Luke and the
men on his boat are able to make their way back to Maine. Each day
I give her the same answer: I do not know.

July 10, 1890
I am not sure I should even write what happened today. It is too fright-
ening. Perhaps it will change my life, or scar it forever. I cannot write
now. I must think. I will tell Mother to turn the wagon away tomorrow
morning, saying my head is paining me. I am not ready to return to
Prouts Neck. I may never be again.

Chapter 32

WAVE. *Black-and-white lithograph of surf, unsigned and undated, but attributed to Alfred Russel Fuller (1899–1980), New England–born painter, teacher, and lithographer known for his coastal paintings. He lived in California during the 1930s, but then settled in Maine, in Port Clyde and Monhegan, in the mid-1940s, where he taught. 11 x 15 inches. Price: $150.*

Maggie put the journal aside. The washing machine had stopped some time before, but she'd been so focused on the pages she hadn't noticed. Now, wondering what had happened to Anna May, she shifted a load of sheets and towels to the dryer and piled dirty clothes into the washing machine.

Giving the journal a longing glance, she realized she'd better focus on cleaning the upstairs for at least a half hour. After all, she'd told Will she'd be putting Aunt Nettie's house in order.

Starting with her bedroom, which was in worse condition than Will's, she sorted through what probably had been in the closet, and then replaced the bureau drawers and their contents. Nowhere did she see the missing morocco leather photograph album. She hung her clothes back in the closet, and cleaned the outside surfaces of the furniture as best she could.

Carolyn's house, too, had been trashed, she thought. Had the upstairs of her home looked the way this house did? Had the same man searched both houses? Aunt Nettie had been quite definite in saying it had been a man, and thank goodness, Aunt Nettie's mind was fine.

She found clean sheets in the bottom drawer of the bureau and struggled to get the plump feather pillow to fit inside a tight pillow-case. She whacked it several times with her hand. Hard.

Life. Death. It all happened too fast. Planning seemed foolish. No matter what you did, life interfered. You planned to be married, but your husband cheated on you, and then had the discourtesy to die before you could even catch him at it. You planned to have children, but your timing was always off. You found a guy who seemed perfect...Maggie looked at a small picture of a grinning ten-year-old Will, sitting on the front steps, wearing a Boston Red Sox cap, that Aunt Nettie had framed and put on her bedside table.

Perfect, except that he didn't want children. His first wife had died during an ectopic pregnancy, and he wasn't willing to risk the pain again. Even for adoption.

Maggie gave the now-lopsided pillow one more solid thwack and glanced around. One more room done. Blood pressure probably up. She couldn't decide if she were angry or depressed. If she was angry, then why was she blinking away tears?

She found a diet cola in the refrigerator, poured it into a tall glass, added ice, and then, in an unusual move, checked Aunt Nettie's limited liquor supply, and added a little rum to her drink. "Thank you, Aunt Nettie!" she toasted her hostess. She checked the dryer. Still another twenty minutes to go, bless energy-efficient but incredibly slow appliances. She went back to 1890.

July 14, 1890

Mr. Homer sent a lovely nosegay for me with Jessie last Friday when I didn't go to pose, and Mother said I had an obligation to go to-day. Even Jessie asked how I was. She knows I don't suffer with headaches. I determined to return to Prouts Neck and see what had changed in the world.

To my surprise, the world was no different than it had been before. Micah brought the wagon to pick me up and inquired about my headache, but did not seem in the least interested in me beyond that. I looked at him so many times to see if guilt or shame were written on his face, but he seemed more interested in seeing to the horses. He scarcely paid me any attention.

I looked up at the windows of the South Gate House from Ferry Beach, where Jessie and I have been posing—together, or alone, as on that frightful day last week when Jessie posed alone for a short while and I foolishly agreed to take a walk with Micah. Now I know what the inside of that grand inn looks like, the dark walls, the bright porches, and the small bedroom, with that narrow bed that must have been for one of the servants, not one of the guests. I am no longer tempted by it. I know it was my fault for having ventured into such a place without a chaperone. Nothing I said or did after entering that room could have stopped what happened.

I am still sore, although it is not my head that is throbbing, and I am thankful for the long skirts and sleeves that cover me, despite the numbness and faintness that I feel when I allow myself to remember what has happened.

Several times during the past few days Mother asked me if indeed I was still feeling ill, since I did not seem to hear her questions. She said I acted as though I were in a dream.

I did not tell her it was not a dream. But I feel I have aged many years in the past week, and no longer see the world in the same way.

How do women live through such experiences? For I am not so naïve as to assume I am the only one to have been treated such. This is why men wish to be married. Why women wish to be married, and how they can stand up in church and say before God and their families that they will endure such a thing, I do not understand. Only a woman who did not know the horrors of it could do such a thing without shame.

I posed today, but I hardly remember doing it.

And Micah ignored me, as though what happened never occurred.

July 16, 1890
Jessie and I have continued posing. Most days we pose as though we are sweethearts, dancing closely in each other's arms, in ways that we would never allow men to hold us. Certainly not in public, as Jessie has whispered to me. Her arms around me feel solid and comforting, though, and I do not mind, although the idea of dancing in such a way with another woman seems strange.

Some days we each posed alone, sitting on that driftwood log, or looking out to sea, or in any of several other poses Mr. Homer has *devised. When one of us is posing alone the other is free to sit in the shade of the trees above the dunes or walk along the beach.*

Micah asked me to walk with him again one day, but I shook my head. I will never do that again. I can tell he is no longer interested in me. He has looked more closely at Jessie. I have told her she should not go anywhere alone with him. She does not listen; she laughs, and says she can take care of herself.

Perhaps she is stronger than I was. But I will be very glad when our trips to Prouts Neck are at an end.

I have saved some money. My mother has said I may use it as I wish. I had planned to buy a new dress or even two. I know Mother would like me to add to the store of linens and blankets put away for my future home.

But I am thinking of leaving Waymouth. I need to get away. I need to think.

If only I had a place to go.

Chapter 33

⸺⊶⊷⸺

HUSSEY'S REAPING MACHINE. *Wood engraving from* The Cultivator *farm newspaper, 1841. Drawing of primitive reaping machine pulled by two horses, with instructions from Mr. Obed Hussey of Baltimore on how to build such a machine "warranted to cut 15 acres of wheat in one day." 3 x 5.5 inches. Price: $35.*

The dryer came to a sudden stop. Maggie put down her now-empty glass. Anna May married Luke; she'd read that at the Waymouth Archives. So she must not have left. Or left and came back quickly. Whatever she did must have happened quickly, since in the journal it was mid-July, and according to the archives Anna May had married Luke in...October? She thought it was October. She'd have to check her notes.

Right now she had to fold laundry. The dryer had been full of sheets, pillowcases, and towels. She refilled it with the clothes in the washing machine, and carried the dry laundry upstairs. Towels went in the hall bureau. She put one set of clean sheets on the bed in the room Will had been using, and folded the other sheets and put them in the bottom drawer of the bureau in that room. Aunt Nettie put extra sheets in bottom drawers, she remembered.

She began at the door of Will's bedroom, and put it back in as much order as she could manage. She hadn't spent any time in this room.

The prints of sandpipers and gulls on the walls were large Morris birds. British vicar and ornithologist the Reverend Francis Orpen Morris had created some of the best drawings of birds in the mid- and late-nineteenth century, all of them hand-colored by his

179

wife. These were lovely ones. Had they been purchased recently? Or had the Brewer family been enjoying them since the 1870s?

Maybe Anna May had visited a Brewer home and admired these prints. It was fun to think so. She made a mental note of which birds were on the walls so she could check those in her inventory. Maybe she could give Aunt Nettie an addition to the collection for Christmas.

Her ringing cell phone brought her back to the present day. Will? She'd been wondering how long he'd stay at the hospital. She took the stairs two at a time down to the first floor where she'd left her phone, slipping a bit on the last stair and almost sliding into the wall.

By the time she'd dug the phone out of her bag it had stopped ringing. She looked at the number that had called. It wasn't Will's number in western New York. It was a Maine number.

She listened to the message.

"Ms Summer? This is Brad Pierce. I'm working on the settlement of Carolyn Chase's estate, and thought you'd be calling me today. I understand you've had some problems this past weekend, but would you please get in touch with me as soon as you can. You have my number."

Right. Brad Pierce. The lawyer. She'd completely forgotten about him. She decided to call Will first, but Will's phone went straight to messages. Either he'd turned it off, or there was no reception inside the hospital. No excuses, then. She called Brad Pierce. "This is Maggie Summer. You called a few minutes ago."

"Thank you for calling back. By the way, I understand Miss Brewer's home was broken into over the weekend and she was assaulted. How is she?"

The grapevine in small-town Maine. You didn't need the Internet or even a telephone here. News reached everyone by osmosis. "Much better, thank you. Will's at the hospital right now, hoping to bring her home today."

"That certainly is good news," replied Mr. Pierce.

"Has there been any progress in finding Carolyn's murderer?" asked Maggie.

"Not that I've heard. I understand the detectives are exploring several different angles. They've completed going through her aunt's home, and finished the autopsy."

"Did they find out anything?"

"Not much from the house, I'm afraid. Hard to tell what might have been missing, since both Susan and Carolyn are dead, and they were the two who might know. The autopsy showed Carolyn died of bleeding into her brain, the result of a blow."

"Was she attacked sexually?"

"Thank goodness, no," said Pierce. "Or if she were, then no one's told me about it. In any case, I don't think we should be discussing police matters. What I called you about was a trunk of family papers that Susan Newall wanted you to have in case of Carolyn's death. She had me write a letter to that effect the day before she died. The letter was signed and witnessed, and acts as a codicil to her will. I don't think any court will question it."

Thank goodness, Maggie thought. Otherwise she'd been walking around with a journal that wasn't hers.

"In Maine an estate isn't settled until six months after someone has died. But I know you don't live here, so I thought you might like to come to my office and look through the trunk to see if you want to take possession in six months. If you do, I'll hold it for you until that time. If you don't, I'll add the trunk and its contents to the list of items to be given to the Portland Museum of Art. That's the institution Carolyn Chase left her estate to."

He was going to give the trunk of documents away! "No! I mean, yes, I'd very much like to come and examine the contents of the trunk," said Maggie. "When would be a good time?"

"My secretary and I will be here tomorrow morning after eight," Mr. Pierce said. "May I assume we'll see you tomorrow morning, then?"

"Tomorrow morning. Yes," said Maggie. "I'll be there."

She'd just put the telephone down when it rang again. Will? No, another Maine number.

"Maggie! It's Rachel."

"Yes, Rachel?"

"When I was at the auction gallery this afternoon I did what you wanted me to. I checked the bids for those two paintings. There was one bid for each of them from the owner of a local inn for two hundred dollars, plus. You know what that means?"

"Yes. I know," said Maggie. A plus bid meant the amount you bid plus one additional bid if someone else bid the same amount you had. If you bid $200-plus, it meant you authorized the auctioneer to go one bid for you over $200. For a low-priced item that might mean $225. If you were talking about a bid of $25,000-plus, you might be authorizing a bid of $30,000, if the bidding was in $5,000 increments. Buyers had to understand the playing field before they placed a plus bid.

In any case, a bid of $200-plus for any oil painting, signed or unsigned, was below bargain-basement. Whoever placed it was hoping everyone else at the auction had their eyes closed.

"No other bids?"

"There was one. An Internet bid. It was for six thousand dollars. Plus."

"What was the bidder's name?"

"That's what's funny. The bid was taken by Lew Coleman. We don't accept 'left bids' of any kind unless there's a credit card to back up the bid and we've checked the card out to make sure it's good for the amount bid." Rachel paused. "I'll admit we don't always check if the bid is, say, under five hundred dollars, or the bidder is a regular buyer. But for a bid that large, the credit should have been verified."

"It wasn't?"

"The note next to it says Lew verified it. But there's no credit card number listed. Just Lew's initials."

Maggie thought for a moment. "Rachel, I assume no one working at the auction house is allowed to bid on items."

"Oh, no. That's against the rules," Rachel said. "If one of us really wants to buy something, once in a while someone has a friend bid for them. But it's against state regulations for the auctioneer to buy anything, and Walter English runs a tight ship."

"The way it should be," said Maggie. "Did anyone see you checking those bids today?"

"I don't think so. Everyone was busy answering phones from people who wanted to pick up their items, or unsuccessful buyers, or people wanting appraisals. With the economy down, a lot of people are de-accessioning, and we always hear from a lot of new clients just after a big auction."

"Good. Thank you, Rachel. You did a great job." She paused for a moment. "And Rachel, did you quit today?"

"I gave notice. I told Walter I'd work through Labor Day, to help with the big auction that weekend, but then I was leaving to plan my new life."

"Congratulations, Rachel! I hope it's a wonderful life!"

"It's going to be, Maggie. I just know it. If I can help with anything else, let me know. I'm going to be working at the library and the gallery for the next couple of weeks, but I'm going to stay as far away from Lew Coleman as I can."

"That's a wise idea."

"Give my best to Aunt Nettie, will you? Tell her I have some of the cranberry-orange muffins that she loves in my freezer. I'll bring some by for her later this week."

"She'll like that. Thank you, Rachel!"

Maggie was beginning to feel pieces of the puzzle coming together. But they didn't all fit yet.

As if in answer, the clothes dryer beeped. She answered its call, folding the mix of her clothes, Will's, and Aunt Nettie's in the kitchen.

Laundry, just like a family, she thought, as she carried the piles upstairs, and put everything away. All mixed together. But it could be sorted out.

What she needed to do was figure out what belonged where.

It was after four o'clock in the afternoon. Shouldn't the hospital have sent Aunt Nettie home by now? And if they released her this late, what would they all eat? Was there any food in the house?

She was checking the refrigerator when the telephone rang again.

Chapter 34

⎯⎯⎯⎯◇◇◇⎯⎯⎯⎯

PETUNIA NYCTAGINIFLORA...PETUNIA PHOENICIA...ETC. *Botanical print illustrating a bouquet of six flowers from Jane Webb Loudon's (1807–1858)* The Ladies Flower-Garden of Ornamental Annuals, *c. 1850. London. Hand-colored lithograph enhanced with gum arabic. Mrs. Loudon, as she signed her books, was the first botanical illustrator to paint flowers that bloomed together rather than illustrate examples of a single specimen or classification. She worked beside her horticulturist husband, even during her pregnancies (which was unheard of at the time), and saw the need for more accessible guides to gardening. She made it fashionable for ladies to work in gardens, and her popular books ended up supporting her family. 8 x 11.5 inches. Price: $160.*

"Hi, lady. It's me." Will's voice was clear and calm.

"What's happening at the hospital? I expected you to call hours ago," Maggie said.

"Sorry. It's been a bit crazy here. The doctors insisted they had to check Aunt Nettie again, and then Nick came to question her once more to make sure she couldn't help identify the man who attacked her. I didn't want to leave her alone."

"Are they releasing her today?"

"Dr. Simpson signed the papers and one of the nurses is helping her get dressed right now. How's the house?"

"Pretty well done," said Maggie, feeling proud of herself. "I've about finished the laundry and our rooms. But we're low on food. I don't know how much she'll want to eat, but you and I will need something for dinner."

As she spoke, Maggie's stomach rumbled. She hadn't had lunch. Diet cola plus rum didn't exactly count as sustenance.

"Don't worry about that. I'll stop on the way home and pick something up. And a locksmith should be arriving any time. Nick suggested we change the locks on the doors and put guards at least on the downstairs windows. He knew someone who could come right away, so I told him you'd be there to let him in."

"Good idea," said Maggie. "We should have thought of that yesterday."

"Even with a food stop, I should be home in an hour."

"See you then. Tell Aunt Nettie it will be good to have her at home again."

"She's anxious to get out of the hospital, but I think she's a little nervous about coming home," said Will, lowering his voice.

"I'm not surprised. I'd be nervous, too, under the circumstances," said Maggie. "I'm glad we'll both be here."

"Exactly," said Will, sounding relieved. "That's what I told her, too. Love you, lady!"

Maggie had barely put down the telephone when a knock on the front door alerted her to the arrival of Butch Osmond, 24-HOUR LOCKSMITH AND HOUSEHOLD PESTS ELIMINATED, according to his orange T-shirt. She authorized his installing deadbolts on both the front and back doors.

It would be good to get as much of that done as possible before Aunt Nettie arrived.

Seeing someone putting heavy defenses on her home would only remind her of what happened Saturday.

In the meantime Maggie refreshed her drink (just a little) and read another journal entry. Once Will and Aunt Nettie arrived there wouldn't be time for reading.

July 19, 1890
What news! Jessie is all in a dither...Luke Trask has returned! Jessie has delayed all of Orin Colby's hints and suggestions, but now that Luke has returned she will have to make a decision. Or Luke will.

I wonder if he received my letter? If so, then he knows of Orin's interest in Jessie, and the challenges he faces.

July 20, 1890

Luke Trask was in church with his family this morning. After services he did not speak with Jessie and her family, as I had expected, but came over and spoke politely to me, asking if he might visit tomorrow evening. Before my mother could respond, I told him that, of course, he was an old friend who was always welcome.

He must have seen Jessie yesterday! We have only one more week to pose for Mr. Homer, but I will see her tomorrow. I can hardly wait to ask her.

July 21, 1890

Jessie told me, with tears in her eyes, that Luke came to call almost immediately upon his arrival Saturday, but her father turned him away, telling him that Jessie was already spoken for.

"What are you going to do?" I asked Jessie.

She just shook her head. "I am going to marry Orin," she answered. "I must. My father has promised him, and I have reasons of my own. You wouldn't understand. You have no beaux."

I would understand better than she thinks, I suspect. But I gave her my handkerchief, which she was in need of. I did try to be sympathetic but, indeed, I could think of nothing but that Jessie had turned Luke away, and that he had asked to call on me!

I have loved him as long as Jessie has, I am sure. Perhaps, for all the strange turns this summer has taken, this might be the turn that will save me.

Now: will he come?

Luke did, indeed, arrive to call this evening, very properly. We sat in the living room, just as courting adults would do. I felt as though we were playing at being man and woman; that we were, inside, still the children who played tag and hide-and-go-seek on the village green and passed notes in school with Jessie. At any moment I expected Luke to reach over and tickle me, or joke about what we were doing.

But he did not, and neither did I. We both played our roles seriously, and I found myself enjoying the grown-up Luke as much as I had hoped to. As much as I had liked the boy. He is very good-looking, as Jessie often said. He is not sophisticated, like Micah, or wealthy, like Jessie's Orin. But I am comfortable with Luke, and I know he works hard.

Which indeed he will have to do, now he has lost all his fishing gear when the sloop went down.

We talked mainly of Jessie, and his months of longing for her, and his disappointment at her being promised to someone else. But he also said he was glad to have me as a friend, and that our friendship sustained him. I told him the same.

It was not precisely a romantic meeting, but he was in the parlor of my home, not in Jessie's or in that of some other young woman. And he said he would call again if I were agreeable.

I said I was.

Anna May had managed to get Luke's attention.

Maggie checked on the locksmith. He had already put new locks on both the front and back doors.

"Tight as they'll get, ma'am, unless someone was to knock the whole door off its hinges. Those hinges won't last forever, you know," he'd unreassuringly pointed out. Now he was putting small locks on each of the first-floor windows.

Maggie hoped they wouldn't make it too hard for Aunt Nettie to open the windows. In New York City and some parts of New Jersey the second-floor windows would need to be reinforced, too, but here in Waymouth... She hoped Nick was right; that wasn't necessary.

Her home had window locks, and so far (she knocked quickly on a nearby pine side table) she hadn't had a break-in. But Aunt Nettie had. Of course, Will had left the back door unlocked and so, technically, the intruder had just walked in. She hoped Aunt Nettie would remember to bolt the locks being installed now.

Will's RV pulled into the driveway a few minutes later. He opened the door for his aunt and offered a hand to help her out as Maggie joined them.

"Welcome home! It's good to see you out of the hospital, Aunt Nettie."

"It's certainly good to be here," said Nettie, as she stood in the driveway and looked around. "I feel as though I've been away years, and aged at least a decade. What's that truck in the street?"

"I called a locksmith to put new locks on your doors, Aunt Nettie," said Will, guiding his aunt to the steps up to the front porch. "How's he coming, Maggie?"

"Almost finished. The front and back doors are done, and he's put locks on almost all the downstairs windows."

"Locks on the windows, too! You'll make me feel I'm in a prison!" said Aunt Nettie. She took the steps carefully, one at a time. A week ago she would have moved three times as quickly. And Maggie noted she didn't really complain that the locksmith was there.

"Let me sit on the porch a few minutes and look at the river," said Aunt Nettie, taking her usual place in her usual chair.

"Would you like something to drink?" asked Maggie.

"Some iced tea would be lovely, dear," said Aunt Nettie. "If it's not too much bother."

"No problem," said Maggie, wishing she'd thought to make some earlier in the day. Will followed her into the house and put his arm around her.

"Thank you, thank you for everything," he whispered. "I couldn't have been at the hospital for Aunt Nettie if you hadn't been here to take care of things at the house."

"Mr. Brewer? The doors and windows are done. You want to pay me now, or should I bill your aunt?" Butch Osborne stood in the kitchen doorway, toolkit in hand.

"Let me look at what you've done," said Will, releasing Maggie with an extra squeeze. "Have you left three or four copies of a key that will fit both doors?"

As the two men left to talk over door and window issues, Maggie heated water and found teabags, lemon, mint, and sugar. Aunt Nettie liked real sugar, not the artificial sort.

With ice cubes added to cool down the hot tea, it didn't take long to make enough iced tea for now and later. Maggie poured one glass for Aunt Nettie and put the rest in the refrigerator.

"Sorry, that took a few minutes," she said, handing the glass to Aunt Nettie on the porch.

The old woman took a long sip, and then handed the glass back to Maggie. "Just put it on the table for me, won't you?" she asked. "I should feel full of energy after being kept prisoner in that place for days, but I don't seem to have any strength. Will stopped to get food for dinner, but I'm not sure I'm up to eating very much of it."

Maggie realized Will hadn't brought anything else into the house. "Food? Is it in the RV?"

"I guess so. I didn't look where he put it."

"I'll check." Sure enough, there were two bags inside. "I'm going to see what he bought, Aunt Nettie. Maybe you can eat a little."

Will must have thought they were going to have guests for dinner. Or he'd been starving when he'd ordered. Maggie remembered the take-out place they'd eaten the summer before. In the bags were fried scallops, fried clams, fried haddock, tiny fried Maine shrimp, and fried onion rings, Will's favorite. At the bottom of one bag was a container of vegetable soup. He'd even bought three Whoopie Pies, the soft chocolate cake with marshmallow filling that was the local most-evil dessert.

Enough food to sabotage two or three diets all in one meal.

Maggie went back to Aunt Nettie, who looked as though she was almost falling asleep on the porch. "Aunt Nettie, do you think you could eat a little vegetable soup? And maybe a couple of scallops?"

"That would probably be good for me, wouldn't it?" she said. "Well, you get it ready, Maggie, and then I'll come in. I don't want to try to eat soup out here on the porch. It's getting late. The sea breezes are coming in and I'm getting a bit chilled."

By the time Maggie'd found Aunt Nettie a sweater to put around her shoulders and set the kitchen table to display all of Will's offerings, he'd sent the locksmith off with a check. "Go and get Aunt Nettie," said Maggie. "She said she's too tired to eat much, but I'm hoping she can manage a little soup and some seafood."

Will helped his aunt in from the porch, and he and Maggie both tried not to watch as Nettie stirred her soup, but ate very little of it, and managed to cut one large scallop into pieces and eat it in tiny bites. They filled themselves with the rest of the vegetable soup and generous helpings of the fried foods.

"I'm sorry. I guess I'm just not hungry," said Aunt Nettie. "Will, could you help me upstairs? I think I'll go to bed early tonight. I'm sure I'll be back to feeling myself in the morning."

"No problem," said Will. "Would you like me to help you get into your night clothes?"

"My dear, no. I'm not an invalid," said Aunt Nettie. "But maybe, Maggie, if you could help me with my shoes and some of my buttons? I always have trouble with buttons when I'm tired."

"I'll go up with you, too," said Maggie.

It was another half hour before Aunt Nettie was tucked into her bed and Will and Maggie were back downstairs finishing their dinner, now cold.

"I hope she has more strength tomorrow," said Maggie.

"She didn't even ask to see the work the locksmith had done, or look at the house," Will pointed out. "Thank goodness we cleaned it up as much as we did. She didn't seem to notice that anything was different."

"She didn't look," said Maggie. "She didn't look at anything. She was depending on you, on us, to help with everything. She couldn't have come home by herself, Will."

"I know," he said. "The doctors said she was fine physically, but I'm not so sure. She certainly isn't the same. We'll see how she is tomorrow."

And the day after, Maggie thought, as she cleaned up the kitchen while Will went to check that his aunt's door was ajar so he could hear her if she called for him during the night. And the day after that.

Chapter 35

——— ⊶ꙮ⊷ ———

FANEUIL HALL, FROM THE WATER. *Hand-colored steel engraving by William Henry Bartlett (1809–1854), printed in London. Bartlett was the best known and most prolific topographical artist in the first half of the nineteenth century. He made four visits to the United States, and also traveled throughout the British Isles, the Balkans, and the Middle East. His engravings were all published uncolored, but some were subsequently hand-colored. This one is from his* American Scenery, *published 1839–1842, and shows a schooner and smaller sailing boats docked near Faneuil Hall in Boston. 8 x 11 inches (image 7.5 x 5 inches). Price: $95.*

"I have an appointment to meet Brad Pierce tomorrow morning," said Maggie. "Carolyn's lawyer. He wants me to see the contents of the trunk she left me. I can't take possession for six months, but he wants me to know what I'm getting."

"Okay," said Will, who'd been pacing the living room in silence for the past fifteen minutes. "When you were cleaning the upstairs today, did you see Aunt Nettie's photo album?"

"No. And I did look for it. All I saw were dirty clothes and bedding and a lot of dust. Fingerprint powder, and the regular kind of dust, too," said Maggie. "And Rachel called this afternoon."

"Did she find out anything about the auction bids?"

"There were two left bids on each of the paintings. We can forget one. It was from the owner of a local inn who only bid two hundred dollars-plus. Way out of the ballpark for any decent oil painting."

"Just looking for Maine scenes to hang on the walls," said Will.

"That's what I figured. But there was a higher bid from some-one approved by Lew Coleman, without identifying information or a credit card number."

Will stopped pacing. "Interesting. What do we know about Lew Coleman, other than that he comes from Waymouth and his father taught math and is now losing it a bit, mentally?"

"I don't think his father is too far down that path," said Maggie. "Remember, I met him. But I suppose he could be in the early stag-es. Rachel said Lew worked in New York before he came home to take care of his dad."

"If he came from Waymouth, no way he didn't know about Hel-en Chase. Rachel said he'd had a call from someone at Sotheby's, right?"

"Right."

"If he'd worked there..." Will pointed out.

"Then he would know people there. And definitely know about Helen Chase," Maggie agreed.

"Maybe he saw those paintings, recognized them, and had someone planted to buy them, so he could resell them at Sotheby's." Will looked as though he'd solved the puzzle.

"Illegal, but possible," Maggie admitted. "But that doesn't explain how the paintings got into the auction at all. If anyone from Way-mouth wanted to sell Helen Chase paintings they could take them to Sotheby's themselves, instead of using a Maine auction house. Or at least have them identified for what they are! Some Maine auction houses get big prices."

"But you said none of Helen Chase's Maine paintings should have been sold. She kept them all, or gave them to Susan. So none of them should have been in any auction house." Will looked at Mag-gie.

"Unless they were stolen. In which case whoever stole them wouldn't want to call attention to what they were. If they were sold, and then 'discovered' as unknown Helen Chase paintings, they could then be sold at high prices," Maggie pointed out.

"Especially if Susan Newall and Carolyn Chase, the only people who could identify them as stolen work, were dead," Will said.

"I have some questions to ask Brad Pierce tomorrow," said Maggie, standing up. "But right now, I'm going to bed. I have a feeling tomorrow is going to be a full day. And I want to read some more of that journal. I still think there are answers there."

July 31, 1890

Jessie's wedding date has been set. She will marry Orin Colby on New Year's Day, and has asked me to stand up with her. She is very excited about the wedding. Much more excited than she is about the pearl engagement ring on her left hand, or the man who placed it there.

She is having ivory satin for her gown sent from Boston, and would like me to wear blue satin, which she says Orin will pay for. They will be married at the Congregational Church, with a reception at her parents' home following the ceremony. It will all be very elegant. She showed me menus from New York and Boston restaurants with recipes for such items as turtle soup and oysters Rockefeller.

I was not sure how those delicacies could be obtained in Waymouth in December, but she assured me S.S. Pierce in Boston could deliver them. She seems to have learned a great deal from our summer on Prouts Neck. Mr. Homer received crates from S.S. Pierce almost every week.

Luke Trask calls on me several times a week. Sometimes now we do not speak of Jessie, but of ourselves. He is not ready to marry, for he has no financial resources, and is but a young fisherman, but I am not ready to marry either, so that is not of concern to anyone but Mother, who sees Jessie's wedding as a challenge for me to also find someone suitable to wed.

She has suggested several men who attend our church and who she feels are eligible, but none are of interest to me, and she has not invited any for me to parade in front of, as Jessie's parents did when they decided Orin Colby was the man they wanted for their daughter. I am grateful for that.

For the most part I try to ignore Mother's suggestions and hints, but some days it is difficult. Although Jessie's wedding will be grand, I do not envy her wedding bed with Orin Colby in it. Or anyone else. Even Luke.

August 20, 1890
Today I looked back at my journal and counted. It has been nearly six weeks since that horrible day in July. I have tried to put it in the past. But, by all signs I have ever heard whispered in women's corners, my body has not forgotten what happened then.

I will not tell Micah Wright. In truth, I feel doing so would accomplish nothing but put myself in the shameful position of asking for something I do not wish under any circumstances to have.

I can see only one chance to save my situation. I have just made a decision that would scandalize Waymouth, but which, if not successful, will result in even more scandal.

As I am, I am ruined, and my family with me. Whatever I do, however degrading it might seem if I were to read it in a penny-dreadful, is what I see now as my only alternative.

There is no one I can talk with; no place I can go. I must use my wits, and whatever charm I can find.

And I do have a lovely yellow dress that I think may do....

August 23, 1890
It is done.

I believe Luke was more surprised than anything else by my sudden overt affection, but if my advances were not polished and knowing, that was as well, since they were to seem naïve and unrehearsed...which, indeed, they were close to being. He was, to my surprise, gentle, and responded kindly and with apologies and gratitude, and held me afterward and told me that, indeed, he loved me.

It was easier accomplished than I had imagined, and despite my nerves, even pleasant. He did not seem to notice anything amiss, thank goodness, and believed my protestations that I was overwhelmed by my affection for him and could not control myself. (Was ever a woman such? But he did not seem to question either my words or actions.)

Now I must wait an appropriate interval to tell him our joyful tidings.

September 10, 1899
Tonight I told Luke of what I feared my condition was. I did cry as I

spoke, more than a few tears, most of them genuine, as he is the first I have trusted with my secret, and no matter what his response, I was relieved to tell it.

He was taken aback, it was clear, but bravely put his arms around me and told me that he loved me and that we would manage somehow and that, of course, we would marry as soon as possible.

Bless Luke!

I confided that I did not want our wedding to compete with Jessie's planned celebration, especially under the circumstances, and Luke readily agreed, because time is of the essence.

He will borrow a carriage from a friend and take me driving Saturday, as we sometimes do, and we will go to Portland, where we will find someone to marry us. We will leave notes for our parents. I have enough money for us to spend our wedding night at an inn in Portland.

The dear man asked if I would like to stay that special night in one of the inns at Prouts Neck, since Jessie and I had journeyed there often this past summer. I quickly assured him that an inn on Prouts Neck was the very last place I wanted to be on my wedding night.

Beyond Saturday, we have no plans. But I do love him. How could I not, when he is saving me from disgrace, or worse? We are not the first to marry in haste and have an early baby.

There are many fates far worse than to have a handsome husband who says he loves me and my child.

Maggie closed the journal, and turned off her light. As she'd read in the Waymouth archives, Anna May and Luke Trask had been married. But it hadn't been the joyful celebration she'd imagined at the Congregational Church on the village green.

Anna May was right, of course, in thinking she wasn't the first bride to get married under such circumstances. Not even the only bride who'd given her husband selective information about the parentage of the child to come.

But that wasn't the end of the journal. Or the story. And what about Jessie?

Maggie was tempted to turn the lamp on her bedside table back on, but resisted. She wanted to be alert if Aunt Nettie needed help during the night. And fascinating though the past was, she had questions in the present she needed to answer. She hoped, tomorrow.

Chapter 36

⎯⎯⎯ ∞∞∞ ⎯⎯⎯

RICHFIELD NONE SUCH. *Hand-colored lithograph by R.H. Pease for Natural History of New York, 1851, "on stone by P.J. Swinton," lithograph of a bright red apple today considered a heritage variety. Nineteenth-century lithographs were made by treating flat stones with a substance that would absorb or repel ink in the required pattern, and then pressing them on paper or vice versa. Large lithographs required large stones. Lithography was the first method of printing that employed color. Engravings, whether steel, brass, or wood, were colored by hand, usually by women working in assembly lines. 8.5 x 11 inches. Price: $85.*

In the morning Aunt Nettie said she felt stronger. If she hadn't slept through the night, she didn't share that with Will or Maggie. She was still "not as limber as she ought to be," though, and reluctantly let Maggie help fasten her bra and pull a long-sleeved T-shirt over her head, while Will scrambled eggs and made toast for breakfast.

"I have to see Brad Pierce," said Maggie, a bit apologetically.

"You go on," said Will. "I have paperwork left from Saturday's show."

There had been no sales at the show, which equaled almost no paperwork. But neither of them was comfortable leaving Aunt Nettie on her own.

"I'll stop at the grocery store and get us some things for lunch and dinner," Maggie volunteered. "Then we won't have to worry about going out later."

"Great idea," agreed Will.

"I could make lasagna for dinner, and we can have sandwiches for lunch."

She checked the refrigerator and cabinets and added coffee, milk, and some fruit to make a tart for dessert to her list. Aunt Nettie might not be up to going out to eat in the near future, and that meant they'd all be eating in. Lasagna would mean leftovers for tomorrow, and bread and sandwich fixings would also do for several days.

Will walked out with her to her van. "I don't know how I could have gotten through the past few days without you, Maggie Summer," he said, gently putting his fingers under her chin and raising it. "I know this isn't exactly the vacation you imagined."

As their lips met, Maggie let herself relax in his arms. Then she pulled back. "We're grown-ups. Grown-ups have to deal with life. Besides which, I really came to Maine for the lobster!" She made a funny face at him and blew a kiss as she backed out of the driveway.

It *wasn't* exactly the vacation she'd hoped for. But their time together wasn't over yet. And Aunt Nettie did seem better this morning.

Onward to see the lawyer.

Brad Pierce's office was in a converted Victorian house just off Route 1. The sign outside listed two lawyers, a chiropractor, a massage therapist, and an acupuncturist. Maggie wondered whether the lawyers referred those in traffic accidents to the chiropractor or the acupuncturist, or whether the massage therapist had accepted clients from all of the above.

She rang the bell labeled BRADLEY PIERCE, ESQUIRE and walked in, as his sign directed. She was greeted and offered coffee by a cheerful woman behind a wide desk ringed with paper folders.

"No, thank you," said Maggie, wondering what the woman would have said if she'd asked for a diet soda. She added her drink of preference to her shopping list. And maybe a bottle of wine to go with dinner. She thought for a moment. How much rum had she added to her soda yesterday? Not much, but there hadn't been much in the bottle to begin with. She should be a good guest and replace it. In Maine, wine and spirits, as her mother had called them, were sold in the supermarket, so that would be easy to do.

"Dr. Summer?" A tall, thin man in his early fifties, with little hair to balance a large nose, had come out of his office.

"Yes. Brad Pierce?"

"Come with me. I've put the chest in my conference room, but I thought we might chat for a few minutes before you look at it."

Maggie followed him into his office.

"I heard Miss Brewer had an unexpected visitor the other day."

"Someone broke in, dumped drawers, and generally messed up most of her house and left her tied up. For a ninety-one-year-old woman it was a very difficult experience."

He shook his head sympathetically. "How is she?"

"She got home from the hospital late yesterday, and is feeling a little better now. But she's far from back to where she was before Saturday."

"Have the police figured out who did it?"

"Not that I've heard. They spent a lot of time at her house, though. Have they made any progress finding Carolyn's killer?"

Mr. Pierce shook his head. "Sadly, no. Her house was left in a similar state, I'm afraid. Was anything of Miss Brewer's missing?"

"We can't say for sure." Maggie hesitated to tell him about the photograph album. It seemed unlikely that it was stolen. "Her nephew, Will, and I don't know her belongings well enough to tell, and she hasn't been able to go through everything yet. Nothing obvious was missing. What about Susan Newall's house, where Carolyn was found? Was anything missing there?"

"Dr. Summer, I understand you were the one who identified two of Helen Chase's paintings that were consigned to the Walter English Auction House for last weekend's auction."

Mr. Pierce had just abruptly changed the subject. Maggie nodded. "I saw the paintings there and wondered why they weren't identified as her work."

"The police feel they may have been stolen from Susan Newall's home, but for some reason all paperwork at the auction house connected with those paintings seems to have disappeared."

"I see," said Maggie. "That seems too coincidental, doesn't it?"

"To me, it does," said Brad Pierce. "But so far no one is talking. Until they know how those paintings got to the auction house there's no proof they were stolen. I once tried to get Susan to make a list of all the paintings of Helen's that she had, but she never did."

"They couldn't have been stolen from the house at the same time Carolyn was killed," Maggie said. "They were listed in the auction catalog that was printed ahead of time. While Carolyn was still alive."

"Quite right, Dr. Summer. So we're looking at a theft that happened before Carolyn Chase's death. Or paintings consigned by Carolyn, or by someone she gave them to."

Maggie shook her head. "I didn't know Carolyn well, Mr. Pierce, but she talked of her mother's paintings with love and respect. She spoke of hanging them in the Newall house when it would be hers, and eventually leaving them to the Portland Museum. I didn't get the impression she was thinking of selling any of her mother's work. Certainly none of the Maine paintings."

"That was my feeling, too," said Pierce. "But of course the police must consider every angle."

"Mr. Pierce, you know everyone in Waymouth."

"Perhaps not everyone. But a good number," he admitted.

"Do you know Henry Coleman and his son Lew?"

"Certainly! Henry taught mathematics for years at Waymouth High School, and coached the basketball team. Good teacher, and darn good coach. He's been retired some time now. His son Lewis graduated from the high school and went on to college, I think at Orono, and then got a solid job in New York. I used to see Henry at the Men's Club at the church on Thursdays for lunch. Henry was so proud of his boy. Said Lewis was doing him up proud, mingling with the rich and famous."

"But Lewis is back in town now."

"The economy, Dr. Summer, has made it difficult for many. Henry told me Lewis lost his job. He couldn't find another, so moved home until he could get his feet on the ground again. Walter English offered him a job at the auction house, as a favor to Henry. The boy does know something about art and antiques. He worked at that big auction place that's on the news sometimes. South something or other."

"Sotheby's?"

"That's it! I knew I'd recognize the name."

"I heard Henry Colman was having some memory problems, and Lew came home to take care of him."

"Oh, Henry's not quite what he was twenty years ago, but he's doing all right. He always was a little absentminded, and living alone hasn't helped. His wife died about five years ago, and he's let himself go a bit since then. But if Lew's been saying that, he's just avoiding telling people what really happened in New York. He doesn't spend much time with his dad. Henry's working on that book of his, and Lew's at the auction gallery all the time. Or out socializing over at the Gull's Way."

"The Gull's Way?"

"A tavern, next town over. A place some of the rowdier young folks from around here, fishermen, lobstermen, carpenters, those who work over to the Iron Works, like to hang out. Not too much eating gets done there, but a lot of dreaming and drinking. I've heard Lew does more than his fair share of both." Mr. Pierce stood up. "But enough socializing. You need to look at the trunk Susan and Carolyn wanted you to have." He shook his head. "Can't say as I know exactly why. There's nothing in it that's of much value, but it was important to Susan, for sure. I don't think Carolyn even got a chance to look through it before she...met her untimely end."

"Where has it been, since Carolyn died?" asked Maggie.

"It was in her car," said Mr. Pierce. "The police brought it to me after they finished searching Susan's house. It's been here ever since."

He opened the side door of his office to a small conference room. Maggie had been expecting to see a large metal or wooden trunk; the kind used by nineteenth- and early twentieth-century travelers that sometimes found new uses as bases for coffee tables or storage spaces for out-of-season sweaters or blankets.

Instead, in the center of an oval cherry conference table was a small pine chest, too large to be a stationery or glove box, but too small to have held clothing. It might have been made to hold sewing supplies. Or dolls' clothes.

On its top, brass carpet nails spelled out the initials SPN. It had belonged to Susan Newall's mother, Maggie remembered. The initials must be those of Sarah Pratt Newall. The married name of Anna May Pratt's sister, Sarah.

"Go ahead. Open it," said Mr. Pierce. "I don't know what you expect, but what there is has been in there a long time."

Maggie lifted the rounded top of the small casket; the leather hinges were still strong. Inside were bundles of envelopes tied with faded ribbons. She picked up one of the bundles and the ribbon broke. The top letter, addressed simply to the Newall Family, Waymouth, Maine, was postmarked "New York City, 1913."

"These must be letters Kathleen Trask wrote back to Waymouth after she married Frederick Chase," said Maggie. She glanced through the pile. They seemed to be divided by years, through the 1920s.

She turned to Mr. Pierce. "I'd like to take a little time to go through these, if I might?"

"You're welcome to," he said. "Put everything back in the trunk when you're finished, and tell my assistant you're leaving. Make sure she has your address in—it's New Jersey you live in?"

"I'll do that," Maggie said. "Thank you." She would have liked to have sat down and read for hours, but there wasn't time.

She wanted to find out whether any papers dated back to the time of the journal. Anything from the early 1890s.

Carefully she checked each stack of letters. Most of them were from Kathleen. Some with later dates were from Helen Chase herself as a girl and then young woman. Some of Helen's letters were decorated with small drawings. (What a find! Maggie thought.) Nothing in the trunk was dated after the 1930s, which must have been when Sarah Newall died and the little casket was left in the attic.

A few photographs were included, but the people in them weren't identified. Their clothing appeared to place them in the 1920s. Maybe Aunt Nettie would know who they were.

There were two envelopes of dried flowers, but no notes as to what memories they held. In one envelope was a pale blue handkerchief embroidered with the initials KT. Maggie assumed it had belonged to Kathleen Trask. Perhaps it had been left behind when she married Fred Chase.

There were also holiday cards: Christmas, Easter, and New Year's postcards and greeting cards from people whose names Maggie did not recognize. Cousins, perhaps, or friends of the family. Casts of stories she could not even begin to know.

In six months these would be hers.

She carefully stacked everything and put them back in the small trunk. She had been left a woman's memories. In any case, they didn't seem to hold any clues to what had happened either in the early 1890s or in today's world.

Maggie left her contact information with the receptionist and walked outside. It was a misty morning, and the fog had not yet entirely burned off, leaving traces of mist in the air as though ghosts were there, biding their time, until...? Until what?

The supermarket was next on her list, so Maggie, her thoughts still lost in the past, turned north on Route 1, planning a dinner menu as well as thinking again about young, pregnant Anna May Pratt, who had lied, but found herself a husband. And Lew Coleman, who'd come home unemployed, and lied, saying he was there to care for his father.

People avoided the truth for so many reasons. Both Anna May and Lew had lied to save face; to protect their image and place in society.

Who else had known about each lie? Had anyone been hurt by their lies? And had they lied about anything else?

Chapter 37

———— ∞ ————

THE LATE ACCIDENT ON THE CONCORD RAILROAD. *Wood engraving, January 1853, from the* Illustrated News. *Not only the engraving (showing a railroad car derailing in Andover, Massachusetts and tumbling down an embankment, killing many of the men, women and children aboard) but also, attached, an eyewitness account. Railroad accidents were not unusual in 1853. This one was historically important because among those on the falling car were General Franklin Pierce, the president-elect of the United States, and his wife and son. The general and his wife were unharmed, but their eleven-year-old son, Benjamin, was crushed and died instantly, the third of their three children to die. Mrs. Pierce never came out of the deep depression the event sent her into. She took her son's death as a sign her husband should not be in public office, casting a shadow over her husband's presidency. Pierce himself later died an alcoholic. 6.5 x 9.5 inches. Price: $170.*

The lasagna was one of Maggie's best, thanks to ripe tomatoes and pork sausage from a nearby farm. Aunt Nettie even asked for a second helping. Although her first portion had been very small, that she was now more interested in food was a positive sign.

While Maggie had been assembling the lasagna, Nick Strait was questioning Aunt Nettie for a third time about the break-in, and going over the house with her. She could find nothing missing. Will and Maggie didn't mention the missing book of photographs, still hoping it would be found. After all, who would break in and attack an old lady to get a hundred-year-old photograph album?

But despite her afternoon nap, a full day at home and dealing with the police was not easy. After a bite or two of Maggie's raspberry-apple tart, Aunt Nettie declared she was ready for bed. "Maggie, would you mind helping me a bit with my night clothes?" she asked. "I hate asking you, but I'm not sure I'm quite up to all the offs and ons yet."

"You ladies get that taken care of." Will announced, picking up dishes remaining on the kitchen table, "Maggie did the cooking, so I'm taking over cleanup duty."

Maggie shot him a "thank you" glance, as she helped a weary Aunt Nettie to her feet, and then to the stairs.

The stairs, so easy to climb a week ago, now looked mountainous. Maggie supported Nettie as the old woman slowly climbed up each step. How much did those machines you could sit on to ride upstairs cost? Would they fit on a narrow, steep staircase in an old house like this one? And would installing one just be delaying the inevitable?

Would Aunt Nettie be able to stay here in the future, with or without help?

She was trying so hard, as she gritted her teeth and pulled herself up each step with Maggie's help. She was better than she had been yesterday. Maybe she would be even better tomorrow.

Maggie helped her into her nightgown and tucked her in ("Not too tight, dear, in case I have to get up during the night") while Will washed pots and pans and dishes downstairs. No dishwasher in this house. There had never been a need for one, and the house had a well, she remembered Will once saying. Would Aunt Nettie be able to take over the chores she had done so easily only a week before? Was today's weakness the result of that minor stroke the doctor had mentioned? Or was it partially an emotional reaction to what had happened Saturday?

Aunt Nettie safely in bed, Maggie rejoined Will downstairs. He said, "I'm about to have a cup of decaf. Cola for you?"

"Please."

They sat at the kitchen table. Like an old married couple, Maggie thought, an old married couple discussing an aging parent. A stage you should get to after the joy of being married and free, having children together, and then gradually seeing your parents age.

Not something you should have to deal with before you'd even committed yourselves to each other.

This wasn't the sort of relationship she had dreamed of having with Will. Nevertheless. Life didn't always work the way you planned it. She thought of Anna May Pratt, who'd dreamed of leaving Waymouth, not of getting married and having a baby so soon.

Dreams changed.

"Aunt Nettie didn't want to talk to Nick about Saturday," Will said. "I don't know if she really doesn't remember exactly what happened, or she doesn't want to remember. She just repeated what she said at the hospital."

"She has no idea who it could be?"

"No idea. And doesn't want to think about it."

"What about anything missing?"

"She kept saying nothing was gone, but, of course, we know she hasn't looked. I got her jewelry box and she looked at what was in it, but said, no, nothing was missing. She has some sterling I didn't even know about, but it was in the dining room, and is still there. Whoever was in the house didn't seem to go into that room. Neither Nick nor I could think of anything else to ask her about."

"It doesn't sound like a break-in by someone looking for valuables to sell for drug money," said Maggie.

"If he was looking for something to sell he would have taken something, even some of her old glass or china ornaments. They're not worth a lot, but there are enough antiques dealers around here that he could have gotten rid of them easily. Few casual burglars would know what would be worth something, and what wouldn't."

Maggie sipped her soda. "We have an antiques show to do this weekend. Setup is Friday."

"I know," said Will. "I've been thinking about that. We can't count on Aunt Nettie's being well enough so we can leave her alone for three full days by then. I'm going to call the promoter and see if he can get a replacement for me. You go ahead and do the show without me."

"But you'd looked forward to doing that show, too!"

"Aunt Nettie is more important than an antiques show. I know it's late, but if I'm lucky they'll have a waiting list of dealers and won't mind my cancelling out at the last minute."

"I'll miss doing the show with you."

"It isn't what we planned, is it?" He reached over and took her hand in his.

"It is what it is," Maggie answered. "It could be much worse. Aunt Nettie does seem to be recovering."

She pulled her hand back and took another sip of her cola. "Would you mind if I went to the library tomorrow morning? After seeing the papers at Brad Pierce's today, I'd like to do a little more research on Jessie Wakefield."

"And she is...? I've been so involved with Aunt Nettie, that journal you've been reading hasn't been at the top of my mind."

"She's Anna May Pratt's best friend. The other girl who posed for Winslow Homer. She's also the connection between Winslow Homer and the Thompson family. So far the journal hasn't led me to any blood connection, just the posing that summer. I want to finish reading it, and then see if anything in the library helps me understand why the Thompsons have been claiming the connection since the 1920s. It also bothers me that Nick Strait hasn't found any clues to Carolyn's murderer. Someone trashed her house, apparently looking for something. Someone trashed this house, too. There could be a connection."

"Maggie: my friend the detective," said Will. "Go to the library tomorrow morning. I have to call about the antiques show. Will you be at the library all day?"

"I don't think so," said Maggie. "I'll take my phone and be in touch. I have some sorting and planning to do for the antiques show that I'll have to fit in some time, too."

"I could help you with that."

"Maybe." She finished her cola. "For now, I'm going to finish reading the journal. I'm close to the end. It might have some of the answers I'm looking for."

September 15, 1890

This is no longer the journal of Anna May Pratt. I am now Mrs. Luke Trask. Our wedding journey to Portland was short, and our ceremony, performed by a justice of the peace, shorter. I had hoped for at least a wedding ceremony in a church. But my dear husband found the justice of the peace first, and the justice did not ask any questions,

perhaps because he smelled somewhat of rum. We were married be-
fore we hardly knew it, with his stout wife and two sniffling children
as witnesses.

I hope our child never has a cold that drips so badly, or if he
does, that he learns to use a handkerchief, and not his mother's skirts.

We spent the night at a small inn off Congress Street. Secretly
I had hoped to stay at the Eastland, which is large and grand, but,
although Luke asked, the price was steep, and we must be careful of
dollars. I could not complain.

We returned to Waymouth by midafternoon, where we discov-
ered our news, although shocking to many, especially our parents, all
of whom were at my home when we arrived, was not the only gossip
of the weekend.

Jessie's engagement and wedding have been called off, and
all in town say it was Orin Colby's doing, and none of Jessie's. I do
not know what happened. Mother says Jessie's family did not go to
church yesterday, and it is said she is crying in her room and seeing
no one.

At first I wondered if it were because I had run off and married
Luke. But perhaps not. Jessie might be upset by that news, but not
Orin. I will try to see Jessie tomorrow. I am sorry about her wedding's
being cancelled. It is scandalous! But I could not have been her maid
of honor under the circumstances, and in truth I have other worries to
think of in my future.

Both Luke's parents and mine were much concerned about our
elopement, as we are young and have no resources. They would
clearly have rather we waited, and that we had a church wedding,
with both families and friends present, in perhaps a year or two.

We told them why we would have another reason to celebrate in
less than a year. They were both appalled and resigned, it was clear.
My mother cried, in front of us all, which was difficult for me to see.
After all, it was not her who was having the baby. I kept thinking how
much worse the circumstances under which she learned my condition
might have been.

After much wringing of hands and consoling each other, our two
sets of parents, almost ignoring Luke's and my presence, decided that
we would live with my parents for the time being, since I have a room
of my own, where Luke could also stay.

He is to look for a job, at sea or on land, as soon as possible, with the goal that we will have our own place by the time the baby is born in the spring.

Both our fathers will inquire of their friends to help him find something, and both prospective grandmothers (as they were already calling themselves) will help me prepare clothing and bedding for the future arrival.

By the time they had all shared glasses of sherry (in celebration of Luke's and my marriage) they had our lives planned.

From being tossed by a storm perhaps stronger than the one that wrecked Luke's ship earlier this summer, I now feel like a child who has been brave enough to go away to school, but has now come home to be lulled with hot chocolate and gingerbread.

The Trask and Pratt families will take care of Luke and me until we can take care of ourselves. Or at least they will help to start us out in the right direction. As I am writing this Luke is at his parents' home getting his things, so we can find places for them here, in the room that was mine alone until now.

I am not one for much praying, but tonight I am going to thank the Lord for my wonderful family, and my husband's family, and then I am going to lie down beside my husband in my own bed, at home, safe from the storms of gossip and condemnation.

Tomorrow I will go to see Jessie.

September 16, 1890
Jessie has gone!

After breakfast this morning, which I prepared with my mother for our husbands(!) I walked over to the Wakefields' home to see if I could talk with Jessie, and perhaps console her on the end of her engagement.

Her mother came to the door. Her eyes were red, and she stood stiffly. "Jessie no longer lives here," she said. "She left early this morning. Her father drove her to the train in Portland. She has gone to live with her cousin Margaret in Boston."

I had never heard Jessie mention a cousin Margaret in Boston, so that news was certainly a surprise. I had thought I knew everything there was to know about Jessie's life. Perhaps we each had our secrets.

"When will she be returning?" I asked.

"I do not know," said her mother, turning, as if to close the door on me.

"Could you give me her address?" I asked. "So I could write to her."

"I don't have Margaret's address with me," said Mrs. Wakefield. "I'll let Jessie know you called when I am next in touch with her."

She shut the door right in my face.

And I am Jessie's very dearest friend.

Why would she leave without saying good-bye to me? She must have been very upset. Clearly her mother was still very upset. The Wakefields had been planning for Jessie's marriage to Orin Colby for many more months than Jessie had been, after all, and no doubt whatever happened to cause him to cancel the engagement, they felt it was Jessie's fault.

Maybe it is for the best that Jessie take some time away from her parents, if not from Waymouth.

How strangely things work out! Only a few months ago it was me who wanted to leave Waymouth, and Jessie who wanted to stay and marry Luke. Now Luke and I are married and settling here, and Jessie has left for Boston.

I do envy her Boston.

I wonder if she envies me Luke.

At this point in the journal there were a number of blank pages. Maggie leafed through them before she found the next entry.

April 12, 1891

I have not kept my journal entries throughout the winter, as I have had neither the time nor the privacy to do so. Being married warms one's bed on cold winter nights, it is true, although when one's body is swollen like a child's balloon larger quilts are more reliable sources of comfort. I have learned a great deal in the past few months.

Luke is a devoted husband. My father found him a job in the mercantile on Main Street, and he has been faithful in working the hours they have assigned him, although the work is clearly not of his choice. He would rather be at sea, and saving for a sloop of his own, instead of saving for a small cottage, and those necessities a wife and child have need of. Perhaps someday he will be able to go back to sea, but it is now clear that will not happen soon. We have not yet saved enough to be able to leave my parents' home.

At the moment what I have most need of is sleep. During the past eight weeks I feel as though I have slept not at all. First, because my body was so large I could not make it comfortable in either a bed or a chair. And now, since the baby has finally been delivered, because I am sore and aching, and because Kathleen cries so.

I gave birth ten days ago, with my mother and Luke's mother and Dr. Bennett present, here in the room where I grew up and where I sleep now as a married woman. My child's name is Kathleen Elizabeth Trask, and all said she was a big baby which, of course, did not surprise me, although, indeed, she was born later than I had thought she might be, thank goodness. She is healthy, for which Luke and I are very thankful, and she has his blue eyes, for which I am also grateful.

In all these months I have never heard from Jessie, which I think strange. Her family says she is in Boston, and having a wonderful time there, attending parties and the theater, and too busy to think of former friends in Waymouth. I hope that is so. I still think it strange that she left so suddenly and without farewells.

I am sure her mother will write to tell her about Kathleen.

I do miss Jessie.

My sister Sarah has grown up a lot since my marriage and has become company for me. When I was seventeen I did not think as much about my future as Sarah does about hers. She has already told me that in three years she plans to marry Enoch Newall, who works in the Custom House. I do not know if Enoch is aware of her plan, or indeed, if he is even aware of who Sarah is! In any case, she has three years to let him know, and being Sarah, I suspect she will do just that.

Imagine. In three years Kathleen will be walking and talking, and will be old enough to be a flower girl in Sarah's wedding, if she should marry.

Time passes so quickly.

After that, although Maggie turned each page carefully, there were no other entries. But at the very back of the journal she found that someone had pasted in two yellowed and brittle newspaper articles.

SOCIAL NOTES

July 1, 1893

Mr. Wesley Thompson and his wife, the former Jessica Wakefield, daughter of Cornelia and James Wakefield of Waymouth, are visiting here in Waymouth for the July holidays with their son, two-year-old Master Homer Thompson. Mr. Wesley Thompson, a director of the Boston and Maine Railroad, is said to be inquiring for real estate in the area, perhaps for a summer home near where his wife spent her childhood. The couple, who reside on Beacon Hill in Boston, will be staying with her parents while in Maine. Mrs. Thompson will be at home to her old friends on Tuesday afternoons during her visit.

CRIME OF PASSION

July 17, 1893

This morning the bodies of Mrs. Anna May Trask, aged 22, and her husband Mr. Luke Trask, aged 23, were found in the bedroom of their home on Water Street in Waymouth. It appeared that Mrs. Trask had been shot by Mr. Trask, who then took the gun and shot himself in the head. No notes were found. The bodies were discovered by Mrs. Trask's sister, Miss Sarah Pratt, who had stopped in to consult with her sister on plans for her upcoming wedding.

The couple's daughter, Miss Kathleen Trask, age 2, was visiting at the home of Mr. Trask's parents at the time of what appears to be a murder/suicide.

The couple, both respected lifelong residents of Waymouth, were not known to have been having any problems. They had been married a little less than three years.

Mr. Trask worked for Northland's Mercantile in Waymouth. The couple were members of the First Congregational Church of Waymouth, where services are to be held Wednesday afternoon next. In addition to their daughter, survivors include Mrs. Trask's parents, Mr. and Mrs. Albert Pratt, her sister, Miss Sarah Pratt, and Mr. Trask's parents, Mr. and Mrs. Caleb Trask, all of Waymouth.

Maggie read the articles a second time and then closed the journal. There were the answers to her questions about what happened that summer to Anna May and Jessie.

It couldn't have been a coincidence that Luke killed Anna May and himself just after Jessie had come back to town, bringing with her a son who was close in age to their daughter Kathleen.

Tomorrow at the library she would check the birthdates for Kathleen Trask and Homer Thompson to be sure.

Chapter 38

―――∞∞∞―――

PRESENT STATE OF THE NATIONAL MONUMENT TO WASHINGTON, AT THE CITY OF WASHINGTON. *Hand-colored wood engraving from* London Illustrated News, *1853, of the partially built Washington Monument. The monument was begun in 1848, but because of political and financial factors was not completed until 1884. This engraving shows masons cutting blocks of stone, and oxen pulling them toward the incomplete tower. Originally black-and-white, it was most likely hand-colored in the late nineteenth century by a Victorian woman as a leisure-time activity. 11 x 15.25 inches. Price: $85.*

Rachel was at the front desk when Maggie got to the library. "Good morning, Maggie! I didn't expect to see you this morning! How's Aunt Nettie?"

"Better, Rachel, but still weak. Her brain seems fine, but her body still needs time to heal. Will's going to try to get out of the antiques show we were planning to do this weekend, to stay home with her. She's not ready to stay alone yet."

Rachel frowned. "It's a shame Will has to miss the show. That's his income." She thought a minute. "I could keep her company on Saturday, and maybe Sunday, too. I'll see if I can rearrange my schedule. You both probably have to set up Friday, too, right?"

"You do know the antiques business!" Maggie said.

"When you work at an auction house you pick up the basics," Rachel said. "I have an idea! Lew Coleman's friend, Joann Burt, is a home health aide. Maybe she could help out."

"Joann Burt..." Maggie thought for a moment. "I've heard that name before. Have I met her?"

214

"I don't know," said Rachel. "She lives here in town. Maybe Carolyn Chase mentioned her? Joann worked for her Aunt Susan last winter. She often comes to the library to pick up books for the people she takes care of, or calls me to pick some out and sends Lew or Josh to get them. Susan liked Agatha Christies. She read the same ones over and over again."

"And Joann's a friend of Lew Coleman? And—Josh? Josh Thompson?"

"She's been with Lew ever since he's been back in town. They were high school sweethearts or something. They were younger than me, so I don't really know. And I guess they knew Josh, too, because sometimes she and Josh would stop in at the auction gallery to see him. That's what made me think of her. Would you like me to help out with Aunt Nettie this weekend?"

"It's a wonderful offer, Rachel. Can I let you know in a few minutes?" Maggie balanced her bag on the counter. "Let me sign in for the archives room. I'll call Will from there and see if he's cancelled out of the show yet. I'll let you know as soon as I find out what he wants to do."

"Not a problem," said Rachel, handing Maggie the key to the archives. "I'll be right here until noon. Then my guy is taking me out for lunch."

"I'll definitely let you know before then," said Maggie. "Do you have Joann's telephone number, if we need it?"

"She works for Waymouth Home Services. I'll look the number up for you." Rachel checked a directory behind the desk, wrote a number down, and handed the slip to Maggie. "Here's her name and the number of the service. They're nice people. If Joann isn't free, they may have other home health aides available. A lot of people in town use them for respite care."

"Respite care?"

"Sort of babysitting for elderly or disabled people who need someone with them all of the time, so their caretakers can go out for the evening, or take a short vacation. It's a great organization."

"Sounds like it," said Maggie, tucking the slip of paper into her pocket. "I'll go and put this stuff down and call Will. Thank you for volunteering, Rachel!"

"No problem. Aunt Nettie's a dear. And she's family. I was planning to stop in anyway."

Maggie opened the Archives door, put her bag down on the table, and telephoned Will.

"Hello!" he answered. "Couldn't stand to be away from me?"

"True," Maggie teased back. "But actually I have a proposition for you from Rachel. I told her you were going to stay home with Aunt Nettie this weekend, and she volunteered to stay with her Saturday and maybe Sunday so you could do the antiques show."

Will hesitated. "That's really terrific of her. I called the promoter, but he wasn't in his office, so I haven't talked with him yet. I'd really like to do that show. My budget would appreciate it."

"And Will, there's more. Rachel knows we'd need someone to be with Aunt Nettie for most of Friday, too, for setup, and she can't come then. But she suggested Joann Burt. Seems Joann was the home health aide who helped Susan Newall last winter. Aunt Nettie might even know her."

"That's an idea," said Will.

"It's two ideas," Maggie continued. "First, if we need someone for Friday, I have the name of the place that Joann works. They have other people who do this sort of work, too. So that's a possibility, for now and maybe for future reference. But, listen: this Joann Burt is Lew Coleman's girlfriend."

"You're saying that the home health aide who probably had her own key and was in and out of Susan Newall's home last winter and spring is the close friend of the guy who somehow lost all the paperwork for whoever consigned the Helen Chase paintings at the Walter English Auction House?"

"Exactly. You got it. And she's also a friend of Josh Thompson's."

Will was silent. "We need to tell Nick."

"Can we wait a couple of hours? I want to check a couple of dates here in the library. They might confirm another idea I have. In the meantime, shall I give you the name of the agency that provides other home health aides?"

"Go ahead," said Will. "I think Aunt Nettie would be fine with Rachel being here over the weekend. I don't know what she'll think about having a home health aide here. But I'd like to try. That last show was such a disaster, I could use a good show."

"Me, too," said Maggie. "Shall I tell Rachel?"

"I'll call and talk to her," said Will. "You go ahead and do your research. Rachel's sitting at the main desk?"

"Right."

"Then I'll talk with Aunt Nettie, and call Rachel directly. Don't you worry. I'll take care of it all."

"I love you, Will Brewer."

"Me, too, Maggie Summer," said Will. "See you soon."

Maggie hung up and went to the file cabinets where the genealogy files were stored. She wanted to know more about Jessie Wakefield, or Jessie Thompson, as she became.

The "Wakefield" folder was empty. Maggie checked the folders in back of it and in front of it to be sure, in case someone had carelessly refiled documents. There must have been information on the family at one time, or the name wouldn't have warranted a listing at all.

An open archives was wonderful for those who wanted to browse through old documents and weren't sure precisely what they were looking for. But it came with the possibilities of source materials being removed.

Maggie went on to the "Thompson" folder. It was full. She paged through newspaper articles from the 1920s and '30s about the Mirage Art Colony, and several notices of Maine gallery openings of paintings by Winslow Thompson in the 1970s. There was no mention of his having shown anywhere south of Portland.

At the back was a two-column obituary for Wesley Thompson from the *Boston Globe* dated 1925. It listed his home as Boston, and his summer residence as Waymouth, Maine.

He'd been eighty-three at the time of his death, and left his wife of thirty-three years, Jessica Wakefield Thompson, his son, Homer Thompson and wife Esther, whose residence was listed as Waymouth.

Wesley Thompson had been forty-eight years old when he'd married twenty-year-old Jessie Wakefield in 1890 or 1891. Clearly a good catch: he'd made enough money as an officer of the Boston and Maine Railroad not only to support his family, but also, she suspected, later to support his son and his daughter-in-law. Although Mirage's condition today might show the money to be drying up, his grandson and great-grandson were still living in that "summer residence."

Jessie's obituary was dated in 1931. It listed her residence as Waymouth. She must have come to live with her son and his wife. It listed one grandchild as a survivor: Winslow, three months old. Jessie had lived long enough to see the stock market crash, no doubt taking a lot of her funds with it, and to see the birth of her first grandchild.

The next clipping was a marriage announcement. Winslow Thompson married Lauren Johnston of New Haven, Connecticut, in 1968. Winslow was thirty-seven; residence, Waymouth. Still living at home with his parents? Maggie did some quick calculations. His parents would have both been over 65. The young couple, Winslow and Lauren, would be at home at Mirage.

Of course. At the family compound in Waymouth. Good thing that house had a lot of rooms.

Lauren had died in the mid-1990s, leaving Winslow free to marry again. Enter Betsy, from somewhere. Fascinating. Basically confirming what she already knew. But what she'd been looking for still eluded her. What was the birth date of Jessie's son, Homer Thompson?

Maggie looked through all of the papers again. Finally, at the bottom of an article about one of his gallery showings, she found it. "Homer Thompson, born in Boston April 10, 1891..."

It didn't take a mathematician to figure out that, even if Jessie had met Wesley Thompson the day she arrived in Boston and married him the day after, a highly unlikely scenario, Homer Thompson was not Wesley Thompson's biological son. He'd been conceived at close to the same time as Jessie's daughter Kathleen. In either Waymouth or Prouts Neck.

If he'd been the son of Jessie's fiancé, Orin Colby, then probably Orin wouldn't have ended their engagement.

The pieces of the 1890 puzzle had come together.

Maggie carefully put the clippings and notes back into the "Thompson" folder and left them on the library table. She was almost to her car when a voice in back of her made her jump.

"Maggie!"

"Hi, Kevin!" said Maggie, turning around. "You startled me. I guess I was deep in thought. On your way to the library?"

"Going to do a little more research," he answered. "It was nice seeing you at Betsy's the other day. But I'd like to talk to you about some of Winslow Homer's wood engravings. I've heard you're an expert on them."

"They're my favorites," Maggie said, pulling herself from 1890 to the world of antique prints. "I've always felt it was a shame that art historians didn't recognize their importance in nineteenth-century art history, or American social history for that matter, until recently."

"I'd love to know more," said Kevin, moving a little closer to allow a car to pass by. "For some reason I've been putting off going down to Prouts Neck to see where Homer lived and painted. I was there years ago, but not since I've learned so much about Homer. Have you been there?"

"No," Maggie admitted. "I've always wanted to go, but never seem to find the time."

"Let's go together!" said Kevin. "I just heard on the radio that last Saturday's nor'easter is still kicking the surf higher than usual, and this is the time in August when there are astronomical high tides. Come with me this afternoon! We can see where he painted, and look at the surf, and you can tell me about the wood engravings."

"You know they were done before he lived in Prouts Neck," Maggie said.

"That doesn't mean we can't talk about them there!" said Kevin. "I'd love you to come with me."

"I'm tempted," said Maggie. "But I'd have to go back and talk to Will about our plans for the weekend first." She hesitated, and looked at her watch. "Give me an hour. I'll meet you back here."

She drove to Aunt Nettie's slowly. Will would be aggravated that she was taking the afternoon and going somewhere with Kevin Bradman, even if she could justify it with scholarly research. If she told him the real reason she was going, Will would be furious. But this was important.

Sometimes a lady had to lie.

Chapter 39

"I Cannot! It Would Be a Sin! A Fearful Sin!" *Wood engraving by Winslow Homer, published in* The Galaxy, September 1868, *story illustration. Gentleman with mustache looks down at a woman seated on the floor who is covering her eyes and crying. 6.875 x 4.875 inches. Price: $150.*

Maggie didn't dare stay long at Aunt Nettie's, for fear she'd say something she shouldn't. Instead, she chatted about the obvious. She'd found what she wanted at the library. She'd run into Kevin Bradman, and she hoped everyone wouldn't mind, but they were going to take the afternoon and drive to Prouts Neck and talk art and history. Two academics, you know.

Will looked dubious, but his mind was on the weekend. He'd spoken with Rachel and had a call into the home health care place. It looked as though they'd both be able to do the antiques show that weekend. There was enough lasagna left for dinner.

Maggie got a sweatshirt from her room in case ocean breezes required one, and slipped Anna May's journal under her pillow for safekeeping. After a moment's hesitation she also left her notebook where she'd written down the family tree information she'd found at the library.

Fresh batteries were in the little tape recorder she always carried in case she had any brainstorms or thoughts for her "to do" list while she was driving. She hadn't used it since she'd walked through her booth at the Provincetown show and made a verbal list of the types of prints she should be looking for in Maine.

Maggie sighed, listening to that list. "Astronomy. Shells. Maps of

New England. Architectural drawings or blueprints. Ships. Fish, especially trout. Don't need any more fashion or nineteenth-century birds or children's. Maxfield Parrish being reproduced too much—not selling well." She hadn't had a chance to do any buying since she'd been in Maine. Would there be any time to do that before she headed back to New Jersey for the fall semester?

For now, she tucked the little recorder into the side pocket of her canvas bag so she could easily turn it on and off.

She braided her hair tightly and pinned it up. A hat might help prevent sun or wind burn if gales were blowing down at the shore. On the other hand, her hats had a tendency to fly off, despite attempts at securing them with the nineteenth-century hatpins Anna May would have recognized as a practical solution. Clearly Anna May and her friends knew tricks to securing hats and long hair Maggie had never managed to master.

Instead, she dabbed on SPF 30. She looked at herself critically in the mirror. Here she was seriously considering murder suspects, and yet was making sure that her nose wouldn't blister in the sun or wind.

On the other hand, appearances were appearances.

She dabbed once more, stuffed her sweatshirt into her bag, and headed downstairs.

"I went to Prouts Neck once, years ago," said Will. "A trail around the top of the cliffs is open to the public, but as I remember it's a mile or two long. Not an easy path, especially if the winds or surf are heavy. Walking it could take all afternoon."

"Thanks for warning me," said Maggie, reaching up to kiss his cheek. "Don't worry. I have my phone. I'll call if there are any problems, or if I'm going to be late." She headed for the door. "I'm going to be just fine."

Kevin was waiting for her at the library, pacing in front of the entrance. He smiled as she pulled up, and reached to open her van door. "Why don't we take my car?" he suggested.

Maggie hesitated. Why not? Kevin was being a gentleman. She was just trying to get some information.

They headed onto Route 1. "Prouts Neck is south of South Portland. We'll drive through Scarborough, and turn east," said Kevin. "Have you read Philip Beam's *Winslow Homer at Prouts Neck*?"

"Many times," said Maggie. "He does a wonderful job of pulling together all the information that was available about Homer and his family at that time. I remember little details. Like, the town of Scarborough was spelled S-c-a-r-b-o-r-o when Homer lived there."

"And people who vacationed at the big hotels on Prouts Neck called the area just Prout's, said Kevin.

"There's also a wonderful book of essays called *Winslow Homer in the 1890s: Prouts Neck Observed*, that has a lot of information on the area. How did you get interested in art history?" asked Maggie. "Did your family take you to lots of museums when you were a child?"

Kevin's hands tightened on the steering wheel. "Actually, no. I didn't have a father, and my mother...wasn't interested in art. I spent a lot of time in the library, though, and loved looking through the big art books. They were more real to me than photographs. I used to imagine I knew the people in the paintings. I made up stories about them."

"That's wonderful," said Maggie. "I know people who escape by reading books. I've never thought of escaping through pictures."

"It can be done," said Kevin, very seriously. "I was in high school before I totally understood there were artists behind the paintings, and started looking for biographies of them. Usually I liked the pictures and my own versions of their stories more than their real lives. Then I got a scholarship to college and studied art history and found you could put it all together: the lives, the pictures, and the way it all fit together in society. I was hooked."

"Have you ever done your own artwork?"

"Never. Well, not *never*. I tried a few times. It was a disaster." Kevin smiled. "I'm a critic. An admirer. An historian. Maybe a professor someday. Not an artist."

"I understand. I can't draw at all. But I admire anyone who can put shapes and colors together, or draw images that pull us into a world we've never seen or imagined," said Maggie. "Homer's work can do that. His wood engravings are like the Norman Rockwell illustrations of the mid-nineteenth century. Without him, how would we know young ladies weighed themselves on country store scales, despite wearing clothing that must have weighed twenty pounds? Or that even then, people scattered seeds for birds in the wintertime?

Or that a former drummer boy would wear his uniform to work in cornfields after the Civil War?"

"By the time he was at Prouts Neck he'd pretty much stopped picturing those sorts of scenes," said Kevin, maneuvering through lanes of summer traffic.

"Yes. Today people remember him most for his oil paintings of surf and ocean scenes. His paintings of Florida and the Bahamas. His Adirondack scenes. But he also did wonderful paintings of a black community in Virginia, and of fisherwomen on the coast of England."

"Did he do any wood engravings of the sea?"

"Only three. My favorite, *Homeward Bound*, is of elegantly dressed passengers on board the deck of a clipper ship. He did that one on his way home from his trip to Paris. But he did quite a few beach scenes, in Gloucester, Massachusetts, Long Branch, New Jersey, and Newport, Rhode Island. The ocean was a theme for him years before he heard about Prouts Neck from his brother, who honeymooned there."

"Winslow lived there more than summer months, didn't he?"

"He was there close to year-round, unlike his brothers and parents. But even Winslow usually left in December or January and headed to New York or Florida or the Bahamas for a couple of months, returning in March or April."

They drove through Scarborough, and followed the signs to Prouts Neck. The road narrowed as they passed swampy land and small modern homes. Maggie thought of the horse-pulled wagon Anna May and Jessie had taken, no doubt on this same road. Not many roads led to Prouts Neck.

Kevin drove past the sign pointing TO FERRY BEACH, as Maggie wondered how far it was from Homer's studio.

He turned left, up a driveway to the parking lot of the Black Point Inn. "I don't remember an inn of that name from reading biographies of Homer," Maggie said, admiring the large white building on a small hill overlooking both the beach and the ocean. The sky was beginning to darken in back of the inn, making its whiteness look even brighter.

"I looked it up on-line before we came when I was looking for directions," said Kevin, turning off the car. "The Black Point Inn is a new name. It's the only one of the old hotels still standing. In Homer's day it was called South Gate House."

The same building where Micah Wright had raped Anna May Pratt over a hundred years ago. Maggie shivered, looking up at the elegant old hotel. How many other secrets did it hold?

"Its website said some homeowners on Prouts Neck got together and bought the old hotel. They tore down part of the building and fixed up the rest. The restaurant is supposed to be excellent."

Maggie just stared, her mind changing the men and women in shorts and tennis attire chatting outside the sheltered entrance into elegant late-nineteenth-century visitors from Boston and New York who would have considered wearing anything that showed their knees, even on a beach, completely indecent.

"We can walk to Homer's studio from here," Kevin was saying. "We can reach the path around the point through the parking lot."

Maggie remembered how long Will had said that trail was, and looked at the brooding clouds. "As I remember from the books, Homer's studio is on this side of Prouts Neck. Why don't we start at this end of the road."

Kevin nodded. "We'll walk down the driveway and along the road to Western Cove, and up past Checkley Point."

"Where the old Checkley Inn used to be," put in Maggie, as they started walking.

"Exactly. Now the hotels and boarding houses are gone, replaced by private homes."

"I remember reading that the Neck was almost bare of trees in Homer's day," said Maggie, as they looked at the thick hedges and trees protecting the private homes and gardens they passed. "In the nineteenth century many towns just felled all the trees. They were used for building materials, or to sell elsewhere, as lumber. No one saw their value until later."

They walked on, admiring the sea view. They passed the Prouts Neck Yacht Club, and then moved off the main road.

"Here's where we join the old cliff walk established back in Homer's day," said Kevin. The trail was above a rocky beach, now swept by the rough sea. High grasses and brambles protected the privacy of homes on the land side of the trail. "The idea was that people wouldn't be able to keep the Neck to themselves. The cliff walk would be open to all."

Maggie scrambled up and down some rough rocks, and made her way across two rotted boards placed across a muddy section of the trail. "This isn't exactly a city sidewalk," she pointed out.

"No, but it's maintained by the people who live here. If it weren't here we wouldn't be able to come and see the places Homer painted," Kevin said.

They stood on the edge of the cliff, looking out at the blue-black ocean topped with foamy whitecaps. Winds were blowing hard, and the surf, true to the reports Kevin had heard, was higher than usual. At low tide it would no doubt have been a quiet scene. Here on the cliff walk at high tide breakers were crashing in, and the air was white with mist.

Maggie stood back. The walkway was only a few feet wide, and in some places less.

She felt dangerously exposed.

"Come this way; you have to see Cannon Rock. It's near his studio," called Kevin, who'd walked ahead of her on the trail.

Cannon Rock! The subject of one of Homer's most dramatic oil paintings. Maggie wondered whether she'd recognize it. Artists altered scenes, and depending on the day, she suspected this path and the ledges and sea-swept rocks below would appear very different.

She caught up with Kevin where the rough trail narrowed above a deep chasm between rock ledges. "See," he pointed at the ledge to the right, "that's Cannon Rock."

Maggie squinted. It was hard to make out the distinctive shape of the furthest rock, pointed out toward the Atlantic. Raging waters and crashing surf almost submerged it.

"At a lower tide, or when the seas were quieter, it would be easier to see, but yes, I can make it out," she said finally. Homer's painting also showed it below the surf. He must have painted it on a day when seas were even rougher than they were now. Perhaps in a fall nor'easter, or after a hurricane that just missed the coast.

She stood watching the wild surf for a few minutes, feeling as though she'd gone back in history, and was seeing the world as the artist had seen it.

"Powerful, isn't it?" said Kevin. "Breakers, crashing into the rocks like this."

"Yes," Maggie answered.

Maggie sensed Kevin tensing. She glanced at him. His expression had changed. On the pretext of zipping the front of her sweatshirt against the wind, she reached into the outside pocket of her bag and turned on her tape recorder, at the same time pulling out a tissue to wipe her face, now wet with sea mists.

Kevin moved a half step closer to her. "Maggie, I want you to give me the journal."

"Journal?"

"Let's not play games. The 1890 journal Carolyn Chase gave you. I don't know who wrote it, but I need it."

"I don't have the journal," said Maggie, adding mentally to herself, "not with me."

"I need that journal," said Kevin again, very calmly.

"Why?" asked Maggie.

"It would be much simpler for you if you just gave me the journal, Maggie. I know a lot of places where it isn't. So either you have it with you, or you know where it is. Carolyn Chase gave it to you. And I want it today. If you give it to me, then no one else will get hurt."

"How do you know I didn't give it back to Carolyn?"

"It wasn't in her house. None of the papers she talked about getting from her aunt were in her house."

Maggie tried to move back along the trail, away from the crashing surf, but Kevin stayed close to her.

"How do you know?"

"Don't play dumb, Maggie! I'm going to get that journal, and the rest of the papers. I don't want to hurt you, but if I have to, I will. I'm already in trouble."

Maggie backed further, talking as loud as she could, hoping the tape recorder would pick up her words, and trying to keep her balance on the trail. And her mind on Kevin's words. "You're intelligent. You have a future ahead of you. Why, Kevin?"

"Have you any idea how much it costs to go to college today?" Kevin followed Maggie's every step. "You teach at a community college. Big deal. I mean a real school. A four-year college with a good reputation. It costs forty thousand dollars and up, really up, to go to college today. Every year. Even with scholarships and grants. I graduated in the hole. A bachelor's degree and over one hundred thousand dollars in debt. Then there's graduate school." He shook his head. "I don't come from a wealthy family like the Thompsons. I worked for every penny. And there isn't a long line of places looking for art historians today, even if I get my Ph.D. and my dissertation is published. No university or museum wants to hire thinkers anymore. They want people who write best-selling books on how Facebook is changing our culture, or how you can get your ten-year-old to love calculus, or what the relationship is between Leonardo da Vinci and fast food, or some other crap like that."

"You're young, Kevin. You're bright. You'll find a way." Maggie moved a little closer to the high bank of dense shrubs in back of her.

"I did find a way! I found Betsy Thompson. Or Betsy Thompson found me. She found me on a listserv about art in New England. She said she'd pay my matriculation fees and a salary if I'd write my dissertation on New England twentieth-century artists, as long as I included her husband and his father in it."

"So you agreed," said Maggie, beginning to understand. A published dissertation including the Thompson artists could add to the value of their art.

"Sight pretty much unseen," said Kevin. "Not the smartest move, but I was desperate. I was trying to get a topic approved. Here were two people no one had written about. And she kept dangling the Winslow Homer connection as an added inducement. If I could prove that, it would pretty much guarantee a book sale. And she'd pay me a bonus. She even offered to put me up at her place for as long as I needed to work."

"Then you met Betsy and her husband. And Josh." Just keep him talking, Maggie thought. He's not a bad kid. He's scared. Just keep him talking. She backed slowly down the narrow part of the trail, away from the deep, narrow ledges above the swirling sea.

Kevin followed her. "The whole family is pretty weird. Josh especially. I had to play their games. And keep my door locked at night. Her husband's work isn't earth-shaking. But *his* father's is passable. Better than that stuff his friends painted that's all over their living room. I could do something with the father's stuff, and with the colony as a way he tried to keep art alive during the Depression. Maine art is a good topic, and I could compare Mirage to other art colonies in Maine. No one had ever written about it."

Maggie nodded. She could sympathize, so far. Getting a dissertation topic approved is not easy. For someone who was young, without income, finding a patron who would sponsor research and offer a place to live and work would be enormously enticing.

"So you moved here." He didn't seem to have a weapon. But he was taller and younger than she was; probably stronger. Just getting away from the higher cliffs made her feel safer. She moved a step with every few words he said.

Kevin didn't seem to notice. "Late last spring I started going through all the papers and paintings at Mirage, and looking through the Waymouth Library archives. That's when I found Helen Chase came from Waymouth. She had nothing to do with Mirage or the Thompsons, but she'd stopped in at the colony a few times, so that was huge. Worth a chapter or so in the book, especially when her daughter, Carolyn, started to come to those meetings at the library and mentioned Helen had painted Maine scenes that no one knew about. Carolyn invited me over to her aunt's house once or twice to look at them." Kevin stopped, remembering. He looked as though he'd seen heaven. "They were incredible. Fantastic. And almost no one had ever seen them before. I had to write about them!"

"So you saw the paintings at her house."

"There were four of them, stacked in one of the second floor rooms. When her aunt was sick they'd rearranged the first floor to make a bedroom for her there. Carolyn planned to hang them all over the house, if the house was hers. I was blown away by those paintings."

"Did she say anything about selling them?" Maggie had finally reached flat land, a part of the trail by a rocky beach. The breakers were close. She and Kevin were both drenched with spray and mist.

"Carolyn? Sell her mother's paintings? No! She wanted to keep them. She said they were family art." He shook his head. "They were only for her to see. And special friends."

"Like you," said Maggie.

"Yes," Kevin agreed. "Remember the night you came with her to the library, and she told us about that trunk full of papers? Betsy was there, too. Betsy said she was sure information in that trunk would prove the Thompsons were Winslow Homer's descendants. The old man, Homer Thompson, had told his friends at Mirage that Winslow Homer was his father, and Betsy keeps repeating that. Homer Thompson said his mother had posed for Homer, and slept with him, and then married the rich railroad guy, Wesley Thompson, as cover, but named him after his real father. It was sort of a joke, from what I could tell. But Betsy took it very seriously, and I think her husband did, too."

"She wanted proof?"

"I told her I couldn't write it in my dissertation as anything but a family legend unless we could prove it."

"What about DNA tests?" asked Maggie.

"She went to a member of the Homer family a few years back and asked, but they just laughed at her. They said Winslow Homer had no direct descendants. Period."

"Why don't we head up toward the road?" Maggie asked, walking in that direction.

Kevin just kept talking, following her, as she stepped off the path and walked across someone's lawn and up a driveway toward a road.

"Betsy wanted me to prove it. She said that was what she was paying me for. To prove the Winslow Homer connection. When Carolyn said she had a journal from 1890, Betsy went crazy. She was sure that was the piece of evidence she needed."

"So?" Maggie kept walking, away from the sea.

"I called Carolyn after the library meeting. I told her how excited I was about the papers she'd found, and she invited me over for a late supper. I'd been there before, so that wasn't unusual. We talked about art, and her mother, and her book, and my research. Then I asked to see the journal." Kevin stopped walking.

"What happened, Kevin?" said Maggie. She could speak quietly now that they were away from the ocean. The pounding waves were at a safe distance.

"She told me you had it, and that no one could see the other papers. She'd decided they were family papers. She was going to use them in writing her biography of her mother, but wasn't going to share them with anyone else."

"How did that make you feel?"

"I was furious! They were American art history! I was her friend. My future depended on writing my dissertation so Betsy Thompson liked it, and it got published. I told Carolyn, she could use the papers first. After all, they were hers! But she owed it to the world to share them. To have them available to scholars in a university or museum archives."

Maggie nodded.

"Carolyn said she didn't think it was any of my business. She said if I were acting for Betsy Thompson, I could forget it. Her aunt had told her Winslow Homer hadn't fathered any children. That she had a journal that included information proving Jessie Thompson hadn't been pregnant with Homer's child, she'd been pregnant with someone else's. And Jessie'd probably breached a confidence and caused the deaths of two of her closest friends, one of whom was Helen Chase's grandmother. So Betsy Thompson had better just shut up about her 'Winslow Homer legacy' because her family's legacy was a nasty one, and Carolyn had decided to write about it in her biography." Kevin just stood, as though reliving the horror of the moment. "I panicked. I knew Betsy would be livid. She might stop sponsoring my dissertation."

"So you killed Carolyn?" asked Maggie.

"No! I wouldn't hurt Carolyn! I did what I had to do. I went back to Mirage and told Betsy what Carolyn had said. I told her we'd better stop pushing the Winslow Homer connection, and maybe Carolyn would soft-pedal what she'd found out from her aunt."

"Betsy must not have been very happy," said Maggie.

"She was furious. She insisted I get the journal and destroy it, so there would be no proof." Kevin hesitated. "You saw her when you came for tea. She sometimes drinks a little too much. That night she had. So I left her and went to bed. I thought she'd go to bed, too, and sleep it off." He stopped again. "The next morning I heard the news about Carolyn."

"You're sure Carolyn was alive when you left her house?"

"Of course I'm sure! Carolyn was doing what she thought was right for her family. I was angry with her right then, I'll admit. And disappointed. I'd hoped that journal would confirm the Winslow

Homer connection to make Betsy happy, and help my dissertation. But I wouldn't hurt Carolyn!"

"Do you think Betsy went to Carolyn's house that night?"

"She was too drunk to get there. But Josh—Josh will do anything she wants, as long as she keeps his allowance going. I heard his car going out later that night."

"Kevin, why did you ask me for the journal back there on the rocks?"

"I want to give it to Betsy, so she can destroy it, and all this craziness can stop! Carolyn Chase is dead, and I heard that old lady, Miss Brewer, was hurt. I don't want anything else to happen," said Kevin. "I don't want anyone else to be hurt. I should never have accepted money from Betsy to write the dissertation she wanted. Now she's angry with me, and at Josh. All she does is drink. Maybe if she had that journal she'd calm down and leave both of us alone."

"You haven't done anything wrong," said Maggie. "You haven't hurt anyone, right?"

"No."

"You weren't the one who broke into Miss Brewer's home?"

"No! I don't even know where she lives! I just met her at the library a couple of times!"

"And you're sure you didn't hurt Carolyn."

"Of course I'm sure!"

Maggie took Kevin's arm. "Let's walk past Winslow Homer's studio. It shouldn't be too far from here, right? Then we'll go back to Waymouth. You and I need to talk to the police."

Chapter 40

---ㅇㅇㅇㅇ---

NEW REGULATION UNIFORM OF THE NEW YORK POLICE. *Wood engraving from* Gleason's Pictorial Drawing-Room Companion, 1854. *Shows men dressed as captain, chief, reserve corps, lieutenant, and private. The uniform is a navy blue double-breasted frock coat, with a skirt extending two-thirds of the way from the top of the hip to the knee with a collar of black velvet, a navy blue cloth cap, and a gold shield or star on the left breast. Police forces were still new in 1854, and an accompanying article suggests that every city should adopt the idea of a uniform. 5.25 x 7.25 inches. Price: $50.*

Maggie sat on the couch in Betsy Thompson's living room, her legs crossed, and a determined smile on her face. "Betsy, I understand you've been looking for the 1890 journal Anna May Pratt wrote. I have it."

"Yes. I want it," said Betsy. Her eyes almost glittered, like a cat's in the darkness.

"Susan Newall and Carolyn left it to me, so it's mine to do with as I please. I know it's worth a lot. To more than one person," said Maggie. She reached into her red bag and pulled out the old journal.

Betsy moved toward her on the couch.

Maggie got up, walked into the center of the room, and stood facing her. "You want it, because of what it says about Jessie Wakefield Thompson. It does not say that Winslow Homer was the father of her son, Homer; in fact, it pretty much names another man as the likely father. But scholars working on the life of Helen Chase will also want this book, because it's written by her grandmother, and tells of how she, too, was a victim of that same man. It also appears, circumstantially, that Jessie Thompson told Anna May's husband he was not the father of their daughter, and he reacted by killing both Anna May and himself, leaving his daughter an orphan."

Betsy stood up and walked toward her, reaching for the book again.

Maggie moved a little further away. "And Winslow Homer scholars would love to see this book, because it describes Homer and his studio, and some of the people around him in 1890, in a first-person perspective not available anywhere else." Maggie walked around the room, perusing the journal. "I could get a very good price for this little book at an auction gallery in New York. If I decide not to publish it myself first."

"No!" Betsy said, reaching again for the book. "I want that journal, Maggie. You don't know what the information in that journal means to my family. I'll give you whatever you want for it."

"Really?" said Maggie, turning abruptly to face Betsy. "Then I want your stepson, Josh."

"What?" said Betsy, sitting down hard on a pine bench near the wall. "What do you mean, you want Josh?"

Maggie pulled her tape recorder out of her bag, put it down on the coffee table, and turned it on. "I want you to tell me how Josh knew you were upset about the journal. How he went to Carolyn's house to look for it, and killed Carolyn. And then, when he still couldn't find it, he went to Nettie Brewer's house, tied her up, and searched her house, too."

"How would I know what Josh did?" asked Betsy.

"You knew because you asked him to do it," said Maggie. "Because you threatened to cut off his allowance if he didn't do what you asked. He also knew that if the Winslow Homer heritage story was proved untrue that would end your dreams of wealth for the family. His family. So it was important to him, too."

"I never told him to kill anyone," said Betsy. "Never."

"Perhaps not," said Maggie. "But you told him to go to Carolyn's house and get the journal, right?"

"I told him we had to have that book. To do whatever he had to do to get it."

"And when he came home without it?"

"We assumed you had it, Maggie. As you do. You told me you'd be at that antique show on Saturday, so he went to Nettie Brewer's house after you left for the show. No one was supposed to get hurt. I told him that! And Miss Brewer is all right. I heard she was out of the hospital. Josh is so stupid. He brought home a photograph album instead of a journal."

"She's better, yes," said Maggie, thinking of the condition Aunt Nettie had been in, and how weak and fragile she was still.

"Now: I've told you what I did. Give me the journal," said Betsy, reaching out for it.

"Not quite," said Nick Strait, opening the back door. "Thank you, Maggie." He walked up to Betsy. "Elizabeth Thompson, you're under arrest for conspiracy to commit murder. We'll discuss the details down at the station house." He turned. "Thank you, Maggie. I think we have all the angles figured out now."

"But I didn't do anything!" said Betsy. "It was Josh! He did it!"

"You'll both have a chance to tell us all about that down at the station," said Nick. "Josh is already there."

"You've already arrested him for murder?" Maggie asked, handing Nick her tape recorder.

"Not yet. We have him and Joann Burt there for stealing two paintings from Susan Newall's home and trying to sell them. Turns out you were right. They're drinking pals of Lew Coleman. Joann was the one who removed the paintings from Susan Newall's house when she was working there as a home health aide. If you hadn't identified the paintings as Helen Chase's, Lew would have sold the paintings to Josh, who was acting as a buyer under another name. They'd already contacted Sotheby's, having established the provenance of finding the paintings at a country auction in Waymouth, Maine. Lew's down at the station, too. They're all talking."

"You have a crowded place today."

"We do. But there's a new prison down the road at Two Rivers. We'll find space for all of 'em." Nick turned. "Come on Betsy, let's go. Give my best to Will, Maggie. Good to see you again. Even if you are from New Jersey."

Chapter 41

_____

THE END. *Last page from Maxfield Parrish's* The Knave of Hearts, *1925. Keyhole-shaped illustration of jester/narrator bowing to audience with"The End" apparently carved in granite underneath him; sky of Parrish blue in back of figure. 10.5 x 12.5 inches. Price: $250.*

Maggie and Will sat comfortably close on the grayed wooden porch swing and looked out over the river. Will was quite proud of himself for having made a salad and steamed the mussels in wine, under Aunt Nettie's supervision, and they'd cut "store bought" raspberry and chocolate and peanut Whoopie Pies in quarters and shared them. Aunt Nettie had retired early.

"It's finally over, isn't it?" said Maggie, snuggling closer. "All the bad guys are in jail, and Aunt Nettie's feeling a little stronger. We have an antiques show to do this weekend. And the light on the river is beautiful tonight."

"All true," said Will. "Thanks to you, and Nick."

"I just wish Carolyn were here," said Maggie. "She died for such a stupid reason. To keep an old lie alive."

"So now you're the keeper of the journal that holds all the secrets, and the trunk full of stories of yesteryear," said Will. "What are you going to do with the papers?"

"I haven't decided yet," said Maggie. "I won't have most of them for six months, so I have time to plan. I'm thinking of taking the sections of the journal that are about Winslow Homer and Prouts Neck and writing an article based on them, so the information will be available to anyone doing research on Homer, not lost in cartons of papers about Helen Chase."

"And the rest?"

"Carolyn mentioned that she'd like me to continue her work writing a biography of her mother, but I'm not sure I want to do that. Someone may, and whoever that is should certainly have access to the papers." She paused. "Kevin Bradman's a nice young man who learned a lot this summer. He may need a new dissertation topic. I think I'll keep in touch with him. Ultimately, I think the papers should go with the rest of Carolyn's estate to the Portland Museum, where they'll be cared for, and available to researchers."

"Sounds like an excellent plan," said Will, nibbling Maggie's ear.

"And Aunt Nettie? Do you think you can leave her here alone?"

"I'm going to stay an extra month," said Will. "I'll see how she is, and what possibilities there are for home care and respite services. I can't totally give up my antiques business; it supports me. But it may be time to consider other options than keeping my house in Buffalo. I'm not there that often anyway."

Maggie looked deep into his blue eyes. She could almost see the stars reflected in them. "You always said that someday you'd move to Maine."

"I did. So, I'll be thinking a little harder about it now." He held her a little closer, and his next kiss was a little deeper. "But not tonight. I'm not going to think about that at all tonight."

HISTORICAL NOTE

Shadows of a Down East Summer is fiction. The town of Waymouth, Maine is a composite of several Maine communities, and the Brewer, Pratt, Thompson, and Chase families in this book grew out of my imagination, not out of Maine coast granite.

However, Prouts Neck, a section of Scarborough, Maine, is a real place, and Winslow Homer did live and paint there in the late nineteenth century. He was fifty-four in the summer of 1890. His studio was owned by the Homer family until 2006, when it was purchased by the Portland Museum of Art, which boasts an excellent collection of Homer paintings and engravings. The Black Point Inn is smaller than it was when it was called South Gate House in the nineteenth century, but it is still elegant, and open for business.

Although Anna May and Jessie did not pose for Winslow Homer, he did hire local Maine women (and men) to pose for him. In the major paintings he did in 1890, *A Summer Night* and *Cloud Shadows*, those models were most likely Mrs. Maude Sanborn Googins Libby and Cora Googins Sanborn. I beg their pardon for borrowing their roles for Anna May and Jessie, and do not mean to imply any improprieties on their parts. Micah Wright is also a fictional character. *A Summer Night* is now in the collection of the Musée d'Orsay in Paris, and *Cloud Shadows* is at the Spencer Museum of Art at the University of Kansas in Lawrence, Kansas.

The description of Homer's studio, attire, deportment, and friends Duck and Sam is, from all accounts that I can find, accurate. The addition to his studio and home that was built in the summer of 1890 he later called his "painting room." He died in that room in 1910.

Bob Thomas

About the Author

Lea Wait is a fourth-generation antiques dealer who has been re-searching, buying, and selling antique prints since 1977. She lived and worked in New Jersey while she was raising the four daughters she adopted as a single parent. Wait now lives in Maine, writes mys-teries and books for children and young adults full-time, and is mar-ried to artist Bob Thomas. Her first mystery, *Shadows at the Fair*, was nominated for an Agatha Award.

Lea Wait may be visited at www.leawait.com and on Facebook.

MORE MYSTERIES
FROM PERSEVERANCE PRESS
🔎 *For the New Golden Age* 🔎

JON L. BREEN
Eye of God
ISBN 978-1-880284-89-6

TAFFY CANNON
ROXANNE PRESCOTT SERIES
Guns and Roses
*Agatha and Macavity Award
nominee, Best Novel*
ISBN 978-1-880284-34-6

Blood Matters
ISBN 978-1-880284-86-5

Open Season on Lawyers
ISBN 978-1-880284-51-3

Paradise Lost
ISBN 978-1-880284-80-3

LAURA CRUM
GAIL McCARTHY SERIES
Moonblind
ISBN 978-1-880284-90-2

Chasing Cans
ISBN 978-1-880284-94-0

Going, Gone
ISBN 978-1-880284-98-8

Barnstorming *(forthcoming)*
ISBN 978-1-56474-508-8

JEANNE M. DAMS
HILDA JOHANSSON SERIES
Crimson Snow
ISBN 978-1-880284-79-7

Indigo Christmas
ISBN 978-1-880284-95-7

Murder in Burnt Orange
(forthcoming)
ISBN 978-1-56474-503-3

JANET DAWSON
JERI HOWARD SERIES
Bit Player
ISBN 978-1-56474-494-4

KATHY LYNN EMERSON
LADY APPLETON SERIES
Face Down Below
the Banqueting House
ISBN 978-1-880284-71-1

Face Down Beside
St. Anne's Well
ISBN 978-1-880284-82-7

Face Down O'er the Border
ISBN 978-1-880284-91-9

ELAINE FLINN
MOLLY DOYLE SERIES
Deadly Vintage
ISBN 978-1-880284-87-2

HAL GLATZER
KATY GREEN SERIES
Too Dead To Swing
ISBN 978-1-880284-53-7

A Fugue in Hell's Kitchen
ISBN 978-1-880284-70-4

The Last Full Measure
ISBN 978-1-880284-84-1

MARGARET GRACE
MINIATURE SERIES
Mix-up in Miniature
(forthcoming)
ISBN 978-1-56474-510-1

WENDY HORNSBY
MAGGIE MACGOWEN SERIES
In the Guise of Mercy
ISBN 978-1-56474-482-1

The Paramour's Daughter
ISBN 978-1-56474-496-8

DIANA KILLIAN
POETIC DEATH SERIES
Docketful of Poesy
ISBN 978-1-880284-97-1

JANET LAPIERRE
PORT SILVA SERIES
Baby Mine
ISBN 978-1-880284-32-2

Keepers
*Shamus Award nominee, Best
Paperback Original*
ISBN 978-1-880284-44-5

Death Duties
ISBN 978-1-880284-74-2

Family Business
ISBN 978-1-880284-85-8

Run a Crooked Mile
ISBN 978-1-880284-88-9

HAILEY LIND
ART LOVER'S SERIES
Arsenic and Old Paint
ISBN 978-1-56474-490-6

VALERIE S. MALMONT
TORI MIRACLE SERIES
**Death, Bones, and
Stately Homes**
ISBN 978-1-880284-65-0

DENISE OSBORNE
FENG SHUI SERIES
Evil Intentions
ISBN 978-1-880284-77-3

LEV RAPHAEL
NICK HOFFMAN SERIES
Tropic of Murder
ISBN 978-1-880284-68-1

Hot Rocks
ISBN 978-1-880284-83-4

LORA ROBERTS
BRIDGET MONTROSE SERIES
Another Fine Mess
ISBN 978-1-880284-54-4

SHERLOCK HOLMES SERIES
**The Affair of the
Incognito Tenant**
ISBN 978-1-880284-67-4

REBECCA ROTHENBERG
BOTANICAL SERIES
The Tumbleweed Murders
(completed by Taffy Cannon)
ISBN 978-1-880284-43-8

SHEILA SIMONSON
LATOUCHE COUNTY SERIES
Buffalo Bill's Defunct
*WILLA Award, Best Original
Softcover Fiction*
ISBN 978-1-880284-96-4

An Old Chaos
ISBN 978-1-880284-99-5

SHELLEY SINGER
JAKE SAMSON &
ROSIE VICENTE SERIES
Royal Flush
ISBN 978-1-880284-33-9

LEA WAIT
SHADOWS ANTIQUES SERIES
**Shadows of a Down East
Summer**
ISBN 978-1-56474-497-5

PENNY WARNER
CONNOR WESTPHAL SERIES
Blind Side
ISBN 978-1-880284-42-1

Silence Is Golden
ISBN 978-1-880284-66-7

ERIC WRIGHT
JOE BARLEY SERIES
The Kidnapping of Rosie Dawn
*Barry Award, Best Paperback
Original. Edgar, Ellis, and Anthony
Award nominee*
ISBN 978-1-880284-40-7

NANCY MEANS WRIGHT
MARY WOLLSTONECRAFT SERIES
Midnight Fires
ISBN 978-1-56474-488-3

The Nightmare *(forthcoming)*
ISBN 978-1-56474-509-5

*REFERENCE/
MYSTERY WRITING*

KATHY LYNN EMERSON
**How To Write Killer
Historical Mysteries:
The Art and Adventure of
Sleuthing Through the Past**
*Agatha Award, Best Nonfiction.
Anthony and Macavity awards
nominee.*
ISBN 978-1-880284-92-6

CAROLYN WHEAT
**How To Write Killer Fiction:
The Funhouse of Mystery & the
Roller Coaster of Suspense**
ISBN 978-1-880284-62-9